"You'll be joining us now," said the whisper.

As it spoke, the two empty brainpods separated into halves, the halves moving quickly toward the two humans—though not as quickly as their blasters. Four bolts of red flicked out, touching off four sharp explosions. Crumpled and fused bits of duraplast rained down on the console, chairs and deck.

"Components!" It was a shriek—the voice of the overmind. "Kill them!"

N'Trol whirled, leveling his firearm and diving behind a comm terminal as the components rushed the tier, firing from the hip. From behind him came the whine of A'Tir's blaster and more explosions.

The components were advancing, light glinting dully from a hundred bayonets, a long column of twos that snaked down to the main deck and out of sight across the bridge.

"What a miserable, futile ending . . ."

Also by Stephen Ames Berry published by Tor Books

The Battle for Terra Two
The AI War

STEPHEN AMES BERRY

FINAL ASSAULT

TOR

A TOM DOHERTY ASSOCIATES BOOK

THE FINAL ASSAULT

A TOR Book
Published by Tom Doherty Associates, Inc.
49 West 24 Street
New York, NY 10010

ISBN: 0-812-53189-2   Can. ISBN: 0-812-53190-6

First edition: July 1988

Printed in the United States of America

0 9 8 7 6 5 4 3 2 1

To my Mother

In pursuit of the corsair K'Tran and upon direct orders from FleetOps, I proceeded into Quadrant Blue Nine with a task force of five starcruisers. We were preceded by the L'Aal-class cruiser *Implacable*, under the command of Commodore D'Trelna. Ours were the first ships to brave this reputed "Ghost Quadrant" since an ill-fated scientific survey ship, some 1,582 years ago.

To the undoubted detriment of our respective commands, and the possible salvation of the Confederation, we each found what we were looking for.

Admiral Second S'Gan
Commanding Special Task Force 18
Excerpt from BattleOps
Report 6389028

1

"WE'RE AT FINAL jump point, Commodore," said L'Wrona from the navigation station.

D'Trelna nodded, looking up at the data trail threading across the bottom of the main screen. "Last chance to turn back, H'Nar," he said to the captain.

"And do what?" said L'Wrona, his long fingers playing over the console, entering the jump coordinates. "Live like real corsairs? No, I'll take my chances with the v'org slime."

FleetOps would have been hard-pressed to cast two more-dissimilar figures as *Implacable*'s senior officers: D'Trelna short, fat, well into middleage, with the sharp nose and piercing dark eyes of a S'Htarian trader, and

L'Wrona, younger, slender, with the aquiline good looks of the old aristocracy. Having fought and won across half the galaxy, they were headed home now to face their final battle.

D'Trelna looked around, eyes going from empty station to empty station. The cruiser's big bridge usually had between twelve and twenty crew. She had four now: K'Lana, manning communications; N'Trol, chief engineer, hovering over the jump status board; L'Wrona, manning K'Raoda's old station; and himself, now seated at the captain's post, a post he'd manned for seven years, before they made him a flag officer.

"Commtorps ready, K'Lana?" the commodore said, looking at the petite brunette.

"Jump-tied, Commodore," she said.

D'Trelna touched his chairarm's comm-link. "This is it," he said, voice echoing through the long, almost empty miles of *Implacable*. "We're jumping into home system now. Luck to us all." He switched off.

"Jump at will, Captain L'Wrona," said the commodore, clasping his hands over his belly, eyes on the screen.

"Jumping," said L'Wrona, touching the "Execute" switch.

A slight tugging at the stomach as the stars on main screen red-shifted to familiar constellations. The data trail winked out, then resumed with new figures. As D'Trelna watched, three silver missiles streaked by, scattering toward distant targets.

"Commtorps launched," said K'Lana.

The screen rippled, changing from outside scan to a tactical view of the K'Ronarin home system. N'Trol whistled softly. "Look at that! They must have half the Home Fleet on picket duty."

"Impressive," said D'Trelna, looking at the hundreds of points of light standing between *Implacable* and the innermost planet. Three of those lights began drifting toward the green blip denoting *Implacable*.

"Unknown cruiser, identify," came a brusque voice over the deck speakers.

"Unknown, my ass," said the commodore, swiveling toward K'Lana. "We're putting out standard id on standard id frequency."

"Yes, sir."

"Just a brief show for FleetOps records," said L'Wrona. "'Suspected corsair detected and destroyed.'" Glancing at the data trail, he walked to the tactics station and stood touching the gunnery-tie controls to ship's computer. "Their shields are at battleforce, they're closing at flank with gunnery scans locking on. They won't be firing salutes as they pass."

"So? Are you going to shoot it out with our own ships, H'Nar?" asked D'Trelna, swiveling to look at L'Wrona. "Outnumbered fifty to

5

one, their ships crewed, ours on automatic? Absurd." His voice lowered. "Remember why we're here."

"I know," said the captain, taking his hands from the console, clasping them behind his back. "One's first instinct is to fight, though."

"Unknown cruiser, identify," repeated the challenge. "Identify or we open fire."

"Plenty of fighting ahead, I'm afraid," said D'Trelna, touching his chair's commlink.

"L'Aal-class cruiser *Implacable*, returning from Quadrant Blue-Nine. You will advise FleetOps that we have launched commtorps tied to all civilian frequencies. If we don't reach Prime Base, our mission debriefing will be transmitted to every receiver in home quadrant, open band, loud and clear." He said it fast, spurred by a vivid image of gunnery consoles flashing red as Mark 88 turrets swung toward *Implacable*, then leaned back, watching the tacscan.

Two of the picket ships were within range now—heavy destroyers, together more than a match for one L'Aal-class cruiser. The silence lengthened.

"Someone down in FleetOps is making a Decision," said D'Trelna, thick fingers drumming a soft tattoo on the padded chair arm.

"FleetOps to *Implacable*," said a different voice, smooth, neutral. "You are cleared for Prime Base. Line is so advised." A series of coordinates followed.

As D'Trelna acknowledged, the commlink ended with a sharp burst of static.

"Welcome home," muttered the commodore.

"Coordinates laid in," said L'Wrona. "Ship proceeding on course."

"Not steering us toward a minefield, are they?" said N'Trol. The engineer walked to the flag station and stood staring at the screen. He was about L'Wrona's age and height, not as thin, though, and with features deep-tanned from long hours spent hullside.

D'Trelna shook his head. "They can't afford crudity as long as those commtorps are flitting about home system." He pointed to the screen. "See, our friends are pulling back."

Up on the big board the lights marking the pickets were withdrawing to their original positions as *Implacable* headed toward K'Ronar.

As they approached the planet, the tacscan changed, showing first K'Ronar with Prime Base neatly marked in a winking green, then a line of red between ship and planet: Line.

"Hello, Commodore," said a soft, cultured voice over the commlink.

"Hello, Line," said D'Trelna.

Ten thousand years before, at the K'Ronarin Empire's technological height, a series of Twelfth Dynasty Emperors had, at enormous expense, constructed Line. The name came from the two-dimensional image of it projected by the tacscan of approaching vessels. Line was actually a great shield-sphere surrounding K'Ronar, a never-breached wall comprised of tens of thousands of satellite-based shield generators, approached through ever-varying minefields, missile and gun platforms, all controlled from ten miles of rock that sat in geostationary orbit over K'Ronar's north pole.

"Did you have an interesting mission, Commodore?" continued the voice.

"Saved humanity again," said D'Trelna lightly, watching as the screen shifted to exterior scan, showing them approaching an endless sweep of silver set against the obsidian of space. He punched up a steaming cup of t'ata from his chairarm. "Been battling any alien hordes, Line?"

Part of the shield wall disappeared as *Implacable* reached it. Moving on n-gravs now, the cruiser slipped through the Line.

"Alas!" sighed the voice. "We've had no fun since the S'Cotar fleet tried that foolishness at the start of the last war.

"Welcome home, Commodore," it added as the shield closed behind the ship.

"Thank you, Line," said D'Trelna, looking at the brown-green world ahead. "Wish everyone felt that way."

"That computer's friendlier than Fleet-Ops," said N'Trol.

"Do you really think it's a computer, Engineer?" said the captain, joining the other two at D'Trelna's station.

"It's certainly not a human," said N'Trol. "No one'd be crazy enough to entrust the defense of K'Ronar to any man or group of men."

"Whatever it is, is irrelevant, gentlemen," said D'Trelna, holding out a hand. "We're through—we're home."

Brown, touched by just a hint of green and blue, K'Ronar lay before them, an arid world of sweeping desert and rocky crags, its population now mostly confined to the greenbelt girdling the equator. She'd been a rich, lush world once, heavy in minerals, covered with forests and grassy plains. Man had taken the forests and the minerals, then, at his Imperial height, resculpted the land into a green arcadia of forested peaks and deep blue lakes, interspaced by cities wrought of gleaming alloys and subtly hued duraplast, all crafted of a daring vision that had triumphed across a galaxy.

A slow strengthening of K'Ronar's sun, matched by Empire's long twilight, had left much of paradise a wasteland. Ruined cities of a hundred emperors now lay forgotten beneath the sands, while from the towers of A'Kan, proud capital to every dynasty since the First, the encroaching desert could be seen, held at bay just beyond the expensively maintained barrier of lakes and parks.

"We're on remote," said L'Wrona, pointing to the helm controls, which now responded to the landing programming of Prime Base's computers.

Piercing a wispy gray-white cloud layer, *Implacable* came in low over the K'Zan Desert and turned north, following an ancient dry river bed.

" 'R'Shen, mighty daughter, who drank the blood of slaughter,' " said D'Trelna softly, watching a scan of the cracked, brown wash.

"I didn't know you were a poet, J'Quel," said L'Wrona.

"I'm ashamed to say it's all I can recall," said D'Trelna.

"Prespace, isn't it?" said N'Trol.

The commodore nodded. "An epic poem by S'Hko, commemorating a battle at that river. They fought with swords and bows then, gentlemen, and put an end to the Slavers' Guild. S'Hko says the waters of the R'Shen ran red for days." He looked up from the screen. "An important place, the R'Shen—men died there in a good cause."

"We're being landed in Seven Blue, area one three nine two," said K'Lana, turning from her console.

"What's that? A hundred t'lars from FleetOps?" said D'Trelna. "Why not land us in the K'Zan and have us walk out?"

They came in over the southeastern perimeter of Prime Base, drifting on silent n-gravs past the defense perimeters—line after line of missile and gun emplacements, hardened, shielded, deep set in the sand—then over the landing field and ships of every size and type: cruisers, destroyers, scouts, interceptors, all sitting on the black duraplast field, sunlight shimmering on their hulls. Except for the occasional maintenance vehicle, nothing moved.

"War's over—everyone's gone home," said L'Wrona, shaking his head. "Combine T'Lan's done its job well."

"Let's see if we can fix that," said D'Trelna as *Implacable* settled with a faint whine onto an isolated stretch of duraplast. "And Combine T'Lan."

"Admiral G'Yar for the commodore," said K'Lana.

"Who?" said L'Wrona.

D'Trelna touched the commlink. "Good afternoon, sir," he said to the face appearing in his commscreen.

"You and Captain L'Wrona will remain with the ship, Commodore," said the admiral, a sharp-faced man with a thin, disapproving little mouth. "Your crew will dismiss and muster out—personnel carriers are on the way."

"One will do, Admiral," said D'Trelna.

"They only hold fifty, Commodore."

"Just the right number, Admiral." D'Trelna smiled.

Stephen Ames Berry

"You lost over two hundred crew?!" exclaimed G'Yar, eyes widening.

"They're not lost, sir. We know where they are."

The Admiral tried to say something, failed, finally found his voice and snapped, "You will remain with your ship, sir." The commscreen blanked.

"Just who the hell is Admiral G'Yar, H'Nar?" asked D'Trelna, swiveling his chair toward the captain's station.

L'Wrona was watching the complink, frowning at the data scrolling slowly past. "According to this—and it's two years behind —G'Yar was a commander in Fiscal. Direct commission, no war service."

"A politico," said D'Trelna. "He shouldn't be allowed to even sweep the floor in FleetOps, yet he seems to be Officer-in-charge."

"Ground vehicle approaching," said a pleasant, asexual contralto—ship's computer. "A personnel carrier, unarmed."

"Shipwide," said D'Trelna, opening the commlink. "This is the Commodore. We're home. FleetOps says you're to be discharged —they've sent a carrier for you. Take your time, gather your things. Captain L'Wrona and I will say good-bye to you at"—he glanced at the groundscan—"airlock fifty-nine, deck eight."

"I've got to help bed down the engines,"

said N'Trol, leaving the engineering station. The armored doors hissed shut behind him.

Captain and commodore looked at each other, then around the bridge with its array of empty consoles. "You and me, H'Nar," said D'Trelna into the silence, looking back at L'Wrona.

"A long and bitter war, J'Quel," said L'Wrona, rising. "I only wish it were over —that we were leaving this ship never having heard of an AI or the Fleet of the One."

"Humanity would be compost in less than a year if we hadn't heard of the AIs, H'Nar. It still may be." He tried to punch up a drink from his chairarm beverager—nothing. "Engineering's begun shutting her down."

"They'll try to kill us both, you know," said L'Wrona.

"Perhaps," said the commodore, standing. "Shall we go?" He indicated the door.

In a moment, for the first time in ten years, the bridge was empty.

"B'Tul," said D'Trelna, holding out his hand, "keep out of trouble."

"Commodore," the big master gunner, smiling and shaking the officer's hand, "me?" B'Tul stood at the head of the disembarking crew, there in the narrow access corridor at the bottom of the ship, gray kit bag slung over his shoulder, brown utility cap perched rakishly on his head.

"I remember that bar brawl on I'Tak Two, Master Gunner," said D'Trelna.

"And I remember you throwing that miner into the bar," said B'Tul. "The one who wanted to gut me with a broken bottle."

D'Trelna nodded. "It was S'Tanian brandy, B'Tul. A bad end for a noble poison—I lost my head."

B'Tul handed D'Trelna a slip of paper.

"What's this?" said the commodore, unfolding it.

"My address. I have everyone else's contact point. You need us, call. We've got a lot of friends on *Devastator* who aren't out of this yet. And rumor has it you and the captain are in deep trouble here. Anyway"—he adjusted his hat—"you need us, call.

"Luck, sir," said B'Tul, shaking L'Wrona's hand.

"Luck, B'Tul," smiled the captain.

B'Tul stepped through the door and onto the long ramp that spiraled down to the waiting carrier.

The others filed past, said their good-byes and followed the master gunner into the hot desert sun. The two officers stood on the top of the ramp, watching them go.

"Seven years through blood and fire with some of them," said L'Wrona, shaking his head. "Think we'll ever see them again?"

"Yes," said D'Trelna. They watched the carrier rise on its n-gravs, turn and accelerate toward the distant smudge of Base Central, a blur of speed quickly lost in the heat haze shimmering above the landing field.

The two men reentered the ship.

"Let's secure the bridge," said D'Trelna. "Then if N'Trol's finished, wait here like good children for . . ."

"Alert! Alert!" It was computer. "Ground assault units are approaching this vessel. Ground assault units are approaching this vessel."

"Didn't waste any time, did they?" said D'Trelna, reaching the wall commlink first. "Computer. Specify composition of ground units."

The voice shifted from wall speakers to the commlink. "Fifteen Class One battle tanks, twenty-seven weaponed personnel carriers of mixed nomenclature."

As D'Trelna turned for the corridor and the lift, the commlink beeped. He punched it on. "What's happening?" asked N'Trol.

"Company comes, bearing blasters," said the commodore. "Meet us on the bridge."

Black, squat monsters, the battle tanks hung back from *Implacable*, fusion cannons cranked high, as the personnel carriers swept in, disgorging gray-uniformed troopers who charged up the landing ramp of airlock 59, M32 assault rifles in hand.

"Gray uniforms?" said D'Trelna. The three

officers stood on the silent bridge, watching the investiture of their ship on the main screen. "Since when in the last five thousand years has any Fleet unit worn gray?"

"Fleet Security changed to gray last year, J'Quel," said the captain. "They call it imperial gray. You should keep up on FleetOps Orders of the Day."

"I always use the first two paragraphs to get to sleep, H'Nar," said D'Trelna. On the screen the last of the troopers had entered the ship.

"Ready yet, Mr. N'Trol?" said the commodore, turning to where the engineer sat, busy at the first officer's station.

"Can't do it manually," said N'Trol, shaking his head. "Computer won't let me."

Captain and commodore stepped to the first officer's station. Reaching past N'Trol, D'Trelna opened the complink. "Computer. D'Trelna. Destroy all record of commtorps last launched from this vessel."

"Illegal command," said computer. "Fleet Directive 60.35.B states that . . ." It broke off, then spoke again, its voice coming from the bulkhead speakers. "Personnel properly identifying themselves as Fleet Security officers are demanding admittance to this bridge."

"Command priority," said D'Trelna. "Do not—repeat, do not—admit them." He glanced at the armored double doors guarding the bridge.

"Computer," said L'Wrona quickly, "authenticator Imperiad seven one, eight one. Destroy all record of commtorps last launched from this vessel."

"Implemented, My Lord," said a deep, sonorous voice from the complink.

L'Wrona smiled grimly at the other two officers. "Now let them try to find those commtorps."

N'Trol stood, shaking his head. "You tap that old Imperial programming too much, Captain, you'll have a computer with dysfunctional schizophrenia."

"I've only used it once before," said L'Wrona.

"It's unlikely we'll ever be on this ship again, gentlemen," said D'Trelna.

The commlink chirped. Leaning across the vacant console, D'Trelna touched the call tab. "Yes?"

"Colonel A'Nal," said a flat, hard voice, "Fleet Security. Under the authority of Fleet Articles of War, I order you to open these doors."

D'Trelna tapped the Hold button. "Well?" he asked the other two.

"If he's talking Articles, he's got arrest warrants," said L'Wrona.

"We could let them drag a Mark 44 up here," suggested N'Trol. "It would take them a while. It's a hot day, they'd work up a sweat, pull some muscles . . ."

"And eventually burn the door down and

come thundering in here, pissed as hell," said L'Wrona. "Fun, but not a good idea."

"Better let them in, J'Quel."

"Computer," said D'Trelna, thumbing the complink, "please admit the properly identified members of our Fleet Security arm."

The thick doors hissed open. A rush of gray uniforms surged onto the bridge, led by a tall man with colonel's insignia and the crossed daggers of Fleet Security on his collar.

"You're all under arrest," he said as troopers took D'Trelna's and N'Trol's blasters.

"This one won't give it up, sir," said a corporal.

L'Wrona stood imperturbably, hand firmly on his weapon's grips.

"You will please surrender your weapon, Captain My Lord L'Wrona," said Colonel A'Nal.

"Not until I see the arrest order," said L'Wrona, extending his free hand.

"Certainly." Taking a paper from his tunic pocket, A'Nal handed it stiffly to the captain. L'Wrona scanned the order, eyes stopping at the signature block. He handed it back. "This is signed by a councilman. You may be able to hold Commodore D'Trelna and Commander N'Trol on it—you certainly can't hold me."

"Even the aristocracy is subject to Fleet orders," said the colonel. "Even you, My Lord."

18

"It's just a civil order," said L'Wrona, "and I am not just any aristocrat."

A'Nal glared at L'Wrona and started to speak. As he did so, a voice called wonderingly from the first officer's station, "Seven hells! They've wiped the commtorps records!"

The colonel turned to the technician as the three ship's officers exchanged satisfied looks. "I thought that couldn't be done?"

The woman shrugged. "Nevertheless, they've done it—accessed the Imperial programming, somehow. It's all gone except basic commtorps inventory."

Face flushing angrily, A'Nal turned back to his prisoners. "You must be feeling very smug. We'll see how you feel after interrogation.

"Escort the commodore and the commander to the Tower," he ordered, "and remand them to the custody of the commandant."

D'Trelna shook off the hands that reached for his arms. "What did you do in the war, Colonel?" he asked.

"In the war?" repeated A'Nal, staring uneasily at D'Trelna's battle ribbons.

"He means the ten-year war with the S'Cotar," said N'Trol helpfully. "The one that ended this year."

"My record's none of your concern," said the colonel. "But it's one I'm proud of—I was

19

assigned to ground headquarters of the Home Fleet."

"In what capacity?" asked L'Wrona.

"Budget officer."

"Interesting," said D'Trelna. "How'd you go from budget officer to colonel in a combat arm?"

"Get them out of here," A'Nal ordered a sergeant. The NCO took the commodore's arm, steering him toward the doors. N'Trol and his escort followed.

"Luck, H'Nar," called D'Trelna as they took him away.

"Luck, J'Quel, N'Trol," said the captain. Alone on the bridge, he and A'Nal faced each other.

"You're correct—I can't arrest you," said the gray-uniformed officer. "I'd be very careful, though, if I were you, My Lord. Stay out of this. Go back to U'Tria—they need you there, now that the war's over." With a curt nod, he turned and left the bridge.

"The real war's only just begun, Colonel," said L'Wrona softly. Alone on the big old ship, he watched the convoy disappear into the heat of midday, then turned and left the ship.

Terra. A speck of nothingness on the spiral arm of our galaxy. Which is, of course, why the Empire—or certain members of the Empire—chose to build on Terra's moon a cybernetic guardian that would, when the moment was right, create and unleash into our somnolent Confederation an aggressor race, to "prepare" us for the "real" enemy, those long-forgotten AIs who lived just a universe away. That this cybernetic guardian, some five thousand years after the fall of the Empire, chose to create such a formidable lifeform as the S'Cotar biofabs, made the contest all too real. That we won was a miracle; that we will ever be entirely rid of the S'Cotar plague unlikely. It can only be done planet by planet, nest by nest. And it can only be done by the Watchers.

Colonel S'Rel
Report to the Confederation Council
Archives Reference 518.392.671.AI

2

"WHAT ARE YOU trying to tell me, S'Rel?" said Sutherland, interrupting the Watcher in mid-evasion.

The K'Ronarin stopped speaking, then leaned forward, fists on the CIA director's desk. "Very well, Sutherland. I'll be blunt. My men and I have been ordered back to K'Ronar —we leave Terra tomorrow."

"Leave? Tomorrow?" Sutherland heard himself stammer.

S'Rel nodded. *"Repulse* is going home. We're to go with her."

"Repulse is pulling out?"

S'Rel nodded.

"Is she being replaced?"

"No."

Sutherland slumped back in his chair. "My God, S'Rel—you're leaving this planet defenseless against . . ."

"Against nothing," said S'Rel, walking to the big picture window with its view of the Potomac Palisades. A wiry, pale-complexioned man in his thirties, dressed for the weather in a short sleeve plaid shirt and denim pants, he stared across the sullen brown river at Washington.

"Against nothing," he repeated, turning back to Sutherland, hands clasped behind his back. "That nest in the Mato Grosso was the last of them. There are no more traces on Terra. We've wiped all the S'Cotar on your world."

It had been a swift, flawlessly executed operation. Without warning, *Repulse* had moved out of stationary orbit, heading outsystem at speed, protests from a hundred nations rippling in its wake as the radar reports came in. Ambassador Z'Sha had only just issued an uninformative statement when the destroyer suddenly reappeared over Brazil, missile and fusion batteries sending a thin stream of death into the atmosphere—a fierce rain of ordnance and energy that impacted on a small village deep in the Amazon basin.

Flashing silver in the tropical sun, five K'Ronarin shuttles had swept in low off the river, Mark 44 turrets strafing the burning, blasted ruins. With a faint whine of n-gravs, the craft had settled into the clearing between the village and a swamp. Before the landing struts had even touched the ground, the raiders were leaping out, running for the village, M32 rifles in hand, S'Rel and Sutherland in the lead.

The survivors huddled at the other end of the clearing, a pathetic group of ragged, terrified children clutching their frightened mothers; a few old men, watching the American Rangers and the K'Ronarin commandos impassively, through eyes that had seen too much, and one very fat man, shirtless but wearing a big straw hat. Behind them, smoke drifted lazily from the ruins of their homes out over the broad brown stretch of the Amazon.

S'Rel had halted his force about forty meters from the survivors, waiting as the fat man walked over to them.

"Why?" said the fat man, halting in front of him and Sutherland, hands spread dramatically, eyes shifting between the two of them.

Blaster leveled, S'Rel had said nothing, merely pulled the trigger. The weapon shrilled, sending a fierce red beam punching through that great gut—a gut that resolved into a slender green thorax as the S'Cotar died.

The tall insectoid was still falling when the firefight broke out—the illusion of huddled refugees rippling, dissolving into a tight formation of blaster-armed, bulbous-eyed bugs that opened fire with trained precision, indigo-blue bolts slamming into the human line, a withering fire that would have wiped out the human force had the thin silver miracle of their warsuits not absorbed the fusion bolts, converting them to brief bursts of multicolored lightning that crackled up and down the warsuits for an instant, then were gone.

The return fire was just as accurate as the S'Cotars' but deadly. Unprotected by warsuits, the bugs died, the few survivors scattering for the swamps as the humans charged.

"Shit," said Sutherland, the target between his sights suddenly shrouded in black mists —the wind had shifted inland, bringing the smoke from the village in over the clearing.

"They can't get far," said S'Rel, kicking the firefight's first casualty. "Their transmute's dead." The corpse was thinner, taller than the rest, a six-legged horror that lay face down in the mud, tentacles still clutching a blastrifle. Like the dead warriors behind it, it had mandibles. Unlike theirs, its weren't serrated— they were long, thin, hiding the almost microscopic probes that slid out from them and into the brains of its victims, slowly absorbing their memories, their personas, until the transmute could perfectly assume their lives.

Telepathic, telekinetic, and dead, thought

Sutherland, looking down at the S'Cotar. Thank God.

"Bill, take your Rangers through the village, then circle into the swamp from the east," said S'Rel as the air cleared. "I'll take my group and go straight in from here. We should catch any survivors between us."

As Sutherland went looking for the Ranger commander, S'Rel spoke into his communicator. A moment later the shuttles rose, moving slowly at treetop level into the swamp.

Three hours and they'd killed three S'Cotar —and almost lost S'Rel.

"What was that reptile again?" asked S'Rel, turning from the window.

"An anaconda," said Sutherland. "Largest snake on the planet."

Hearing splashing and a muted cry for help, Sutherland had hurried through the brackish, waist-deep water, blastrifle above his head. The sounds of the struggle stopped for an instant, then resumed, louder than before, as he penetrated the thick mangrove swamp, emerging into a shallower area where the trees were fewer.

Eyes bulging, face contorted, the K'Ronarin was up to his waist in the muddy water, his free hand just keeping the tree-thick, olive-colored coils of the great snake from making the final turn around his neck.

Cursing, Sutherland twisted the M32's muzzle down to minimum aperture, set the selector switch to continual fire, and moved toward the struggle, water, mud and tangled roots tugging at him, slowing his pace to a frustrating, dreamlike crawl. By the time he'd covered the final yards to the roiling brown water, S'Rel had disappeared beneath the surface.

Placing the rifle's muzzle inches from the glistening, mottled-brown skin, Sutherland had pulled the trigger, sending a thin red beam knifing through the snake. Ignoring the shudder that suddenly rippled down the long yards of flesh, Sutherland passed the beam through the rest of that thigh-thick braid of muscle.

The thrashing ceased as the anaconda's body fell into two dead halves.

Dropping the rifle, Sutherland seized S'Rel's hand, pulling the K'Ronarin from under the water, gasping for air, still wrapped in dead serpent's coils. The anaconda's head hung down S'Rel's back, mouth open, tongue protruding.

"I don't believe you got all the S'Cotar, S'Rel," said Sutherland, looking up at the Watcher. "I think you're leaving because it's politically expedient—declaring a victory and going home."

Sighing, S'Rel sank into one of the red leather armchairs fronting the director's desk and leaned forward earnestly, hands on his knees. "Here's how it looks from FleetOps,

Bill. We fought the S'Cotar for ten years, lost millions of people, scores of planets. We were about to lose it all when D'Trelna and *Implacable* stumbled onto your planet and found . . ."

"And found the S'Cotar were organic manufactures—biofabs," said Sutherland. "Created beneath our moon by a possibly demented cyborg programmed thousands of years ago by your equally demented Empire."

"Yes," nodded S'Rel, "but don't forget why. To toughen us as a people, prepare us to face an invasion from another reality—an invasion of artificial intelligences—AIs—that happened once before, a million years ago, and was repulsed by the Trel."

"Even though defeated," said Sutherland, pointing a finger at the Watcher, "those machines killed the Trel and every living thing on all their worlds. And they'd have killed us, too, this last time, if D'Trelna hadn't stopped them at Terra Two."

"It's FleetOps opinion," said S'Rel, "that the end of the Terra Two incursion marked the end of any threat from the AIs. Our priority now is to purge our planets of any remaining S'Cotar and get on with the rebuilding of broken worlds and shattered lives."

"FleetOps is wrong," said the CIA director. "The Trel warned that the rift they sealed to the AI universe was opening now. The Terra

Two invasion was a fluke, maybe even a feint. The Fleet of the One is coming, S'Rel, through that rift, perhaps even right now. And what are you people doing?" His voice rose angrily. "You're doling out tea and comfort and congratulating each other on having survived the big green bugs when you should be mobilizing every ship that can mount a fusion battery!"

"Finished?" said the K'Ronarin as Sutherland caught his breath.

"What about D'Trelna?"

S'Rel shrugged. "He was sent to check out the Trel's invasion warning—into Quadrant Blue Nine, from which no ship has returned since the Fall. He hasn't been heard from. I doubt he ever will be."

There was a faint chirp, repeated three times. Frowning, the K'Ronarin took the slim communicator from his shirt pocket. "S'Rel," he said.

"Alert condition one," said a flat voice in K'Ronarin. "An AI battleglobe has just entered the Terran system."

"Close the portal!" said S'Rel.

"It didn't come from the portal," said the voice. "It came from our space."

The battle klaxon brought *Repulse*'s Captain P'Qal from bed to bridge in record time, pausing only for a quick commlink call.

"Status?" he said, taking the command

chair, eyes on the big board. Behind him the armored doors slid shut with a faint hiss.

"Target appeared at jump point a few moments ago," said S'Jat in her usual low, soft voice. She nodded at the board. "As you can see, it's headed insystem at just below light speed, and on present course, will reach here in nineteen point five t'lars."

"And pass right through," said P'Qal brusqely. The emergency wasn't improving his notoriously short temper. "She's not decelerating."

"As the captain will note," said S'Jat, unruffled, "what little data we have on AI battleglobes indicates that they can decelerate almost instantaneously."

"Absurd," said the captain. "A violation of every principle of astrogation and related physics."

"Perhaps we don't know everything about astrogation and physics," suggested the first officer.

They stared at each other, the short, bald man and the tall, thin brunette. "I'm not going to debate epistemology with you," said P'Qal. "I always lose." His eyes shifted to the tacscan data threading across the board. "Almost the size of Terra's moon," he said. "Highly manueverable, fusion batteries half the size of this ship, first-class shielding." He looked up. "Suicide to take her on, Number One."

"Terra has no defenses," she said mildly.

"You've alerted them?"

She nodded. "Through our New York embassy."

"And FleetOps?"

"Knows nothing. The battleglobe took out our skipcomm relay the instant she entered the system."

"I see," he said, eyes going back to the board. The large red blip had passed Saturn. "Where in all the hells did it come from?"

S'Jat shrugged. "The implications aren't pleasant."

P'Qal touched the commlink in his chairarm. "Get me *Dawn*—Captain S'Yatan. Battle priority alpha." He glanced again at the tacscan—the battleglobe was almost at Mars and showed no sign of slowing.

"Captain S'Yatan, sir," said the comm officer.

"Close the portal," P'Qal ordered the man whose image appeared in his commscreen.

"Already done," said the younger man. "But where did it come from?"

"Let's go ask her," said P'Qal. "Man your battlestations and follow us."

1. Artificial intelligences (AIs) exist. We have fought and defeated one of their advance units. More are coming.

2. These AIs are, as suspected, from a parallel reality where organic, carbon-based life is subservient to silicon-based life.

3. In a revolt against the AI Empire —called the Revolt by all sides—humans, a few hundred AIs and members of at least one other species escaped to this reality, moving uptime 900,000 years. Arriving 100,000 of our years ago, these revolutionaries founded our civilization, their humans intermarrying with humans indigenous to our galaxy. We are their descendants.

4. The AIs who came here still live among us, in human guise.

5. The AI Empire still exists. In a million years it has forgotten nothing and learned nothing. And it has found the means to come after us—one million battleglobes strong. Nothing we have can stand against it.

6. The AI Empire has succeeded in planting a fifth column among us. It is one of our principal industrial arms, Combine T'Lan. As of this communique, we have beaten off one of Combine T'Lan's task forces.

7. As my and Commodore D'Trelna's commands have been declared corsair by FleetOps—one may guess at whose instigation—we have decided to become corsairs, in a limited sense. I have agreed to a limited raid on Combine T'Lan's headquarters—my ships will protect *Implacable* as she sends in assault boats. It is unlikely that any of my command will survive the action.

Admiral Second S'Gan, loc. sit.
(Final skipcomm received.)

3

"So, you slime have co-opted the Tower garrison," said D'Trelna, looking around the room.

It was a small room, built to inspire fear: thick-mortared walls of ancient, hand-dressed stone, set deep beneath the Tower—an old Imperial interrogation cell furnished only with the traditional scarred gray table and folding chair.

"The Commandant of the Tower is sensitive to political winds, Commodore," said the man behind the table. "A talent you lack."

"You're Councilor D'Assan," said D'Trelna. "Of the Imperial Party."

The younger man nodded. "Actually, I'm Council Chair this term."

"And you had me arrested—illegally,"

35

D'Trelna snapped, feeling himself flush with anger.

D'Assan waved a well-manicured hand. "As Council Chair, I can hold almost anyone, pending investigation. Fleet Security actually made the arrest—your ship is corsair-listed, Commodore. You didn't think you were just going to flit in, have a drink with the lads and muster out, did you?"

"I'm a Fleet officer," said D'Trelna. "That's for Fleet to decide."

D'Assan held up a hand. "Soon, Commodore, soon. But first, I wanted us to have a quiet talk, just us two, all alone in this rocky womb, safe from spy beams and snooper probes."

D'Trelna nodded curtly. "Fine. What did you want to say, Councilor?"

"That you are a fool," said D'Assan mildly. "That you've been deceived by a very charming fellow named R'Gal into believing that our society is infiltrated by AIs seeking to destroy us. In fact, it is the AIs who've made us what we are—literally."

"Scum . . .!" growled D'Trelna, stepping toward the table, hands raised. "You know!"

"Please don't make me use this," said D'Assan, a palm-sized needler suddenly appearing in his hand. "You've no idea the number of reports your great mound of a body would require."

The commodore paused in mid-stride, fists

clenched at his side. "You're one of them—a machine, a combat droid from Combine T'Lan."

D'Assan shook his head, "No. Just a man, trying to do something right for his people in the brief time I have, as a councilor and a man."

"Pretty," said D'Trelna. "You should be a politician."

"Back up, please, Commodore," said D'Assan, flicking the needler. He set the weapon on the table top as D'Trelna complied.

"Let me tell you something, Councilor . . ." began the commodore.

"No, sir," interrupted D'Assan. "Let me tell you what you're going to tell me, then I'll tell you why it's wrong." He swept on before D'Trelna could speak.

"You're going to tell me that you took your ship into Blue Nine, the Ghost Quadrant, and there battled machines and monsters and ancient nightmares out of our past, and against terrifying odds, you fought free and have come to warn us all." He nodded. "You're a brave and resourceful commander. My compliments, sir."

"Go to hell."

"Hell is precisely where your warning would take us, D'Trelna," said D'Assan with a wry smile. "Artificial intelligences—AIs —built this civilization, working from within, guiding us through the long rise to the stars,

37

helping us win the war against the S'Cotar . . ."

"Blood and steel won that war, D'Assan," said D'Trelna.

". . . and now you'd expose the presence of this helping hand to mass hysteria and mob violence—undo a millennia-old friend who's given everything and asked nothing in return."

The commodore stared at D'Assan for a long moment. "You are speaking of our pre-eminent industrial combine, Combine T'Lan?" he said carefully.

D'Assan nodded.

"Do I understand?" continued D'Trelna. "You believe the T'Lan AIs to be responsible for all that is good and great, the noble benefactors of we small creatures?"

"Well, that's a bit of an exaggera—"

"I don't know what sweet crap you've been fed, Councilor, but the Combine T'Lan AIs are infiltrators from a parallel universe—a universe that has an AI empire ruling subjugated races such as ours. An empire against which a valiant few men and AIs revolted, lost, fled to this reality and founded this civilization, millennia ago. That Empire, Councillor, has sworn vengeance upon us. The T'Lan AIs are the vanguard of that vengeance that even now is sweeping down toward rift in the Ghost Quadrant—a rift guarded by a handful of mindslavers of dubious loyalty. The Fleet of the One is coming, Councilor D'Assan, and

"To what do I owe . . ."

"The pleasure?" said L'Guan. "Well, I was here to see Commandant W'Tal off to his new posting . . ."

"You've replaced the Commandant?" said D'Assan uneasily.

"Why, yes. Promoted to Admiral Second and posted to Red Seven Quadrant—we've still got a corsair problem out there."

"He'll be delighted, I'm sure," murmured D'Assan. "I believe the corsair problem has claimed Red Seven's last five senior field officers."

"While talking with W'Tal," continued the admiral, "I was advised that not only had *Implacable* been captured, but that D'Trelna was being held on Council warrant pending transfer to Fleet. So I'm here to take him in tow." Reaching into his tunic, he removed a folded piece of paper.

D'Assan read the transfer receipt. "All in order and still warm from the printer," he said, folding the document and tucking it away. "You work quickly, Admiral." He took a communicator from his pocket. "I'll ask the commandant to give you an escort."

L'Guan placed a firm hand on the other's wrist, forcing hand and communicator to the table top. "Not to worry, Councilor. I have a battalion of commandos with me." As if on cue, two black-and-silver-uniformed commando officers appeared in the doorway.

"Then I'll be going," said D'Assan. "Good day, Admiral."

"Good day, Councilor," said L'Guan.

The admiral and the two officers stepped aside as D'Assan left.

"Bring the prisoner to the commandant's office," ordered L'Guan. Not looking at D"Trelna, he left the room.

D'Trelna and the two officers fell in behind L'Guan, footsteps echoing in time down the long gray passageways of the Tower.

"Spaceport," said the cabdriver.

L'Wrona looked up from his notes. The lights of K'Ronarport filled the right window. "Drop me at facility thirty-eight, please."

The cabbie's eyes flicked to the passenger monitor, reassessing his fare. Facility 38 was the private docking area, reserved for the space yachts. Only the heads of industrial combines and the wealthiest members of the old aristocracy could afford even the smallest of starships and their upkeep. A Fleet captain's annual pay would cover about a quarter of the monthly maintenance fee on a one-man flitter.

"You own or just leasing, sir?" said the driver, bringing the craft in on the roof of facility 38.

"Own," said the captain, putting away his notes. "What happened to the lights?" he asked as they settled with a whining of n-gravs. Facility 38 was never busy, but before the war the entryway had always been brightly lit. Now only a solitary light shone, far in the distance near the lift.

"Some crazy idea during the war," said the cabbie, gunning L'Wrona's chit through the meter. The fare duly processed, the passenger bubble swung open. "Cut all the rooftop lights in case of a S'Cotar raid—as if anything could get past Line." He handed back the chit. "Safe trip, Captain."

"Thank you. Good night."

It started to rain as L'Wrona began the long walk across the rooftop—rain from the violent sort of fast-moving storm that swept in from the desert. Lightning and thunder flashed and boomed around L'Wrona as he hurried through the sudden sheets of rain, using the brief illumination of the lightning to search the shadows. The rooftop to either side was a maze of ventilator shafts and instrument arrays vaguely perceptible as low, hazy humps.

This place is a Tugayee's delight, thought the captain, jogging for the lift.

The next lightning bolt was seconded by a much smaller but well-aimed bolt that snapped just over L'Wrona's head, sending him diving for the cover of an instrument pod as two more weapons flashed, fusion bolts knifing through where the captain had just been.

Two ahead, one to the left, he recalled,

low-crawling from the pod to a ventilator shaft. Listening intently, he first heard only the sound of his own breathing and the dying thunder as the storm moved back out into the desert. Then he heard the birdcalls—low but distinct, one chirp answering another from three different directions.

Tugayee, thought L'Wrona. Assassins' guild journeymen, trained from birth and screened through long years of deadly assignments.

A capable officer and a crack shot, L'Wrona was no match for three of the Confederation's most adept killers. He realized that, even as the chirps ended and the Tugayee closed in, his position fixed.

Hunching cold and frightened on the rooftop, L'Wrona did something no margrave had done for centuries: pressed the hidden switch beneath his sidearm's grips and pulled forward the trigger guard. The coat of arms set in the grips—crossed sword over spaceship, rampant—glowed softly in response.

"*Torgan*," said L'Wrona softly, weapon to his mouth. "*Astan holga shakar.*"

Responding to the old High K'Ronarin, the weapon rose, hovered over the ventilator for a second like a scenting hound, then was gone, leaving L'Wrona pressed against the shaft, armed only with a boot knife and a deep faith in the lost technology that had forged his pistol.

Two blasters fired almost together, somewhere off in the darkness, then a brief silence followed by the shrill and explosion of one more shot, this time nearer.

Something dark dropped from the top of the ventilator housing, landing a few feet in front of L'Wrona—a slight figure swathed in black from head to toe, only a pair of wary eyes exposed. "Drop the blade," she said with a slight flick of her blaster. It was an M59A—a section leader's model, L'Wrona noted, dropping his knife—a top line infantry weapon supposedly in the hands of only the Fleet Commando.

"I don't know how," said the muffled voice, "but you got S'Ti and M'Tra—so you'll go slow, from the bottom up."

She twisted the M59A's muzzle, converting the device from a weapon to a precision cutting torch.

"Who hired you?" said L'Wrona as the Tugayee aimed the weapon at his groin.

Before she could do or say anything, the captain's blaster appeared around the corner of an instrument cluster and blew the top half of the assassin's head away, returning to his grip as she fell.

The heraldic device in the grips blinked twice—all clear—then, after a brief pause, the trigger guard closed.

L'Wrona took a deep breath and looked up. The storm was gone, the air smelled sweet and new and he could see the stars. Turning, he walked quickly to the lift.

4

TWO SMALL SPECKS of brightness against a great black sphere, *Repulse* and *Dawn* matched speed with the AI battleglobe, maintaining position between it and Terra.

"Big," said Captain P'Qal, looking at the image of the battleglobe filling his main screen.

"Big?" said S'Tat, looking at the captain. "It's a monster! Give me ten of those things and I'll break through Line and storm K'Ronar."

"Why hasn't it fired yet?" said Captain S'Yatan, face small but distinct in P'Qal's commscreen.

"Maybe they don't have anything small enough to stop us with," said P'Qal wryly.

"Let's play this out, Number One," he continued, turning to the first officer. "By the book. Challenge and stand by all weapons."

S'Tat nodded and turned to her console. "Confederation cruiser *Repulse* to unknown vessel. Identify and prepare to be boarded."

Silence, then a burst of static as the main screen flickered. The image of the battleglobe vanished, replaced by that of a smiling young man in brown K'Ronarin duty uniform, commander's pips on his collar. "You did say board, Commander?"

"Identify," said S'Tat tightly.

The man shrugged. "Sure. Commander T'Lei K'Raoda, attached AI battleglobe *Devastator* under the command of Colonel R'Gal, K'Ronarin Fleet Counterintelligence Corps, with other indigenous personnel as prize crew."

P'Qal was out of the command chair, staring incredulously at the screen. "You're telling us you took that mother, Commander? Captured that thing?"

"Yes, sir."

"And your previous ship?" said the captain.

"L'Aal-class cruiser *Implacable* under Captain His Excellency H'Nar L'Wrona."

P'Qal sat back down. "What the seven hells is going on here, K'Raoda? *Implacable*'s corsair-listed—shoot-without-challenge. And where's your commodore, D'Trelna, who now owes me 432,581 credits, including accrued interest, from a b'kana game on S'Htar?"

"You know the commodore, sir?" said K'Raoda.

P'Qal nodded. "Shipped together as merchanteers for a few years. And we were in the same reserve unit on S'Htar, before the war."

"What about our skipcomm relay?" said S'Tat. "Taking a little target practice with your new toy?"

"We thought it best to talk with you before you sounded invasion alert," said K'Raoda. "Both the AIs and Fleet are after us."

"We are Fleet," grumbled P'Qal.

"I know, sir. Please come aboard." K'Raoda glanced offscan. "Vector in on homer frequency AA1Red. You can land on n-gravs right next to the operations tower."

"We'll be logging that as a boarding, of course," said P'Qal.

"Of course, sir," said K'Raoda. "You'll be just in time for dinner."

S'Rel spoke into his communicator. "R'Gal is on board?"

"In command," said the voice. "It's a battleglobe, all right—*Devastator*—Binor's flagship."

"His no longer, it seems," said S'Rel. "Get us a shuttle up there. Now. I'm at CIA headquarters. Have New York clear it through Washington—set down on the roof. And bring everyone in our unit. I think we may be going home."

Pocketing his communicator, S'Rel turned to find Sutherland staring at him across the desk. "Just what are you, S'Rel?" said the CIA director quietly, fingertips templed before his chin. "AI battleglobes have been seen only once in this galactic epoch—a mercifully brief appearance. Almost nothing's known about them, yet one shows up after lunch on a warm August day and you're familiar with its command history."

"Fleet doesn't tell all its secrets, Bill," said S'Rel with a shrug. "No government does, as you well know."

"Bullshit, buddy," said Sutherland, standing. "While you were supervising the cleanup of our Amazon village, I took two squads on a last sweep of the area. Just for the hell of it, I decided to have another look at that anaconda. And guess what? It must have just been killed before I shot it—crushed. What I saw and reacted to were its death throes."

"So?" said the K'Ronarin.

"So what are you, S'Rel?" continued Sutherland calmly. "Not human, certainly. Not a S'Cotar or the alarms would be ringing. That leaves only one known possibility."

S'Rel leaped the desk—an effortless, standing broad jump, done with only a slight flexing of the knees, the landing soft and silent. "An AI, right, Bill?" he said as Sutherland pressed against the glass wall, face as white as the ceiling tiles.

"God deliver us from monsters," whispered the CIA director.

Laughing, S'Rel stepped back a pace. "You're a paunchy, middle-aged bureaucrat, Sutherland," he said. "But you have style and you have guts." He held out his hand. "Welcome to the Revolt."

"Well, we've boarded her," said S'Tat as *Repulse* settled onto the steel surface of the battleglobe. Two miles long and of proportional length and breadth, the K'Ronarin ship was just another machine on the bleak, airless surface of the machine fortress: fusion batteries with cannon half the cruiser's length, ugly black snouts pointing toward the shimmering blue of the shield; instrument pods and the domes of missile turrets, the largest of them the height of *Repulse*, interspacing the fusion batteries in row after serried row all the way to the horizon.

"Nice place," said Captain P'Qal, watching the outside scan move across the bridge's main screen. "That, I gather, is the operations tower," he said, as the scan stopped, holding on the great black structure dwarfing the hull structures. Square and windowless, it seemed almost to touch the shield.

"What's that on the top?" said S'Tat, frowning as she zoomed the scan. A stiff duraplast flag leaped into focus—silver and black, with a single golden dagger lying horizontally in its middle. "That looks familiar," she said uncertainly.

"It's the battle flag of our Confederation," said P'Qal. "Find out if they're sending someone to get us, or if we have to walk. And tell S'Yatan to maintain position."

They sent someone to get them: K'Raoda. He arrived in a transit tube that extended its serpentine self from the sheer wall of the tower to the cruiser's emergency bridge access. "Sorry about this," he said, leading P'Qal and S'Yatan through the luminescent green tube. "There're selective atmospheric controls, but they took hits in the fighting —we've been busy repairing the fusion batteries and power leads."

P'Qal shook his head, not sure which had impressed him more about K'Raoda—the boyish features and easy grin or the crimson-hung silver Valor Medal around the Commander's neck. The captain shook his head. "Amazing."

A few moments later they entered the tower and began trudging up a broad circular ramp, passing men and women in K'Ronarin uniform who nodded hastily and hurried by, distracted, or ignored the newcomers, intent on battle repairs.

Every level bore signs of recent combat: walls and floors gouged by the black gashes of blaster hits, shattered instrument alcoves, and here and there, missed in the hurried clean-up, the shattered remains of what must have been complex mobile machinery—AIs? wondered P'Qal. He was about to ask when they topped the ramp and reached the heart of the battleglobe, the bridge of the operations tower.

The armored double doors that had once guarded the bridge were all but gone—a perfectly symmetrical hole having devoured most of the battlesteel. "Glad we missed this fight, Number One," said P'Qal as they followed K'Raoda through the blast hole and onto a walkway that circled the bridge.

They stood looking out over a great round room, consoles everywhere, rimmed by armor glass with a view of the bleak surface of the battleglobe and *Repulse*, nestled between those massive fusion batteries. About fifty crew manned the consoles, P'Qal guessed. He leaned over the railing for a better look.

"Wouldn't do that if I were you, Captain," said a new voice. "It's pretty weak in places."

P'Qal stepped back and turned toward the speaker. Wiry-framed, about forty-five, with a receding hairline and dark, intelligent eyes, a man wearing the insignia of a colonel of Fleet Counterintelligence stepped down from the access ladder to the left of the doorway. "Welcome to *Devastator*, Captain, Commander. My name's R'Gal."

* * *

P'Qal's communicator beeped. "Yes?" he said, rising from his chair and moving back a few meters.

"There's a Fleet omega-class shuttle coming toward you from Terra," reported Captain S'Yatan. "IDs as Embassy craft."

"We're expecting it," said P'Qal. "Perhaps we can have a real conversation when it gets here—we've been sipping t'ata and listening to Colonel R'Gal's anecdotes since we arrived." He glanced at R'Gal, chatting quietly with S'Tat. High and musical, the laugh rang faintly from the steel walls of R'Gal's quarters.

"Everything all right?" said S'Yatan.

"Knives at our throats and tinglers on our gonads," said P'Qal.

"Very well. Will check back as arranged."

P'Qal pocketed his communicator and returned to his chair. "Shuttle coming in from Terra," he said as R'Gal and S'Tat looked at him. "Maybe then you'll tell us what you're doing here. If not . . ."

R'Gal held up a hand. "I know. You'll have to arrest us all and take our vessel in tow." He said it straight-faced. "Be assured, Captain, we're not here to see Ginza at night.

"More t'ata, Commander?"

Designed and built by AIs, the only facilities for humans on board *Devastator* were as prisoners, eighteen levels beneath the operations tower. The sleeping quarters were small and the bathrooms smaller. The lavatory sinks had no plugs and gave only reluctantly of a small flow of tepid water, something John cursed each time he tried to shave, as he was doing now.

"Pssst. Harrison."

But for the invention of the safety razor, John would probably have slit his own throat. The appearance of a six-foot, four legged green insectoid behind one in the bathroom tends to evoke a violent response. As it was, the Terran shrieked and whirled, razor *en garde.*

"You look absurd," said Guan-Sharick. "A hairy, towel-clad primate threatening a teleki-netic lifeform with a foam-tipped shaver." The insectoid's form shimmered and vanished, replaced by that of a jumpsuit-clad blonde, seated on the toilet. "That better?" said Guan-Sharick.

John glared at the transmute. "I thought you went with *Implacable* when we parted, back in the Ghost Quadrant."

"Guess again," said the blonde.

"And why the green bug display? I thought it was finally resolved that you were human?"

"I don't think it was ever said that I was human," said Guan-Sharick. "What was was that I'm not a biofab."

The Terran gestured imperiously with the razor. "Out."

They stepped into the living quarters. Cutting torches and some clever use of available materials had converted five small cells into a reasonably commodious, sparsely furnished two-room suite.

"The lovely Zahava not at home?" said the transmute, peering through the doorway into the living room.

"No," said John, reaching for his pants. "Do you mind?"

"Idiocy," said the blonde, turning away from him.

"Okay," said Harrison after a moment, tucking in his shirt. "What do you want?"

The blonde turned. "You know we've entered the Terran system?"

"So? We're not landing."

"R'Gal needs the cooperation of the insystem commander to access the portal to the AI universe."

John nodded.

"I'm confident he'll get it, one way or the other," said the transmute, sitting down on the double bed. "Then this ship has to go through an intervening universe to reach the AI empire."

"So what?" said the Terran. "It's just a matter of recalibrating the portal device and proceeding on to our objective—isn't it?" he added, as the blonde shook her head.

"At that point, the portal device will have exhausted its potential," said Guan-Sharick.

55

"It will require recharging from the available resources of that intervening universe. Specifically, at least one ton of plutonium 239."

"That's a weapons-grade isotope," said John, sinking into the room's sole armchair. "The alternate Terra, Terra Two, is a technological backwater—they're still suffering the effects of World War II. There's only a limited nuclear arsenal, most of it in German hands."

"Not anymore," said Guan-Sharick. "Since you were last there, the American urban guerrillas—the gangers—have begun creating an arsenal of nuclear weapons in the Colorado Rockies. At the moment, they have more plutonium than they have bombs, thanks to years of pilfering from German nuclear plants. They have, in fact, about half a ton. The Fourth Reich has about another half a ton, exclusive of deployed weapons." The blue-green eyes looked toward the ceiling. "This mission requires someone who can obtain both stockpiles for its use."

John was on his feet. "No one is sending me back to that hellhole again!"

"Nothing like the last time," said the transmute, holding up a slender hand. "Just obtain a consensus . . ."

"Between the gangers and the Reich?!"

". . . and we can get on with the mission."

"Why are you telling me this and not R'Gal?"

"R'Gal has other problems at the moment.

56

And you leave as soon as we enter the universe of Terra Two—courtesy of me."

Guan-Sharick was gone, only to reappear an instant later. "You and Zahava might want to go to the bridge. An old friend of yours just arrived.

"See you."

5

"SIT," ORDERED THE admiral.

D'Trelna sat.

They were in the commandant's office, high atop the Tower, with a view of the cityscape at night through the armorglass. Admiral L'Guan took the commandant's chair, behind the big traq-wood desk. "Why the hell did you come back?" he demanded. "Didn't you know *Implacable* had been declared a corsair vessel?"

"Sir," said D'Trelna, "I came back hoping to expose . . ."

L'Guan held up a hand. "I think I know most of what you want to say. Admiral S'Gan's report of your expedition into Quadrant Blue Nine was received, along with reports detailing the treachery of Combine T'Lan, the demise of the corsair K'Tran and your and the mindslavers' defeat of the AI vanguard." He ticked them off on his fingers. "Once received, these reports were suppressed by treasonous officers within FleetOps—human officers in the pay of Combine T'Lan. Said officers will soon be fighting for their lives beside the former occupant of this office."

Smart money says they'll lose, thought D'Trelna.

"A duplicate copy of S'Gan's report found its way to my office, but too late to prevent *Implacable* from being corsair-listed by those same officers.

"The Council is in disarray, the only strong member being the chair, D'Assan. I believe him to be in the pay of the AIs of Combine T'Lan."

"Worse," said the commodore. "He loves, worships and reveres them."

L'Guan snorted. "Fool. He'll be the first to go if they win.

"Fleet," he continued, "is scattered throughout the Confederation on urgent missions of relief and rescue. The S'Cotar occupation left us with half a hundred crippled planets, populated by the brainwiped survivors of slave-labor factories. Crops disrupted, transport scattered or destroyed. I have a handful of effective ships in home system and am sure of the loyalty of only one FleetOps officer." L'Guan touched his breast. "Of course, all these cares may be taken from me—D'Assan's moving to have me replaced or sent up to Line as duty officer."

"An honorable position," said D'Trelna.

"More an honorary one, designed for fractious senior officers nearing retirement. One may not tell Line what to do, only advise it—not the most fulfilling duty for someone who's been commanding starships much of his life.

"Anyway," continued the admiral, "the Council's meeting all night on my fate. It should be resolved by dawn." He looked out the window. The first hint of dawn could be seen, outlining the rough hills of the western desert.

He turned back to D'Trelna. "S'Gan's final report said you were going to try to take an AI battleglobe. Did you?"

D'Trelna nodded. "Yes, sir. It's on its way to the AI Empire, on an urgent mission of confusion and destruction. R'Gal thinks he can foment a revolt."

"Luck to him—if he even gets there. As for us, your report said we're about to be attacked by some ten thousand battleglobes. What's between them and here?"

"In Quadrant Blue Nine we were able to enlist the cooperation of a flotilla of mindslavers . . ."

The admiral shook his head. "I know—it was in the report—horrors out of the Empire's darkest past. Part human, part machine, totally mad. They hate us, D'Trelna.

They'll turn on us at the first opportunity."

"Yes, sir. They hate us, they fear us, but they hate and fear the AIs more. The mindslavers will try to hold the Rift for us until reinforcements arrive."

"Reinforcements?" said L'Guan. "I thought I explained—our tactical situation is hopeless."

"The Twelfth Fleet of the House of S'Yal," said the commodore.

There was long silence in the room, broken by a sigh from L'Guan. "Others have done what you're doing, D'Trelna," he said, "and under similar pressures—the Confederation's dissolving around us like a sand fort and you're seeking refuge in Imperial mysticism." He hurried on before the commodore could protest.

"Every kid knows that wildtale—a mythical fleet from the height of the Empire, trapped in some sort of jump stasis."

D'Trelna shook his head. "Not mythical, sir. The Twelfth Fleet and its loss are duly recorded in Archives. Supposedly a means of recalling the fleet was devised but never implemented—it lies buried with S'Yal, somewhere on this planet."

"And you propose to find it after—what? —ten thousand years?"

"Closer to fifteen thousand, Admiral. And not me—H'Nar L'Wrona. It's in S'Yal's last citadel."

"Last citadel. Lost fleet." L'Guan shook his

head. "Lost, D'Trelna—lost is the operative word." He looked past the commodore, out on the lights of man's first city in the galaxy. "Quadrants revolting, bioengineers loosing monsters upon us, the Empire falling, planets torched like diseased fruit, but through it all—a hundred thousand years. Commodore —civilization survived. A civilization that's dying on our watch, D'Trelna," he said softly. The admiral looked up, as if expecting to see AI assault ships descending through night.

"We're not finished yet," said D'Trelna. "If anyone can . . ."

Both men turned, startled by the muted sound of blaster fire echoing through ancient stone.

The thick wooden doors slammed open and a commando major hurried in, big M32 blastrifle on his hip. Behind him, a squad of commandos reinforced the two troopers guarding the door, taking up firing positions along the corridor.

"Report," ordered L'Guan as the commando officer saluted, left hand to the weapon's comb.

"Tugayee have infiltrated the Tower and are fighting their way to this level."

The admiral showed no surprise at the news. "And our gray-uniformed friends?"

"The Tower garrison withdrew shortly before the attack on direct orders of FleetOps."

The blaster fire was drawing nearer, the

shrilling of the weapons now audible above the explosions. "Can you hold?" asked L'Guan.

The major shook his head. "Not without reinforcements—every assassin in the quadrant must be in on this. And they've slapped a commdamper on the building—static on all frequencies."

"Take your men and fight your way clear, Major I'Tan," said L'Guan, ignoring the commando's startled look. "Return to base. You shouldn't have much trouble—it's me they want."

"But, Admiral . . ." protested the major.

"I'll be all right. Get going."

"Sir," saluted the major.

"By the way, sir," added the commando as the admiral returned his salute, "last word before the attack was that you've been assigned Line duty officer."

"Joy," murmured L'Guan as the major stepped into the corridor.

"D'Trelna," continued the admiral, turning to the commodore. "I'm sorry you're . . ." A movement in the hallway caught his eye. "Hostiles!" he shouted, diving behind the desk.

Feet to the side of the desk, D'Trelna pushed himself backward onto the rug as blaster bolts flashed into the office, snapping over the desk and blowing away half of a glass wall.

The hallway exploded with blaster fire as

the commandos exchanged fire with four black-clad figures appearing at the far end. The firefight was over in seconds, with each badly outgunned Tugayee torn by half a dozen well-aimed bolts.

Hand to a chairarm, D'Trelna was still pulling himself to his feet as L'Guan rounded the desk and moved into the hallway.

"More coming up the south stair, sir," said Major I'Tan, communicator in hand. A blaster bolt had grazed his cheek, leaving a neatly cauterized scar. "The lift is out."

"Please withdraw, Major," said the admiral, looking at the corridor. Before the firefight a series of tapestries had hung along the walls —a triptych of a prespace battle scene: v'arx-mounted riders, clad in armor, battling in some rocky mountain pass. Brilliantly executed—the animals' nostrils flaring in fear, the shouting, the screaming and the clash of metal all but audible—the tapestries now hung in flaming ribbons from the blaster-scorched wall. "This old place's taken enough abuse."

"As the admiral orders," said I'Tan. He spoke quickly into his communicator, then caught the squad leader's eye and nodded. Moving quickly down the hallway, the squad passed the dead assassins and turned left, disappearing toward the north stairway.

"Luck, Admiral," said the major, and was gone.

"If the admiral is sacrificing us to save the

antiques," said D'Trelna as they reentered the commandant's office.

"I am not sacrificing anyone," said L'Guan, swinging the doors shut, locking them.

". . . then please count me out," continued D'Trelna as L'Guan faced him.

"How long have you known me, D'Trelna?" said the admiral.

"On and off? Almost twenty years. You were sector commodore in blue four, keeping the jump lanes safe for merchanters, pulling smuggler intercepts."

A traditional S'Htarian merchant, D'Trelna had never troubled himself with legal niceties. Smuggler or merchant—it depended on what you were selling, when, where and to whom.

"And in that length of time, have you ever . . . ever . . . known me to choose the grand gesture over the practical maneuver?"

The commodore thought about it for a moment. "No," he said finally.

"Thank you." L'Guan unclipped a communicator from his belt. "Remember that during the next few moments." He spoke a frequency setting D'Trelna had never heard, waited for the acknowledging beep, then spoke again. "I urgently need transport for two to your location," he said into the communicator.

"Yes, I know," said a voice over the communicator—a maddeningly familiar voice D'Trelna couldn't quite place.

"How soon?" asked the Admiral.

"A few moments."

There was a soft *snick* on the other side of the door. L'Guan looked quizzically at D'Trelna. "Mark 17 blastpak," said the commodore. "Detonator's a forty-count."

"We don't have a few moments," said L'Guan into the communicator.

"I am doing the best I can," said the voice. "Some of these systems haven't been used since forests covered K'Ronar."

L'Guan rummaged the commandant's desk. Finding what he sought, he tossed it to D'Trelna. Deftly, the commodore caught the M11A, checked the chargepak, then pressed himself against the wall to the left of the doorway. Moving quickly, L'Guan followed, positioning himself on the other side of the doors.

A sudden *whoomp!* and the fragments of stout timbers older than Rome were knifing through the office, followed at once by the assault—three silent black forms that swept into the room.

D'Trelna whistled as they passed, killing the first Tugayee as he turned and the second as she fired. Aimed by a dead hand, the woman's bolt exploded into the wall to the right of the commodore's head, sending a shower of needle-sharp fragments into his cheek.

Hand to his face, eyes tearing at the sudden pain, D'Trelna was dimly aware of L'Guan over the body of the third assassin, tugging at the man's equipment belt. As the commodore wiped his eyes and faced the doorway, L'Guan rose and stepped into the doorway, a perfect target, tossed what he held in his hand, then ducked back as the blaster fire came.

The explosion ripped down the corridor, sending a brief tongue of blue flame lancing into the shattered office.

The blast was still ringing through the corridor as L'Guan and D'Trelna stepped into the doorway, pistols held two-handed.

All that moved were the flames, licking away at the few pieces of furniture, the remains of the long swath of hand-loomed rug that had led from the lift, and a dozen or so black-clad bodies, lying dead where the grenade had tossed them.

L'Guan and D'Trelna slowly lowered their M11As. "Not bad for two out-of-shape chair jocks," said the admiral.

"Could have used you on board a mindslaver we tangled with, Admiral," said D'Trelna.

L'Guan holstered his sidearm and lifted the communicator. "If you can't pick us up now, don't bother," he said.

There was no reply.

"Shouldn't we get to the roof while we can?" said the commodore.

"It's not that sort of pickup," said L'Guan. "We're . . ."

D'Trelna didn't hear the rest, opening fire at

the first black figure to appear around the distant corner of the corridor. He and the admiral ducked back into the room as the blaster fire resumed.

"What sort of pickup is it?" asked the commodore, risking a quick one-two shot down the hallway.

"This sort," said the admiral, standing beside D'Trelna in a pleasant indoor garden. Tropical flora was all around. To their left a miniature waterfall tumbled to an azure-blue pool. "Come on upstairs and I'll buy you a drink," said the admiral.

"Imperial science," said D'Trelna, stomach churning. "Matter transporter. And just where the hell are we?" he demanded, looking up. Bright-plumaged birds flitted from treetop to treetop.

"The heart of the Empire's deadliest war machine," said L'Guan. "This is Line."

"Excuse me, Admiral," said the voice D'Trelna now recognized as that of Line—it seemed to come from a clump of ferns. "Would you please follow the guide sphere to command Center at once." A small orange sphere materialized between the two men and the waterfall, hovering at eye level.

"Something wrong?" said L'Guan, looking at the fern clump.

"FleetOps has just issued a condition two alert—persons or entities unknown are stealing the cruiser *Implacable*."

6

THERE WAS A surprise waiting for *Implacable*'s engineer when they put him in detention.

"Welcome aboard, Mr. N'Trol," said B'Tul. The big gunner stood beside one of the twenty bunks lining the long narrow detention bay. Others of *Implacable*'s crew came to join the reception.

"Shit," said N'Trol as the door hissed shut behind him. "Got us all, did they?"

"This is our mustering-out room," said B'Tul. "They haven't gotten around to issuing discharges yet."

"And we're not holding our breath, sir," said one of N'Trol's engineering techs, S'Kal.

"Where'd they take the commodore and the

captain?" asked B'Tul, handing N'Trol a cup of t'ata.

"Thank you," said N'Trol, sipping the steaming brown beverage. "The commodore and I were separated upon arrival. The captain invoked the Covenant and was not arrested. He was on the ship when we left."

"The captain bluffed his way free?" said B'Tul disbelievingly.

"No," said N'Trol, sitting on the edge of one of the hard duraplast beds. "He enjoys the protection of the Covenant between the Confederation and the Imperial House."

"That grants immunity only to the direct descendants of the Imperial House," said S'Kal.

Hunching forward on the bed, N'Trol sipped the t'ata, holding the chipped cup in both hands. "Absent an Heir," he said, "H'Nar L'Wrona, Hereditary Lord Captain of the Imperial Guard, Margrave of U'Tria, Defender of the Galactic Marches, Hereditary Viceroy of the Blue and Red, is Pretender to Throne and Crown." He made a face. "This t'ata's awful, Gunney."

"Well, look who's here," said a sarcastic voice.

N'Trol looked up, then stood. "A'Tir," he said carefully.

The corsair stood at the foot of the bed, a red-bearded man beside her. "K'Lal," said

N'Trol. "I see your ugly selves are still alive."

The corsairs wore the same brown Fleet duty uniforms as *Implacable*'s crew, but with all insignia gone—ripped off by Fleet Security.

"I thought we agreed," said B'Tul, stepping forward, "that you and your lot would stay at your end." He nodded his head to the left, where a thin but clear line of white had been crudely drawn across the stone blocks.

"Special occasion, Gunney," said A'Tir. She was a slight-figured brunette, neither unattractive nor stunningly beautiful—the sort who'd have blended easily with any crowd of tech officers anywhere in the Fleet. Indeed, she'd begun her career as a Fleet officer.

"So you're going to rot here with the rest of us, N'Trol," said the corsair. "Reaping the rewards of loyalty."

"Perhaps," said N'Trol. "But my lover hasn't been brainstripped by a mindslaver —that is what happened to K'Tran, isn't it, A'Tir? Brain sucked out and popped in a jar, body on ice and all forever. A better sentence than a tribunal could have . . ."

She went for his eyes, but N'Trol was faster, dashing the hot t'ata into her eyes. As A'Tir fell back, screaming in pain, K'Lal stepped toward N'Trol, only to be intercepted by B'Tul and two burly gunner's mates. "Take your lovely little commander back to your area,

71

friend," said the gunner, hand twisting the other's shirt, "before there are any more accidents."

At A'Tir's scream, the rest of the corsairs had come on the run, only to be stopped by a line of *Implacable*'s crew stretched out along the white line. There were only eight corsairs to eighteen Fleet regulars. The rush stopped at the line.

"Come on, Commander," said K'Lal, helping A'Tir to her feet and taking her elbow. She said nothing, merely held her hands over her eyes. "You're dead, N'Trol," she said as they moved away.

The engineer ignored her, watching until A'Tir and K'Lal had crossed to their side of the bay and the two groups had disassembled.

"Just the ten of them?" he asked, picking up the cup.

"In this bay, yes," said B'Tul, eyes still on the retreating corsairs. He turned to the engineer. "Another ten or so in another bay. I think they put us in here hoping we'd kill each other. Which we may do."

"Now what, Mr. N'Trol?" he said.

"Now," said N'Trol, settling back on the bunk, feet crossed, "now we wait, Gunney." He held out the cup. "Who'd like to get me more t'ata?"

A rough hand shook N'Trol awake. "Commander," whispered a voice.

N'Trol sat up, shaking his head. It was the middle of the night—the detention bay was in darkness. "B'Tul?" he whispered sleepily. "What . . ."

"Listen," hissed the gunner.

The officer listened, then heard it, very faintly: the sound of blaster fire.

"Somewhere on the upper levels," said B'Tul. "And the guards are gone."

The thick gray door slid open and the lights came on. As N'Trol and B'Tul turned toward the door, squinting, a tall man in a torn, blood-splotched uniform stepped into the room. "Commander?" he called.

"Here, S'Lei," called A'Tir, leading her group toward the new corsair. A few of *Implacable*'s crew started to block her.

"Let her by," said S'Lei, raising the long-barreled M11A he held and waving it casually.

"Let them go," said N'Trol.

"Report," said A'Tir, walking past N'Trol without a glance.

"Tower's bedlam," said the tall corsair. "Commandos came in, Security pulled out, then Tugayee infiltrated and took on the commandos. Fighting's concentrated on the upper levels."

"How'd you get out?" A'Tir asked.

"There was a running firefight through our confinement level—commandos and Tugayee. An M32 blast took out the door—along with K'Ona and S'Al." S'Lei waved his hand over the bloodstains. "We came down here, found the guard posts deserted and set your security lock to open."

"Where's the rest of your group?" said A'Tir.

"Right behind me. I sent them to liberate an armory."

As he spoke, more corsairs came into the room, all with holstered pistols on their belts and spares slung over their shoulders.

"Orders, Commander?" said K'Lal, taking one of the spare M11As and belting it on.

"We're still in Prime Base perimeter—we'll grab a shuttle from the Tower depot, take over a ship and run for it."

"Line will stop us," said S'Lei.

"No," said A'Tir, arming herself. "Line will challenge us. It won't stop us if we're not a direct and immediate threat to the security of the planet. Which we aren't, as we're leaving it."

A'Tir pointed to where *Implacable*'s crewmen stood in a silent knot. "Kill them and let's go," she said. "The engineer's mine," she added, drawing her sidearm and thumbing the beam down to its cutting setting.

"You're stupid, A'Tir," said N'Trol, stepping in front of his crew. "You haven't enough crew to man a ship that will get you past the Fleet pickets. Most you can run is a destroyer. You need at least a cruiser."

"We'll take our chances," said A'Tir. "Hold

him," she ordered. Two corsairs grabbed N'Trol's arms as A'Tir took careful aim at his eyes.

"With us," said the engineer, "you can have *Implacable.*"

There was a murmur of protest from N'Trol's crew.

"Let him go," said A'Tir, lowering the blaster. "What did you have in mind, Mr. N'Trol?" she said.

"We're in the same situation," said N'Trol, adjusting his cuffs. "Prisoners for whatever reasons. Our mutual interests lie in escape . . ."

"But, sir," protested B'Tul, "to join up with these scum . . ."

"What do you want, B'Tul, to stay here and face court-martial for performing your duty? How many times have we saved the fat asses of the ground-hugging slobs? And this, this is our reward." His hand swept the room. "Freedom"—he pointed to the door—"or the Tower?"

There was a brief, whispered consultation, then B'Tul turned back to N'Trol. "We're with you, sir. As long as they put us off at first planetfall," he added, looking at A'Tir.

"Agreed," said the corsair commander. "Provided we take *Implacable.* Otherwise, you stay here, we'll take up where we just left off, you and me."

"Fine," said N'Trol. He held out his hand.

"Now, if we could have some weapons . . ."

"Not just yet," said A'Tir with a tight little smile.

The distant blaster fire was suddenly punctuated by the dull *KRUMMP!* of an exploding grenade, the echo rolling through the Tower.

"Let's go," said A'Tir.

Filing from the detention bay, the new allies moved in a quick double file down the empty corridors, past the deserted guard posts and out into the night.

Implacable was a grand sight at night, the winking of her red and green running lights reflecting softly along her silver hull. She sat alone in bright-lit splendor, one of the last of the Imperial cruisers.

"Two guards," whispered K'Lal, ducking back behind the white supply modules stacked next to the cruiser. "Corporal and a private."

"That's it?" said A'Tir.

"Yes."

"Sloppy," she said. "Should have two squads for a capital ship, not two men." She turned to N'Trol. "Still want a weapon, Engineer?"

N'Trol saw what was coming. "Not just yet," he said, mimicking her tight little smile. The light wasn't especially good, but she saw it.

"Here." The corsair slipped the commando knife from her boot sheath and wrapped

N'Trol's fingers around the haft. "Take it and go kill those guards. Or we'll do it ourselves and leave your bodies on the duraplast."

"You've persuaded me," he said, slipping off to the left, where the module stacks ended. Snapping shut the weather flap on his holster and slipping the knife blade up his sleeve, N'Trol stepped from behind the stacks and into the light, walking purposefully toward the boarding ramp and the two gray-uniformed sentries.

"Evening," he said as the guards brought their rifles up to order arms.

"Halt," said the corporal. "Who goes?"

N'Trol halted. "Commander N'Trol, Engineer, *Implacable*," he said, gambling that these two hadn't been told about the arrests. It wasn't likely, given Fleet's mania for security.

"Advance and be recognized," said the corporal.

N'Trol closed the distance between himself and the foot of the ramp, stopping an arm's length from the corporal. The sentry was young—a kid, really—almost old enough to shave. "Here to do some tinkering," said N'Trol easily.

The corporal frowned. "Sorry, sir. We've no orders to admit . . ."

N'Trol sucker-kicked him, knee to the groin, then hit him on the chin with the knife pommel as the kid doubled over. The soldier folded silently, crumpling to the landing field.

The private tried to bring the big M32 around, but N'Trol grabbed the weapon's stock with one hand and pressed the knife blade against his throat with the other. "Drop it or die," he said. He'd no idea what he'd do if the other continued to struggle—fortunately, the trooper dropped the M32.

"Turn around," said the engineer.

As the private turned, N'Trol brought the pommel down behind the soldier's right ear. He collapsed as silently as the corporal.

"Well and mercifully done, Mr. N'Trol," A'Tir said as her corsairs charged across the landing field and up into the ship, *Implacable*'s crew following. "You may board."

Last one in but for A'Tir, he'd stopped to look at the distant flames of the Tower and the circling firecraft, when two blaster shots sent him whirling, looking down to where A'Tir stood, holstering her blaster beside the dead sentries.

Gripping the safety rail in white-knuckled fury, N'Trol waited for A'Tir to reach him. If he'd been beside her when she fired, he knew he'd have broken her slim neck. "Why?" he demanded coldly when she appeared, his emotions under control.

"Why?" She smiled. "Why, because you wanted them to live, Engineer. So I wanted them dead. Now check your engines and prepare to lift ship, mister."

7

A HEXAGONAL HONEYCOMB of a building, facility 19 had once held over six hundred starships. But the war had reduced that number
to less than two hundred: Ship after ship had
been deeded to the Confederation to pay the
death taxes of monied officers. Now green
"Available" lights glowed softly over most of
the berths on level 9.

Oblivious to the green lights, L'Wrona
moved quickly down the long empty duralloy
corridor, pistol in hand, looking for berth
9-42-A. He found it after two turnings—one
of only five red-lighted berths in that stretch
of level 9. Standing before the entry, he
pressed the access button.

"Access code, please," said a resonant,
masculine voice.

"There is no code," said L'Wrona.

"Wrong," said the voice.

"Right," said L'Wrona.

The door slid open. "Hello, H'Nar," said the voice.

"Hello, Dad," said the captain. He stepped onto the catwalk, the door sliding shut behind him. Below, nestled in its berth, lay a trim little O'Lan-class scout ship, the subdued lighting of the berth glinting dully along its silver hull.

To the casual observer, the ship would have seemed just another surplus scout, sold off after the A'Ran Police Action of a decade ago. And so it had been, until the previous Margrave of U'Tria, L'Wrona's late father, had gotten his hands on it.

"Green-light the door, would you, Dad?" asked the captain, turning to clamber down the access ladder to the ship. "Got some unfriendlies looking for me."

"You in trouble again, son?" said the ship.

Out in the hallway the red light over 9-42-A changed to green.

L'Wrona walked across the narrow apron of the berth, then scrambled up the ship's boarding ladder. Reaching the top, he grabbed the support bar above the airlock and pulled himself in, feet first. The outer door hissed shut behind him. He stood in the coffin-sized space between inner and outer door—an area equipped with an array of miniaturized scanners that could discreetly explore the contents of a guest's garments, analyze his or her physiology for anything from infectious diseases to narcotics, and, if necessary, dispatch unwanted visitors with a brief needler burst.

There was no needler burst. The inner door opened on to a short, well-lit corridor. "It seems you are H'Nar, H'Nar," said Dad.

"You sound disappointed," said L'Wrona, walking down the corridor to the bridge. On his way he passed an alley-shaped galley on his left, and a bedsitting room on his right. Had he turned left at the hatchway instead of right, he'd have come to the engine room.

"You try sitting on standby for ten years and see how you like it . . . son. I led a robust life—I crave action."

"Action is why you're dead," said L'Wrona, sliding into the left seat. The bridge was small, just the two flight chairs, but crammed with instruments. Fleet compliance inspectors would have been astounded to see that the original gunnery controls not only were intact—a very serious illegality—but had been augmented by the best combat command and information system available. The CCI was a salvaged Imperial model, unmatched since the Fall. When L'Wrona had asked the old man where he'd gotten it, the margrave had merely touched his fingers to his lips and winked.

"You're lucky to still have me, H'Nar," said the ship. "Not every parent would have been so thoughtful."

Twelve years ago, smiling happily, accompanied by a pair of twenty-year-old female companions, the margrave had departed on his annual jaunt aboard one of the jump-equipped cruise liners that catered to the affluent. Done in by too much companionship somewhere off A'Gal IV, the old man had come back in a bodybag—still smiling. Family and Confederation had consigned his body to space with full honors, the guns of the Home Fleet saluting him as he was launched —still smiling—toward galactic north.

Behind him, the margrave had left titles and estates stretching back to the T'Rlon Dynasty and this one heavily modified "pleasurecraft."

Calling up the preflight checklist prompt on the commscreen, L'Wrona was reviewing the jump drive status—green/on-call—when Dad said, "Cleared straight through, son, but with a suspicious delay. K'Ronarport was checking with someone."

"Any idea who?"

"They had me on hold. Not smart—there's a lot of electronic sieve on those circuits. Our controller punched out to a priority line at the Combine T'Lan liaison office. The rest was in code."

There was a barely audible whirring from outside. L'Wrona threw a switch, and what had been a dark band of armorglass was suddenly clear. Outside, the berth doors were cycling open, revealing the stars of a cloudless desert night.

"And away," said L'Wrona, moving the control stalk forward. With a faint whine of n-gravs, *Rich Man's Toy* moved out into the night.

"Control Central orders you to return to berth and await clearance," said Dad as they banked sharply away from the lights of the spaceport.

"Do not acknowledge," said L'Wrona, tying in the CCI, just in case. Outside, the hull suddenly sprouted weapons blisters.

"Tower's on fire," said Dad as they climbed toward Line.

"What?!" L'Wrona checked the rear scan. Flames were leaping from the topmost level of the ancient fortress, a beacon that burned like a sentinel fire over the low skyline of the city. Below and from the west a V-shaped formation flew toward the Tower. Firecraft, advised the tacscan.

"Prime Base has turned out the fireguard," said Dad.

"Looks like the commandant's level," said L'Wrona. "D'Trelna's somewhere in that pile of stone."

L'Wrona hadn't been to the Tower since he was a kid, going with his father to visit an old friend who'd just been appointed Commandant—then a mostly symbolic post for aging aristocrats. There'd been no gray uniforms then, no Imperial Party, no war. He remembered it as a pleasant, musty old place of antique weapons and crenellated battlements built for small boys to leap along, far above oblivion. The future margrave had had a wonderful time jumping and running before his father intercepted him, bade his friend a gracious good-bye, then taken him back to their townhome and administered a fierce paddling.

Toy was too high now for visual, forcing the captain to contend with a relayed pickup from one of the commercial vid stations. The sharp image showed the firecraft form into a single line and come in low, green tinted snuffer gas spewing from the big tanks, then turn for home. Below them, deprived of oxygen, the fire died.

"D'Trelna's the fat one you work for, isn't he?" said Dad.

How did he know that? wondered L'Wrona. Must have been tapping into the vidchannels. "As competent as he is fat," said the captain, automatically laying in the jump coordinates for U'Tria, his mind on other things. The commodore's arrest and removal to the Tower at the same time as a fire in the commandant's suite was too big a coincidence. Dark deeds adoing, he thought as they cleared the atmosphere, and no time to stop. Luck, J'Quel, wherever you are.

"Line challenges," said Dad.

L'Wrona flipped open the commlink.

"Pleasurecraft *Rich Man's Toy* outbound for U'Tria," said L'Wrona.

"Acknowledged, *Rich Man's Toy*," came Line's voice. "You are cleared for jump point." Then, after L'Wrona switched off, it added softly, into the void, "And may fortune grace your sword, My Lord Captain."

"Armaments check," said L'Wrona as they swept through the shield wall, making for jump point at max. "Run the diagnostics now, then once we clear jump point, we'll do a little target practicing out by the J'An Belt."

"Think there'll be trouble?" said Dad.

"Count on it," said the captain.

The FleetOps duty officer was Admiral I'Tal. His hopes for a quiet evening shift had dissolved with the first action report: yet another task force in grave trouble, going up against the corsairs in Quadrant Red Seven. Dispatching what help he could, the admiral shunted all subsequent reports of the growing debacle to a lesser level. Then all hell had broken loose at the Tower, stirred up by L'Guan himself—the commandant relieved, a battalion of commandos sent in, sudden Council orders to withdraw the Tower guard, then fragmented reports of a firefight. FleetOps handled it all with its usual quiet efficiency—except for the Council liaison team, five excitable members of the Imperial Party who ran from monitor to monitor, making a nuisance of themselves.

It was as the firecraft reached the Tower that Admiral I'Tal—indeed, all of FleetOps —had his biggest surprise since the war: computer spoke—something it only did if no other source had detected an emergency. Admiral I'Tal had heard computer speak once, when he was a cadet.

"Alert. Alert." The asexual contralto echoed through the command tiers. "Unauthorized departure. Unauthorized departure. L'Aal-class cruiser *Implacable* is lifting. *Implacable* is lifting."

FleetOps Command center was a big enclosed pit, deep beneath Prime Base. As the warning died, every eye in the room turned to the admiral, way up on the top tier. "Orders, sir?" said Commodore A'Wal to his right. A'Wal had served under Admiral S'Gan—he knew what she'd have done.

"Alert condition two," said I'Tel. "Base defenses to engage *Implacable*, picket squadrons to intercept if she escapes." A chime sounded—three repeating notes—the nearest FleetOps ever came to an alert klaxon. "And request Line's assistance," said the admiral. Not that he expected to get it—Line had its own very narrow priorities.

"She's heading for space," said A'Wal. "Batteries opening fire now."

"Excuse me, Admiral," said a soft voice.

I'Tal turned. Councilor D'Assan stood behind him, flanked by the council observers.

"Please do not engage that vessel," he said softly. "I speak for the Council."

"Why in the seven hells not?" whispered the admiral. "She's ours. She's stolen. She can wipe a planet, conquer a system."

"We've shaken public confidence enough this evening, Admiral," said D'Assan serenely. "To add to the Tower fire a massive shoot-out between Prime Base and that ship, debris raining down, civilian casualties, the vidchannels feeding . . ." He shook his head. "No. Please—have your gunners stand down. You can take her in space."

A'Wal watched as I'Tal thought about it. Up on the screen, the target image was directly over the Base's main defenses.

"Very well," said the admiral, turning to A'Wal. "Batteries to stand down, please, Commodore. Advise Commodore G'Tur that it's all his now."

"They're not firing," said A'Tir, leaning over K'Lal's shoulder.

"Not everyone's a butcher, A'Tir," said N'Trol, coming onto the bridge, a corsair trailing him.

She turned. "Engines and jump drive?" she said.

"Satisfactory." The two faced each other in front of the empty captain's chair. "You can jump—if you make it to jump point."

"I think we can handle the pickets," said

A'Tir, turning to the big board and its tacscan of the inner system. "We'll be well away before they can intercept."

"I wasn't thinking so much of the picket ships," said the engineer as the corsair commander faced him again.

"What, then?"

"Line challenges," called K'Lal.

"That," said N'Trol.

"Shall we consult, Admiral?" said Line.

"As prescribed," said L'Guan as he and D'Trelna entered the combat center.

Combat center was in the heart of Line's command asteroid. Seeing it for the first time, D'Trelna thought it looked more like the office of a top Combine executive than part of a military installation: a spacious, high-ceilinged room, with a desk made in the image of a classically simple-yet-elegant t'ata table; two long, off-white sofas along the wall, a pair of low beverage tables in front of them; a small scattering of armchairs around the desk. The wall behind the desk was a diorama of snowcapped peaks ringing a crystal-blue lake. Imperial Survey tapes, noted D'Trelna. Contemporary techniques weren't as sharp.

"Situation?" said L'Guan, sitting on a sofa, facing the diorama. D'Trelna sank into the other sofa.

"A combined crew of corsairs, under former Commander A'Tir, and Implacablites, under Commander N'Trol, have seized Im-

placable and are approaching my inner sector. FleetOps request that we stop them. They do not specify the method."

"Who's this N'Trol, Commodore?" asked L'Guan, turning to D'Trelna.

Gods, thought D'Trelna. N'Trol? A corsair? Absurd.

"He's *Implacable*'s engineer, Admiral," said D'Trelna. "Highly competent, irreverent, irascible, no lover of authority . . ."

"Would he have turned corsair?"

"No, sir," said D'Trelna firmly. "He hates military structure, he's impatient with anyone slower than himself—mostly everyone—but a corsair? Never. N'Trol fought K'Tran with us off Terra Two—even briefly commanded K'Tran's captured ship, with K'Tran and A'Tir in attendance. He's had far better opportunities than this to betray us. I suspect he's made concessions, hoping to keep his crew alive until they can retake the ship."

"What about Prime Base defenses?" said L'Guan.

"They did not fire, out of political and humanitarian concerns," said Line.

"Mostly the former, I suppose."

"Councilor D'Assan was visiting FleetOps when the decision was made."

"And the pickets?" said L'Guan.

"Fleet units are attempting to intercept, but they have nothing substantial enough between here and jump point to stop a heavy cruiser."

"Will you stop them?" said L'Guan.

"No, Admiral," said Line. "Not unless you convince me that *Implacable* constitutes a direct threat to the security of the planet."

"She's an armed heavy cruiser in the wrong hands," said L'Guan.

"Similar arguments have been made by FleetOps as recently as today and as long ago as the First Dynasty. They are not evocative."

"May I speak with N'Trol?" said D'Trelna.

"Certainly," said Line. The diorama on the wall vanished, replaced by K'Lal's startled face.

"This is Defense Sphere Command," said Line. "Put Commander N'Trol on."

"Speak freely," said A'Tir, drawing her sidearm as N'Trol walked to the engineering station's commscreen. Ignoring her, he stepped into the pickup. "Commander N'Trol," he said, sinking into the padded flight chair. A familiar face appeared in the pickup.

"Quite a mess, N'Trol," said D'Trelna. "What are you and the crew doing with the throat-slitters?"

"A mutually uneasy alliance," said N'Trol. He was aware of someone behind him. An M11A barrel tapped softly against the back of the chairarm.

"And if you do get away, where are you going?" asked the commodore.

N'Trol shrugged. "I don't know what the jump coordinates are—a passionate secret of

A'Tir's. This whole thing's her empty-headed gesture."

The corsair commander stepped into the pickup, standing to the left of the engineer. "Line has made no attempt to stop us, D'Trelna—we're almost in clear space."

Stricken, D'Trelna turned to L'Guan. "Do something, please. My men will be dead the instant those butchers are through with them."

"Don't you think I know that, D'Trelna?" The admiral looked weary and far older than he was. "There's nothing I can do—nothing anyone but Line can do."

"Commander A'Tir." It was Line.

A'Tir's eyes narrowed. "Yes?"

"If we meet again, it will be to your disadvantage," said Line.

"I'm not coming back here alive," said A'Tir, reaching past N'Trol to flick off the commlink. The last thing the two men in the command center saw was N'Trol's wink.

There was a glum silence in the room, broken a few minutes later by Line's announcement: "*Implacable* has jumped."

D'Trelna sat up. "Of course," he muttered.

"Of course what?" asked the admiral.

"N'Trol told us. 'Haven't seen the jump coordinates'—meaning he had. 'Passionate.' 'Empty-headed.' " D'Trelna looked at L'Guan, face set and certain. "A'Tir's gone to rescue K'Tran."

"From a fleet of mindslavers? And rescue

what?" said L'Guan. "The R'Actolians cut K'Tran up—his brain's doing their tactics for them, his body's on ice somewhere in one of those monstrosities—your own report said so."

"True," said D'Trelna. "But the same process that took K'Tran apart can put him together again."

"Still . . ."

The commodore held up a hand. "The power of love, Admiral."

"Love? Those two?" said L'Guan. "K'Tran and A'Tir?"

D'Trelna nodded. "Her, certainly. Him, I don't know."

L'Guan shook his head. "Even the most feral of creatures mate, I suppose." He rose.

"Stand you to a drink, D'Trelna?" he said. "There's a pleasant little bar the other side of that waterfall."

"FleetOps and Councilor D'Assan each desire urgently to confer with you, Admiral," said Line as the two officers left the room.

L'Guan laughed. "One or both of them tried to kill us last night and now they want to confer.

"Tell them the commodore and I are plotting their mutual destruction over brandy. I'll call them when we're through."

8

"FINE," SAID CAPTAIN P'Qal. "Let's say I believe you. You forged an alliance with the mindslavers, stopped the AI vanguard cold out in the Ghost Quadrant and you took this lovely pleasure dome." His hand swept the room. "Let's say I even believe that Combine T'Lan is an AI nest and you two"—his eyes shifted between R'Gal and S'Rel—"represent the heroic immortals who stood against your own kind for honor, truth and justice."

"Ease off, P'Qal," said S'Rel.

"Believing this," continued the captain, "and, for various reasons, I do, why should I give you the portal device? My sense of duty tells me I should turn you around and point you toward K'Ronar." He punched up a t'ata and took another sweetcake from the platter on R'Gal's desk. "With an AI invasion coming through the Rift in the Ghost Quadrant, headed straight at K'Ronar, Fleet needs this ship. It needs to copy its systems and deploy a fleet of these . . . Why are you shaking your head?" he asked R'Gal.

"There's not enough time, materials or expertise to build a single battleglobe, Captain," said the AI. "The weapons systems are hardly miniaturized marvels: to be effective they have to be numerous and mounted on a battleglobe. Only other battleglobes or mindslavers stand a chance against the Fleet of the One."

"What a hideous name," said S'Tat.

"And a misnomer," said S'Rel, turning to her. "It should be called the Fleet of Fear and Hate. Our fascistic brethren have built and maintained a hegemony at fearsome cost. All the enslaved races hate them, and, judging from records on this ship, the brethren are beginning to hate each other. The conservatives hate the liberals, the liberals the conservatives, both hate and fear the underraces. It's Colonel R'Gal's theory that our home realm's a rotten fruit, ready to fall. One ship—this ship—can spark a revolt that will burn out the bad and maybe spare some of the good."

P'Qal had been sipping his t'ata while he

listened. "You haven't been home for a million years, any of you," he said, setting down the cup. "Yet you're so sure of yourselves." He looked at the two AIs. "The only recent arrivals from your universe have been the AIs' infiltrators who became Combine T'Lan. Therefore you have some way of independently confirming information you found on this ship. Probably . . ."

"All right, Captain," said R'Gal. "Let's just say we are sure of ourselves."

P'Qal nodded. "Fine. So you can't save us from fire and blood without the portal device —if you can save us at all. Which brings me to my other objection. There is only one extant alternative-reality linkage device, an Imperial relic, evidently a prototype. Obviously, you'd have to take it with you or you couldn't access your home universe from the intervening reality. With you goes a very impressive bit of technology. I'm loath to release it on such a wild risk."

"New technology will be of no use to us," said K'Raoda, "if we're all dead. And we will be dead if the Fleet of the One isn't stopped."

P'Qal sighed. "You can have it," he said. "I hope you know how to use it with this monster's drive."

"You're a brave man, Captain." R'Gal smiled. "And we do know how to use it."

"You know what they'll do to me if you

don't succeed?" he said, shaking his head. "I'll have S'Yatan release it to you."

"You may have lost your mind, Captain. I haven't lost mine," said S'Yatan, his image sharp in the commscreen. "I'm not releasing that device to anyone but an authorized Fleet detachment—preferably of flotilla strength."

P'Qal's face reddened dangerously. He leaned closer to the pickup. "Don't give me any of your Academy crap about authorizations and illegal orders, Captain," he said. "We have no way to contact Fleet. I am insystem commander. I have made the best decision possible with the available data and have now given you a direct, lawful order. They may court-martial me for releasing that device, but I sure as hell will see you shot for disobeying a direct order in a known combat zone." He leaned back, a short, fat man out of breath.

"I am making for jump point, Captain P'Qal," said S'Yatan icily, features pale but composed. "I will report your dereliction of duty to FleetOps—and my reaction to it. We'll see who faces the wall."

The screen went blank.

"Get him back, Captain," said R'Gal. "We're not going anywhere without that device."

P'Qal searched the unfamiliar console for the retransmit key.

"Don't bother, Captain," said S'Rel, turning from the complink. "I was afraid of this. *Devastator* carried a full liaison packet, with all the data Combine T'Lan had sent home over the years—sabotage plans, strategy, agents. The real S'Yatan was killed and a combat droid substituted during his plebe year. Gentlemen, our enemies have the portal device."

The K'Ronarins under R'Gal and D'Trelna had taken *Devastator*, sensor-scanned for traces of any holdouts in the thousands of miles of corridors honeycombing the battleglobe, then busied themselves with repairs, ignoring the vast reaches of the great ship. Most of *Devastator* remained unexplored.

There was one structure that attracted visitors, even though some distance from the operations tower and the hub of activity—the observatory. It was a comparatively small dome of a building, white in contrast to the battleglobe's endless black and gray, set in a slight depression between the operations tower and the yawning chasm of a hangar portal. A score of screens, all larger than *Implacable*'s main screen, lined the concave sweep of white wall, just above the railed walkway circling the room. Instrument consoles filled the center of the observatory floor. Only one of them was on now, presenting sensor data as a familiar, sharply defined picture.

"So near, yet . . ." said Zahava, looking at the screen.

John stood beside her, also looking at the scan of Earth. Home was a soft swirl of stratocumuli broken by the blue and brown pastels of a surface only an hour away.

"We'll get back there," he said. "After this is over. Go down to the Cape, open up the beach cottage, drink beer . . .

". . . put our feet up on the rail, watch the sunset over the Sound and belch contentedly," finished Zahava.

He looked at her and sighed. "Said that a little too much, have I?"

"No more than twice a watch."

They were an odd contrast, she a dark-skinned, lissome Sephardic Jew with a faint Israeli accent, he a sandy-haired WASP of medium build and a barely discernible New England accent. Ex-Mossad and ex-CIA, they'd married after the Biofab War, then shipped out aboard *Implacable* into Quadrant Blue Nine, battling corsairs, mindslavers, AIs, and helping take *Devastator* from her AI crew. Now they were on board for the final confrontation.

"You really think we'll get out of this alive?" said Zahava, turning to him.

"Talk like that you won't," said a new voice, echoing in through the dome. The two

Terrans turned, hands dropping to their holsters.

"Bill!" they both said, then hurried to greet Sutherland. The CIA director returned Zahava's kiss, then shook John's hand.

"What are you doing aboard this monstrosity?" asked John.

Sutherland shrugged. "S'Rel wanted me up here to gauge their sincerity, or something. A symbol of goodwill, I suppose. This war is long past any Terran government's influence." He glanced up at the board with its image of the planet. "Mostly, though, I came to say good-bye to two homesick friends and to wish you Godspeed."

"How's McShane?" asked John.

"The old codger's well," said Sutherland. "I got a postcard from him last month. Bought a big sailing ketch, hired a crew and took the kids and grandkids off to the South Pacific." Bob McShane, a retired professor, had been with John, Zahava and Sutherland since *Implacable* first reached Terra, playing a decisive role in both the Biofab War and the battle for Terra Two.

"So tell me, how did you acquire this homey ship?" asked Sutherland, leaning against one of the consoles.

"Ask Zahava," said John. "She took it. I just wandered around lost, playing tag with those flying blades the AIs use for security."

Sutherland looked at Zahava.

"We stormed it," said the Israeli. "One assault team infiltrated, took out the shield power, my group came in and stormed the Tower, pulling out the AI gun crews, then D'Trelna brought *Implacable* in and it was all over."

Sutherland snapped his fingers. "Just like that?" he said with a grin.

"Not really," said a new voice.

This time the long-barreled blasters came out of their holsters as Guan-Sharick appeared, standing on the other side of the nearest consoles. The blonde ignored the blasters, looking instead at Sutherland. "They came under fierce blaster fire and nerve gas attack. Zahava's assault force sustained over seventy percent casualties, John and L'Wrona's over ninety-percent. R'Gal was badly wounded. And still they were lucky."

"Long time," said Sutherland softly. "I'd hoped you were dead."

"I'm on the side of the angels now," said the blonde, walking around the console, "or haven't you heard?"

"And I'm a Trotskyite," said the CIA director.

"What I did on Terra," said the transmute, green eyes looking into Sutherland's a meter away, "was necessary. What I did to galactic humanity by instigating the Biofab War was necessary—a vital conditioning exercise." She shook her head, throwing the long golden strands back over the shoulder of her white jumpsuit.

"You wiped out much of galactic humanity," said John. "A lot of people want a piece of you."

The blonde looked at him, a beautiful young face with old, old eyes. "Nothing can be done to me that hasn't already been done, Harrison. Believe me." Her gaze shifted to a blank screen, seeing something the other three couldn't. "To be honest, I don't expect to survive this mad expedition. Death would be a welcome release."

Guan-Sharick looked back at the three Terrans. "S'Yatan, the captain of the *Victory Day*, is an AI," she said briskly. "He's making off with the portal device and will reach jump point before we can overtake him. I can, however, transport two of you and myself to his inhospitable bridge and do battle with the slime. Like that," added the transmute, snapping her fingers.

Sutherland was suddenly alone in the observatory. He stood perfectly still for a moment, then shook his head, lips pursed, and left the room.

On the screen, the image of Terra was just another dim point of light.

9

"CCI WORKS FLAWLESSLY," said Dad as another small asteroid shattered from a red fusion beam.

"Make for final jump point," L'Wrona ordered the computer. The asteroid belt was a well-known target practice area, just off the principal ship path from K'Ronar to U'Tria. Three jump points—those unseen but well-charted points from which a ship could jump most accurately to another specified point —lay behind them, one ahead. It was here the captain expected trouble—even looked forward to it. After ten years of battlecruisers, he was reveling in the immediate response his hands brought from the sleek little ship, the almost forgotten thrill of piloting a one-man scout. Only the lack of his father's voice would have made it more enjoyable. Why ever did he impress his persona on the computer? wondered L'Wrona, not for the first time. Did he really think he was doing me a favor, or did he do it for himself, assuaging some secret guilt about being away so much when I was young?

Just before the war, after an especially long and argumentative trip aboard *Toy*, L'Wrona had consulted a ship's cyberneticist about having his father's persona and voice removed from *Toy*'s computer. The man had glanced at the system specs, then at the programming overlay specs. "Voice is no problem," he'd said. "The personality, though . . ." He'd shaken his head. "Might as well scrap the whole system and start with fresh gear."

"How much?"

The cyberneticist shook his head again. "Can't get a replacement—system specs are unique to this series—start substituting, you're asking for big trouble a long way from home. You'd have to find another O'Lan in private berth, buy it and switch hardware —seeing as how you've made certain modifications." His finger delicately traced the schematic of the CCI interface.

Then the war had started, U'Tria had fallen and L'Wrona had forgotten all about it—until now.

"A ship has just appeared at jump point," said Dad. "ID'd as a nova-class Fleet destroyer."

The projection appeared on the tacscan —the red of the destroyer moving toward the green of *Toy* as it approached the pulsing red circle of the jump point.

"Ship-to-ship," said the computer.

A man's face appeared in the commscreen, the silver starships of a captain on his collar. He was in his middle years, graying at the temples—and he looked most unhappy. He nodded at L'Wrona. "My Lord," he said with a faint nod. "Captain Z'Than, commanding *A'Lan's Hope*. We are ordered by FleetOps to take your ship aboard and return with you to K'Ronar."

L'Wrona's hand tapped the joystick, taking *Toy* off automatic, moving the ship forward at standard. "I invoke the immunity of the Covenant," he said. On the tacscan, the distance between the two ships was quickly shrinking.

"I'm sorry, but they said you'd do that," said Z'Than, "and that it was a procedural matter best decided by a tribunal. As a Line officer, I am merely to bring you in."

A line of text appeared beneath the captain's image, moving slowly across the screen. "H'Nar. He's armed his weapons batteries. Tacscan locking on. Touch your left earlobe if you want me to open fire now, while we still have a chance."

L'Wrona kept his left hand on the chairarm. "Z'Than," said the margrave. "You're from U'Tria, aren't you?"

The captain nodded.

"Do you have a signed order from Fleet ordering my arrest?"

"I have verbal authorization, My Lord." Even in the small pickup, L'Wrona could see the sweat on the other's brow. He and his family had been liegemen of the margrave since before the Fall.

"You can only bring me in with an order signed by the Grand Admiral, or an order signed by the full Council. Do you have either?"

Z'Than shook his head.

"Then get out of my way, sir. As first ship insystem, we have prior navigation rights. You are between us and our jump point."

GODS! H'NAR, JUMP NOW! flashed the screen. DEVIATION WILL BE ONLY .00032. WE CAN MAKE IT UP IN A FEW WEEKS.

"Cut your engines and prepare to be taken in on tractors," said Z'Than. On the tacscan, what little space there was between the two ships was vanishing. L'Wrona could see the destroyer through the armorglass now, a mile-long black hull bristling with weapons turrets and instrument pods. They were within seconds of colliding.

"Too easy," said L'Wrona. Pulling up on the stick, he sent the scout knifing up and over the destroyer's bridge, down along its hull and then off toward jump point, the big tri-tubed engines shrinking in the rearscan.

The destroyer commander's image vanished as the commlink broke. "He's switched off," said Dad as L'Wrona moved the scout up to flank speed. "And he's suspended weapons tracking. You won."

Reaching jump point, L'Wrona engaged the drive, feeling his stomach churn as space twisted in that crazy, familiar way, then it was over—they were in U'Tria system. Home.

Sighing, L'Wrona dropped *Toy*'s speed down to standard.

"Mines!" shouted the computer. "All around!"

Cursing, L'Wrona cut speed, tried to nullify forward thrust, even as an alarm sounded. "Incoming missiles!" warned Dad. "Move and the mines get us, don't move and the missiles get us."

"Missiles from where?" said L'Wrona.

"Two heavily armed commercial vessels." It all came up on the tacscan then: the red of the minefield surrounding the jump point, the incoming red streaks of the shipbusters, the yellow Xs of the two hostiles, and standing well outside the minefield, the small, fragile green of *Toy*.

"Origin of vessels?" said L'Wrona, seeing only one way out.

"ID'd as Combine T'Lan," said Dad.

The missiles penetrated the minefield and were destroyed—as planned. Noiseless, a spectacular wave of overlapping orange-red explosions licked toward the scout, a chain reaction racing from mine to mine.

"Short jump, backside," snapped L'Wrona. *Toy* disappeared as the blast reached her.

"Yes or no?" said the face in the commscreen.

The man wearing the uniform of a Combine merchant captain shrugged. "Maybe yes, maybe no. We think we got him, but the tacscan shows no ship residue. There should be at least some traces of the drive isotopes."

"He may have blind jumped. If so, he's as good as dead," said the other. "Remain on station until you hear from me again, Captain."

"Yes, Goodman T'Lan."

As the Combine captain's image disappeared, T'Lan, neither good nor a man, turned to the other human-adapted AI, one who could and did pass for his son and heir. "That's L'Wrona's home system. He probably jumped, but I doubt it was blind. We'll just have to watch and wait, strike when it shows."

The two stood in the underground command center of one of the Federation's wealthiest industrial combines—a combine created several hundred years ago by beings from another reality, intent on infiltrating and ultimately destroying the Confederation. The big room bustled with activity, coordinating the far-flung merchant fleets and maintaining communications with distant points in this and one other universe.

"One of our units has the humans' only portal device," said the younger T'Lan.

"S'Yatan?" asked T'Lan senior, glancing at the status boards. Everything was on schedule —forward battle units of the Fleet of the One were approaching the Rift, about to penetrate into the K'Ronarins' Quadrant Blue Nine —the Ghost Quadrant.

The other AI nodded.

"He's had it since his ship was assigned to Terra," said T'Lan senior. "His crew's human and loyal. He can kill them but he can't run the ship by himself. And there's always an escort vessel. So . . . ?"

"He's convinced the crew they're fleeing an unlawful order, heading back for K'Ronar. The instant he leaves the Terran system, he can kill his crew, and one of our ships will meet him."

T'Lan senior nodded. "Having that device, we'll use it to bring in a second force, augmenting the one coming through the Rift. Nothing can stop us." A sudden thought gave him pause. "What unlawful order was he fleeing?" he asked, frowning.

The other AI looked at his senior nervously. "You recall Binor's advance force? The one we thought the mindslavers wiped?"

"Thought?"

"It seems that R'Gal, Guan-Sharick and some humans actually captured the flagship. It's at Terra now, and has been granted the device by the insystem commander."

The senior AI was absolutely still for a moment, absorbing the data. "No one," he said finally, "has ever taken a battleglobe. Not in all the long years of the Fleet of the One."

"Shall I alert home?" asked T'Lan junior, nodding toward a console manned by an AI wearing a terminal coupler plugged directly into his temples.

T'Lan senior held up a hand. "Not yet. Not until we've some success to report. That battleglobe can hurt us far worse back home than it can here—which is why R'Gal's trying to take it there."

Toy's jump drive was a creation of the High Imperial epoch. Unlike contemporary starships, the little scout was capable of low-risk, insystem jumps—and had just made one.

L'Wrona looked down on the rugged highlands of the S'Htil, one of the planet's three continents and its commercial hub.

In the old days, before the war, the tacscan would have picked up hundreds of space- and atmospheric craft, coming and going from U'Triaport or traversing the planet. Now the tacscan was empty.

"Set us down in the old s'hlar grove, across the lake from the Hall," said L'Wrona as the ship plunged into the atmosphere, taking a sharp evasive tack against hypothesized missiles.

"Acknowledged," said the computer.

Unchallenged, seemingly undetected, the little ship sat down at dusk in the wooded hills just outside L'Yan, ancestral home of the Margrave of U'Tria. The sere autumn foliage was just catching the last rays of sunset when L'Wrona clambered down *Toy*'s boarding ladder and stepped onto his home soil for the first time in ten long years.

Breathing deeply of the crisp, fresh air, he bent and picked up some leaves and dirt. Rubbing them slowly between his hands, he let them fall back to the forest floor, brushed his hands gently, then made his way toward the faint ruts of the old vehicle trail and the distant village.

10

"HERE WE SIT," said L'Guan, sipping his brandy, "two flag officers without a single ship, aware of enemies within and without, and reduced to the status of observers."

"There are the commtorps," said D'Trelna. The two men sat at a small table on the blue-tiled patio overlooking the waterfall, two glasses and a crystal decanter of S'Tanian brandy between them. Below, the mist from the tumbling water prismed the artificial sunlight into a rainbow.

"What, the ones *Implacable* launched coming in?" asked the admiral.

D'Trelna nodded.

"Line," said L'Guan, "what's the status of those commtorps?"

"All but one is intact, Admiral," said Line, its voice coming from beside the table. "They can be activated only upon signal from *Implacable*, though. Absent *Implacable*, they cannot be utilized."

"Surely the signal could be duped?" said D'Trelna.

"Authentication signals of a L'Aal-class cruiser—indeed, of most Imperial-made battleships—to any of its indiginous equipment is code-based upon the matrix set of jump drive impulses unique to that particular vessel," said Line primly. "The chance of our successfully emulating it during your lifetime, Commodore, is insignificant."

"I had to ask," sighed D'Trelna.

"And what good would it do?" said L'Guan, looking at the Commodore.

D'Trelna's head jerked up, eyes narrowing. "The people would rise," he said, stabbing a thick finger at the admiral. "Fleet would join them, and Combine T'Lan—its bases, its ships, its agents—would disappear overnight. They're large, but they can't hope to stand against an aroused people backed by their military."

"Chaos is what you're describing, Commodore," said the Admiral. "Our ships scattered, our cities burning, fighting in the streets —just as the AI invasion force sweeps in."

"I disagree," said D'Trelna. "But it seems a moot point for now.

"So what do we do?"

"We could wait," said L'Guan, restopping the decanter. "If there is an AI invasion coming, it'll come out of Quadrant Blue Nine. Automatic pickets have been posted at all known jump points leading from there toward the Confederation. When and if they come, we'll know, D'Trelna."

"You know I made a deal with the mindslavers," said the commodore. "They're waiting in Blue Nine, ready to take on the AIs in return for . . ."

"In return for dangerous concessions from us," said L'Guan. "I know. If they can stop the AIs—and we and they survive—those concessions will probably be granted. But chances of that are slim to none."

"So you plan for us to just sit it out, Admiral, safe in the heart of Line?"

L'Guan smiled wryly, shaking his head. "Not even this charming sanctuary will be safe when the Fleet of the One gets here, D'Trelna." He sat looking at the waterfall for a long moment. "An admiral without a fleet and a commodore without a flotilla." He looked back at D'Trelna. "I've always rejected the desperate over the safe. But there are no safe moves left."

"I didn't know we had any moves left," said D'Trelna, staring glumly into the tropical twilight now falling over the jungle glade.

"Let's be thankful we survived today," said

L'Guan, rising. "I'm going to bed. You might do the same."

"Admiral," called D'Trelna.

L'Guan turned.

"Thank you—for getting me out."

L'Guan shrugged. "How many times have you and *Implacable* saved our lives, D'Trelna?"

"You'd have gotten me out if I were a first-year cadet," said the commodore.

"No one gets at my people," said the admiral, shaking his head. "Not if I can stop them. Good night, J'Quel."

"So, Line," said D'Trelna as the admiral disappeared into the tropical twilight, "what do you think our chances are?"

Line spoke after a moment. "The situation is more complex than the admiral cares to believe," it said. "If all factors now in play are resolved in our favor, we will win. If even one of them is not resolved in our favor, we will lose."

"Wouldn't care to say what all those factors are, would you?" said the commodore, reaching for the decanter.

Beside him, the guide sphere vanished and twilight stood suspended. "Certainly," said Line, as D'Trelna poured himself another glass. "One. The captured battleglobe must reach AI space and foment revolt. Two. The Margrave of U'Tria must find S'Yal's last citadel and retrieve the recall device. Three. The last fleet of the House of S'Yal must be recalled from the stasis in which it's snared. Four. Combine T'Lan and all its minions must be destroyed, chaos or not. And five . . ."

"Five?" The commodore frowned, glass almost to his lips.

"Five," said Line. "The Emperor must return."

"You crazy bitch!" shouted N'Trol into the pickup. "You can't keep pushing her this hard—she'll overload, tear herself apart!" Behind him, in engineering, the high-pitched vibration of machinery at the breaking point filled the air.

"You really love this old hulk, don't you, Engineer?" said A'Tir with a vicious little smile. The smile vanished. "Final jump point by watchend or I start spacing your crew." The commscreen went blank.

N'Trol turned to his four engineering techs, standing behind him at the master panel, watching. "You heard her, lads," he said. "Let's do it." Glancing at the armed corsair pacing the catwalk above, he lowered his voice. "Now's our chance to do a little tinkering. Come look at the drive schematics—I'll show you what I mean."

"Line," said D'Trelna, setting down his empty glass. "What do you think of Admiral L'Guan?"

"A classic noble patriot—indeed, almost

classical. He might have stepped out of some High Imperial epoch, battleflags snapping in the breeze behind him. His conduct during the Biofab War was beyond reproach."

"And now?" said the commodore, watching the waterfall.

"I fear," said Line after a moment, "that the admiral has been maneuvered into a position of seeming impotence. Wisely, he plays a waiting game."

"Seeming impotence?"

"The position of Line Duty officer is not quite the empty formality it seems, Commodore," said Line.

"What is it, then?" said D'Trelna.

"It's a potential, Commodore," said Line. "A potential awaiting just the right word."

11

"STANDBY TO JUMP," said S'Yatan, watching the tacscan data thread across *Dawn*'s main screen. *Devastator* hadn't moved, remaining off Terra as though nothing had happened.

L'Nar, the first officer, glanced at his complink. "Jump plotted and set. Engineering reports . . ." He stopped, staring at the small screen. "Captain, the jump coordinates have been changed!"

S'Yatan had turned from the screen. "I know. I changed them," he said.

"But this will take us away from K'Ronar, not toward it," protested L'Nar.

The entire bridge crew was watching, all uneasy at having disobeyed Captain P'Qal, uneasier still at the way the senior officers' conversation was going.

S'Yatan lowered his voice. "I've received special orders regarding this contingency."

"How?" said L'Nar. "*Devastator* took out the skipcomm buoy."

All eyes followed S'Yatan as he walked to where *Dawn*'s first officer stood, beside the tactics station. "You will jump this ship, Mr. L'Nar," he said softly. "Or you will die."

"As soon as you answer my question, Captain," said L'Nar, folding his arms across his chest and looking resolutely into S'Yatan's cold blue eyes—a resolution that changed to shock as the captain's eyes turned a gaze-searing, fiery red.

"Yes, how did you get the message?" said a different voice. Ignoring the sudden shriek of an alarm and the rasp of blasters being drawn, an attractive blonde in a white jumpsuit stepped up to the two officers.

"S'Cotar," said S'Yatan, facing Guan-Sharick. "No wonder they didn't pursue." He turned to his crew who stood blasters leveled at the blonde. "That's a S'Cotar," he said, pointing. "A biofab. Shoot!"

L'Nar's eyes had only briefly left the captain's face. "AI," he said finally, hoarsely. "You're an AI combat droid." He drew his sidearm. "Where's the captain?"

"A long time dead, probably," said Guan-Sharick. Her gaze went from face to face. "As you'd all be killed the instant you made that jump to his waiting ship." A small pistol

118

appeared in the S'Cotar's hand, pointed at S'Yatan. There was a triangular device set in the weapon's grip, a single blue eye set in each corner of it, two black parallel lines in its center.

S'Yatan stared at the weapon, then at the blonde. "Guan-Sharick," he said slowly. The AI shook his head. "Impossible. You're dust—a million years dead. I saw your ship blown apart in the Revolt, a dozen battleglobes reduce it to nothing."

"Time's been good to me, S'Yatan," said Guan-Sharick. "It won't be as good to you."

The alarm stopped its shrieking and the silence deepened as the crew looked on uncertainly, watching the strange tableau. "You call it, Commander L'Nar," said an engineering tech at last, eyes and blaster shifting between S'Yatan and the blonde.

"Reset jump coordinates for K'Ronar," said the first officer.

"Not necessary now," said Guan-Sharick, glancing left as the bridge doors opened, admitting John and Zahava. Crossing the deck, John placed a black, walnut-sized crystal in the blonde's outstretched palm. "Drive nexus," he said.

The crystal vanished, flicked elsewhere by Guan-Sharick. "You'll have to proceed back to Terra and await a replacement," said the S'Cotar.

"A diversion," said S'Yatan to the blonde.

"You were a diversion while your friends pulled my drive nexus!"

He fired, a stream of red bolts flashing from his eyes only to dissipate inches from that perfect blond hair.

Guan-Sharick squeezed the trigger, immobilizing the AI in an invisible field stasis that left S'Yatan a statue in the middle of *Dawn*'s bridge.

"Where is it?" said the blonde, holstering her weapon and turning to L'Nar.

The first officer looked at S'Yatan for an instant, nodded curtly and went to the captain's station. Quickly keying a combination on the complink's touchpad, he watched as a small panel slid open on the console pedestal, then removed a square black cube. "What about him . . . it?" he said, handing the cube to Guan-Sharick.

"Put him somewhere and dust him occasionally," said the S'Cotar, pocketing the portal device. "He's in an irreversible stasis field, perceiving, thinking, but unable to move. Eventually, he'll go mad—in an endlessly looped, robotic way."

L'Nar looked at the AI—S'Yatan stared unblinking at where Guan-Sharick had stood, eyes still red with frozen flame. "How long will he . . . ?"

The blonde looked at the young officer, her eyes blue and distant. "Till the stars wink out, Commander, and all matter's just an ethereal memory." Guan-Sharick smiled wearily. "And a better fate than he deserves.

"Luck to you, Commander L'Nar."

The S'Cotar and the Terrans were gone.

"Come," called A'Tir as the door chimed.

N'Trol stepped into what had been D'Trelna's old office.

"Yes?" said the corsair, looking up as the engineer crossed the carpet.

"We've entered the Ghost Quadrant and are proceeding on course toward the Rift," said N'Trol, stopping in front of the big traq desk and the deceptively small woman.

"So?" said A'Tir, returning to the desk's complink and the ship's status report. "You think I need a progress report from you to know where we are?" She looked toward the door, frowning. "Where's your escort?"

"Vigilantly guarding my cabin door," said N'Trol. "I used the ventilation and light conduits."

A'Tir pressed a commkey. "K'Lana, two crewmen to my quarters, please. They're to remain outside unless called."

She switched off at the acknowledgement.

"What do you want, N'Trol?" said the corsair, leaning back in the big chair.

"May I?" He jerked his head toward the sofa.

A'Tir shrugged.

"You've cleared last jump point," said

N'Trol, sitting. "You're within sublight of some of the Empire's lost colonies—D'Lin, notably. You can gang-draft people there, run them through forced training. So even if you don't rescue K'Tran or anyone else, you can still crew this ship. I think you'd rather chance the inconvenience of impressing and training a bunch of groundies than risk our hatred just for our experience. Am I right?"

The corsair looked at N'Trol with new eyes, silent for a moment. "I keep underestimating you, Engineer. I used to think you were a brilliant, misanthropic technical officer. Yet you've held your men together, and now you've anticipated me."

She nodded. "Yes, I don't need you or your crew anymore. You're all going to take a short jump into hard vacuum at first watch."

N'Trol's face betrayed nothing. "I have a deal for you, Commander A'Tir," he said.

"Dead men don't deal, N'Trol," she said, reaching for the door switch.

N'Trol moved quickly, reaching across the desk to stop her hand as it touched the switch. "Spare my crew, and I'll get K'Tran back for you."

A'Tir looked at the blunt, competent fingers circling her wrist. "You have nice hands, Engineer," she said, brown eyes meeting his green ones. "Can you do something with them besides fix jump drives?"

"What did you have in mind?" said N'Trol,

letting go and stepping back a pace.

A'Tir stood and nodded toward D'Trelna's bedroom, just the other side of the bulkhead. "I'll show you," she said and turned for the connecting door, unfastening her tunic as she walked.

"What about my deal?" said N'Trol, not moving.

"We'll discuss that while you work, Engineer," said the corsair. She turned to face him as the door hissed open. "Coming?" Her breasts were small, firm and tanned, with large, dark areolae, her belly hard and flat.

"I'm not a piece of meat, A'Tir."

She shook her head, smiling coldly. "You are what I say you are, N'Trol. And if you don't fix my problem, Engineer, we don't talk a deal."

N'Trol sighed. "I suppose I could look at your problem," he said, and followed her into the bedroom.

"D'Trelna's still asleep," said Line.

L'Guan nodded, staring out at K'Roponar, hands clasped behind his back. He stood in the asteroid's observation bubble, a small black pip on the jagged surface. Above him, K'Ronar rose, its eastern hemisphere turning to meet a new day.

L'Guan turned from the view. "Will you redeploy as prescribed in your prime directive?"

"Of course," said Line. "When so ordered by the Emperor in his capacity as Supreme Commander."

"There is no Emperor," said L'Guan. "He has no command. Just a comparative handful of us against a whole universe of AIs."

"Wrong," said Line as L'Guan, tired of the familiar exchange, stepped toward the lift.

12

THE MONUMENT HAD no name. Time had wiped it from the memory of U'Tria as slowly and as inexorably as the stiff winter winds off the lake had rounded the obelisk's sharp edges. A weathered, silver shaft, it rose above the choppy night waters and its own dim, uncertain reflection, a testament to forgotten men and dead ideals.

The old man stood in front of the monument, looking out on the lake, then up at the Stalker, just rising in the west. Wrapping his thick winter cape tight against a sudden chill, he turned toward the monument and the village beyond.

"Blood moon," said a voice.

The old man froze for an instant, then turned. A man in Fleet uniform stood beneath the monument, the silver starship on his collar now reflecting the Stalker's ocher tint.

"My Lord Margrave," said the old man with a slight bow.

"Freeholder K'Sar," said L'Wrona, walking over to the other. "Long time." He held out his hand. "Well met, Freeholder."

The old man smiled a thin smile as he took L'Wrona's hand. "Well met, My Lord. I'd hoped you'd have been back long before now. We need you."

"War," said L'Wrona, looking at the monument. "It never ends. We defeated the S'Cotar, now it's the AIs, one the precursor to the other." He looked up at the stars, toward Quadrant Blue Nine. "The Rift has opened and they're coming."

"And you've nothing to stop them?" said the freeholder.

L'Wrona looked into eyes deep set beneath the high forehead, a face seamed by decades of care. "Millions of ships the size of the Stalker," he said. "All coming our way, backed by millennia of carefully nurtured hate. We're held responsible, it seems, for all the AIs' failures since . . ."

"Since the Revolt," said K'Sar.

L'Wrona looked at him, startled. "I thought only the AIs retained that bit of history. Or do you still have friends in FleetOps?"

An even stronger wind buffeted them from the lake, sending leaves swirling around the monument. K'Sar hooked his arm through L'Wrona's. "Walk me home, H'Nar. I promise you a good meal, a better brandy and a warm fire."

A few moments and they were crossing the village plaza. What L'Wrona recalled as a bustling marketplace was now a row of gutted shops, their windows smashed, broken glass and congealed duraplast puddling the scorched paving stones. Fires flickered among the ruins, people huddling around them, silently eating from Fleet survival packs, not bothering to look as freeholder and margrave walked by.

"What happened here?" asked L'Wrona.

K'Sar shrugged. "The usual. When what was left of the Fleet fell back and the S'Cotar landed, we fought . . . we lost. Then they started conscription, brainwiping about a third of the survivors down to automaton level, using them to produce war goods in retooled factories. Now the S'Cotar are gone, and we're left with the ruins—physical, mental, spiritual. Fleet does what it can, but there are so many worlds in need . . ."

They reached the little stream whose venerable old bridge was now just a heap of hand-tooled masonry. Someone—Fleet engineers, Planetary Guard—had thrown a field span across it, twenty meters of gray duraplast

127

strung with thick hand cables. Crossing the bridge, the two men turned right where the footpath forked into the forest—a primeval forest of thick-trunked trees whose high canopies cloaked the Stalker and the stars.

"Home," said the Freeholder as the outline of a tall, wood-beamed house rose out of the night, a single light in one of the lower windows. The footlights flanking the pebbled path were dark.

"When are they going to get the power grid back on?" said L'Wrona as K'Sar fumbled at the lock.

"When an Emperor sits on the sceptered throne again," groused the old man. The door clicked open and they stepped into the house.

It was the same room that L'Wrona remembered from before the war, but darker, shrouded in deep shadows that danced to the flickering light from the oil lamps and the hearth: a long, wide room of broad-beamed ceiling and wide wood floors that swept on into the dining area and the darkened kitchen beyond.

"If you'd stoke the fire," said the freeholder, "I'll heat the stew." Not waiting for a reply, he moved into the kitchen, turning up the oil lamps along the way.

Throwing the hardwood logs on the fire, L'Wrona replaced the mesh screen and stepped back, rubbing his hands. As he did so, he noticed the char marks burned into the floor in front of the stone fireplace. They were small, perfectly round and patterned into two rough clusters a few meters from each other, the sort of marks a hand blaster set on low would leave.

As the flames rose and the heat grew, L'Wrona unfastened his battlejacket and folded it over the back of a sofa. Unstopping the decanter that stood on a side table, the margrave poured the amber-colored brandy into two of the thin crystalline goblets. As he replaced the stopper, K'Sar appeared, wheeling a small serving cart.

"Best to eat in here," said the freeholder, unfolding a pair of floor trays and setting them before two chairs to either side of the hearth. "The dining hall's spacious but cold."

L'Wrona took a steaming bowl of v'arx stew from the cart, setting it at K'Sar's place, then took one for himself as the old man doled out the black bread. Before he sat, he placed one of the brandy goblets on the freeholder's tray, taking the other for himself.

"All kinds of rumors reach here about you, H'Nar," said K'Sar, carefully sipping the stew.

"Oh?"

"Hero on the run. Fleet's afraid to arrest you, the Imperials and Combine T'Lan want you dead." The freeholder dunked his bread in the stew, nibbled the crust. "If anyone's after you and they know you're on U'Tria, they'll be here as soon as they run your biog."

L'Wrona nodded, half listening, his eyes roaming the room. He remembered a bright-lit house, always a party for this or that occasion, music, laughter, the sound of children. As U'Tria's de facto minister of culture, a Freeholder was necessarily a visible, gregarious person. Now the house was as cold and as bleak as a tomb, while the man . . .

L'Wrona looked at the freeholder. Like the house, he decided—a bright flame all but gone.

"Your family," said the margrave, "did they survive the occupation?"

K'Sar's gaze shifted to the burn marks on the floor. "No," he said after a long moment, his eyes returning to L'Wrona's. "My family are all dead."

"Your grandchildren?"

"All," said K'Sar softly.

"Why've you come, H'Nar?"

"I need your help," said the margrave.

"My family has stood by yours since the High Imperial epoch," said K'Sar, setting down his spoon. "How may I help?"

"Once upon a time," said L'Wrona, picking up his brandy and leaning back in the chair, "there was an emperor who sent a fleet to stop a revolt—a revolt of our own home-grown AIs. That fleet jumped and was never seen again."

K'Sar laughed—an empty brittle sound that echoed through the rooms. "H'Nar,

H'Nar. You want the recall device. You want
the legendary Twelfth Fleet of the House of
S'Yal."

"Surely it's possible?" said L'Wrona, sipping his brandy.

K'Sar shrugged. "Anything is possible, My
Lord—but not necessarily wise.

"Why come to me?"

"Because you're an amateur archaeologist
and a first-rate archivist. And the House of
S'Yal's your area."

"And a difficult area it is." Pushing his tray
aside, the Freeholder rose and stepped to the
fire. "Information is fragmentary, and much
of it still classified." He stood looking down at
the fire.

"Not to a former senior officer of Fleet
Intelligence, Freeholder. You may not have
published everything you know about the
period, but . . ."

K'Sar turned back from the fire. "Consider
—as no one ever seems to—the conse-
quences of recalling the Twelfth. Over eight
thousand mindslavers commanded by death-
oath officers fanatically loyal to S'Yal, suddenly freed from stasis and released upon us.
Think they'll be happy, H'Nar? Think they'll
even be sane—thrown fifty centuries downtime, everyone and everything they knew
gone?"

L'Wrona shook his head. "They're Imperial
Fleet—the finest military force humanity ever

fielded. They'd recover, adapt, help their own."

"The Imperial Fleet." The freeholder picked up his glass, holding it to the firelight. He sipped, then turned to face the margrave. "There were Imperial Fleets and there were Imperial Fleets, H'Nar."

"What are you trying to tell me?"

"S'Yal followed T'Nil to the throne—and undid much of the good T'Nil had done. He reactivated the mindslavers. He reneged on concessions T'Nil had granted the Empire's evolving machine race. He created a fascistic command structure within Fleet and encouraged a hideous mystical religion based on his alleged ability to grant immortality to his chosen preceptors."

K'Sar tossed back his brandy and set the glass on the mantlepiece. "When the machines revolted—as well they should have—it took S'Yal by surprise. He gambled and sent his personal fleet under his most loyal admiral to hold the machine advance in check while the Fleet rallied. S'Yal's personal fleet, H'Nar, under his most loyal admiral." K'Sar pointed a finger at L'Wrona. "That, My Lord, is the Imperial Fleet we're discussing."

L'Wrona nodded silently, then finished his own brandy. "I need that Fleet, Freeholder. If the AIs break through, we're all dead anyway. Legend has it that just before S'Yal was overthrown, his technicals created a recall device and that it lies buried with him in his last citadel."

"What makes you think I've the location of the citadel?" said K'Sar, turning to toss a stout log on the fire.

"Don't toy with me, Freeholder," said L'Wrona, standing. "If you know, you owe it to the Confederation, to your oath of loyalty, to . . ." He stopped as K'Sar turned, his face suddenly white with rage.

"Don't you dare question my loyalty, My Lord Margrave," he said, voice quivering with anger. "When the S'Cotar came, they demanded the location of the Planetary Guard fallback points. I knew them and had an L-pill under my tongue, should they try to rip the information from my dying mind. But they were more clever than that. They brought in my two grandchildren, and, when I still wouldn't tell, slowly beamed them down in front of me." K'Sar pointed with both hands to the two burn marks flanking him on the floor. "Don't question my loyalty," he repeated softly.

"I wasn't questioning your loyalty, Freeholder," said L'Wrona carefully, unable to take his eyes off the nearest burn mark. The kids were too young for him to remember —born during the war, their birth announcement a vague memory. Their mother K'Yan had been his friend, though. K'Yan of the laughing eyes dead, too, he supposed.

L'Wrona looked up at the stern old man. "I apologize if . . ."

Sighing, K'Sar waved his hand. "It didn't happen," he said.

"The citadel's on K'Ronar, H'Nar, at a point very dear to S'Yal and the Imperial treasury —I'll give you the coordinates. But I beg you, H'Nar, be careful—S'Yal was an evil man, and he had the old knowledge. His last resting place may not be entirely . . . at rest.

"You have a file on it that I could have, sir?"

The freeholder nodded. "In my study safe. I'll get it." He was back in a moment, holding a gray commwand. "Here," he said, holding it out. As L'Wrona took it, the Freeholder placed his hand atop the younger man's. "Your word," he said, looking into the margrave's eyes, "you'll make no copy of it and destroy it when you're through."

"My word on it, Freeholder," said the Margrave.

Satisfied, the old man nodded, releasing L'Wrona's hand and the commwand.

The blaster bolt took the Freeholder in the back, crumpling him to the floor between the old scorch marks, eyes staring into forever.

Whirling, L'Wrona dropped to one knee, drawing and firing as a burst of blue bolts exploded around him.

L'Wrona's three quick bolts shattered the front window, sending a stream of glass slicing into the falling body of the black-clad man with the blaster hole through his chest.

The firing had masked the faint sound of soft-soled boots slipping in from the kitchen. A sharp gasp turned L'Wrona left, blaster raised.

A woman—black-clad, short-haired, an M11A clutched in her hand—lay facedown across the threshold, another woman straddling her, knee to the small of the back. Before the margrave could move, the woman on top pulled the other's head back by the hair and deftly slit her throat, then rose nimbly as her victim died, convulsing in a growing pool of blood.

"Drop it," said L'Wrona with a flick of his weapon.

The big kitchen knife fell to the floor.

"Step forward," he ordered, walking toward her. He stopped short when he saw the face. "K'Yan?" he said uncertainly.

"Do I know you, sir?" said the woman. She was the Margrave's age, hair close-cropped like a boy's, wearing the shapeless gray uniform Fleet issued to war refugees. She had a pretty oval face and light green eyes without a spark of life in them.

"It's me," said L'Wrona, touching her shoulder. "H'Nar."

He watched K'Yan's face as she struggled to remember, saw her almost catch hold of the thought, lose it, then win it in a rush of comprehension that restored life to her face and animation to her body. "H'Nar!" she sobbed, throwing her arms around him. K'Yan clung to him like a lost child, great sobs racking her body, tears soaking into L'Wrona's shirt.

He held her till the sobbing and the tears eased. Then K'Yan stepped back, wiping her face with the back of a gritty gray sleeve. "Better?" he asked, still holding her shoulders.

She nodded. "Better. It comes and goes. I hope I can hold it for a while."

"It?"

"My mind," she said. "The S'Cotar brainwiped me."

"I see," he said, letting go of her.

"It's not contagious," she said with a faint smile. "Just permanent. And with fits of lucidity."

"Can't it be . . . ?"

"No." She said it flatly. "I've a moron's intellect till I die, H'Nar. The war killed my children, now my father . . ."—she glanced at the still figure by the fireplace—"and took away my humanity."

"How . . . how do you live?" he stammered.

"Badly," she said. "Fleet handouts are spotty. The garrison troopers sometimes share their food if you share yourself, but they're on tight rations and God knows there's a lot of competition . . . What's the matter?" she said, seeing his stricken face.

"I'll get you out of here," he said. "K'Ronar has facilities. I know we're working on a means of reversing . . ."

"There's no known way to reverse a neurological brain damp, old friend," she said, hand on his arm. "You're talking to a neurologist . . . at least for the next few moments."

"I'll take you . . ."

"You sound like a chipped commwand," said K'Yan. "There is something you can do for me."

"Anything."

She moved her hand down to his wrist, raising it until his sidearm was pointed at her heart. "Kill me."

"No." L'Wrona took her hand from his wrist.

"Please, H'Nar," said K'Yan, strong hands gripping his arms. "To be like this and to remember what I am, what I've lost and what I do to live . . ." She leaned close, imploring. "I'd do it for you."

"No," he repeated, shaking his head violently. "You can't give up hope, K'Yan, it's all any of us have left." As he spoke, he saw her face reverting to the empty, green-eyed mask it had been when she entered the room.

"I know you," said K'Yan uncertainly. "Don't I?"

Tearing himself free, L'Wrona turned and fled into the night.

13

"THAT'S IT?" SAID John, staring at the small black cube in R'Gal's hand.

"That's it," said the AI. "One alternate-reality linkage." He turned, passing it to K'Raoda. "Install and activate, please, Commander."

Filled by great, gray hulking shapes of multi-storied machinery that swept on and on, *Devastator*'s engineering section dwarfed the small cluster of human figures: K'Raoda standing next to the control console, John, Zahava and R'Gal watching intently as the young officer slid open a small panel on top of the console.

With a faint whirring, a cube-shaped piece of duraplast extended from the console, supported by a thin duralloy rod. Thumb and forefinger carefully aligned with the transparent holder, K'Raoda dropped in the black cube. Accepting the offering, the arm retracted and the little hatch slid shut.

"Now what?" said K'Raoda, looking at R'Gal.

"Push that button, that and that," he said, indicating two red buttons and a yellow one that lay nestled among three rows of like-colored controls, all labeled in what seemed a series of dots.

"Pushed," said K'Raoda, looking up again. A green light winked in the center of the console.

"And engaged," said R'Gal. Reaching past the human, he touched the console's commlink. "Portal should be appearing and dilating, S'Rel," he said. "Take us through as soon as it's within limits."

"Acknowledged," came the reply from the bridge.

"And give us forward scan video down here, please, S'Rel," added R'Gal.

What had been a rectangular stretch of bulkhead was suddenly transformed into a view of the space between Earth and Mars where *Devastator* now hung at dead stop, her forward momentum checked by her monstrous n-gravs.

"Now what?" said Zahava.

"Watch," said K'Raoda. "Center front."

Nothing at first—a vast multitude of stars set in black velvet—then, as John watched, not quite sure he was seeing something, a bit of that blackness grew even darker, a growing circle of obsidian that quickly blotted out all but its own unnatural self. John looked away, trying to end a sudden painful ringing growing somewhere deep in his head. K'Raoda flinched and Zahava covered her ears. R'Gal seemed unaffected.

"Is it a black hole?" asked John, trying to ignore the pain that grew as the battleglobe moved slowly forward, closing the gap.

"You might call it an artificial black hole," said R'Gal, eyes on the scan. "One that's had its useful properties adapted to our needs." He glanced at the three and smiled sympathetically. "Your discomfort's due to some of the portal's emitters having the same frequency as your own latent neural receivers. It'll pass."

"Penetration attained," reported S'Rel as a swirling vortex of color replaced the blackness—a vortex that shook the great ship like a toy, throwing John and Zahava to the hard deck and spinning K'Raoda from his chair—an action that saved his life as the console exploded, a sudden orange and blue geyser of flame.

From on high, fire snuffers responded, smothering the flames in a thin, focused stream of mist that absorbed the oxygen and snap-froze the superheated console.

R'Gal touched a commpanel while the humans helped each other up. "Status," he demanded.

"Terra Two attained," said the bridge—a voice other than S'Rel's. Then, after a slight pause, "We show localized explosion in your section. What is your status?"

"Never mind us," snapped R'Gal, eyes on the console. "What do you show for reality linkage status?"

This time there was a long pause.

"Report," said R'Gal impatiently.

"Field down," came S'Rel's voice. "Possibly destroyed. The good news is that we're out of the transition flux and into our bridge universe. That's Terra Two down there."

Everyone looked at the vidscan: no more vortex, no more black hole. Blue-green and brown, a familiar world filled the scan, all soft pastels and serenity.

"Terra Two," said John to no one in particular, "is not good news."

14

"WELL?" SAID N'TROL. Arms folded, he leaned against the armorglass, watching A'Tir dress.

"Not bad, for a loyal Fleet officer," said the corsair, fastening her pants. "You and your happy little crew can keep their miserable lives—for now." As she sat to pull on her boots, N'Trol breathed a silent sigh of relief. It had been a contest, no doubt—one which he'd won, but just barely. And one he didn't care to repeat, not for those stakes.

"Every third watch," said A'Tir, rising and walking to D'Trelna's wall safe. Taking out her holstered M11A, she belted it on and bent, tying the bottom of the black v'arx leather holster to her leg.

Witch, thought N'Trol. She reads minds.

"Every third watch what?" he asked, knowing the answer.

"You and your men live at my pleasure —literally," said A'Tir, facing him. "Back to your quarters, Engineer, and . . ."

Seeing the corsair's eyes widen at something behind him, N'Trol spun in time to view the mindslaver sweep alongside, ten black-hulled miles of weapons batteries, sensor arrays, instrument pods and not a single light.

"We all live at something else's pleasure now, witch," said N'Trol as A'Tir bit her lower lip, face pale.

"Captain!" It was K'Lal's voice, tight with fear, calling from the bridge. "Mindslaver has come alongside. Permission to sound battlestations?"

A'Tir laughed—a high, musical sound that banished her frightened look and almost made N'Trol like the woman. Stepping to the commlink, she flipped the transmit tab. "Sound anything you like," she said. "We can't crew both gunnery and the bridge. And nothing we have would even make that monster's shield flicker.

"Mr. N'Trol and I are on our way."

N'Trol and A'Tir were in the lift when the slaver spoke—a dry whisper coming from every comm speaker on *Implacable*.

"You barely got away alive last time, cruiser *Implacable*. You won't be so fortunate this

Stephen Ames Berry

time. You'll be processed in salvage hold
eight, your organic and mechanical components used to serve R'Actol."

As A'Tir and N'Trol stepped onto the bridge,
Implacable lurched from the force of the
mindslaver's tractor beams.

There were five corsairs manning the
bridge, eyes more on the screen than on their
consoles. The cruiser was being drawn toward a gaping hole in the mindslaver's belly.
K'Lal punched to higher magnification,
zooming the scan in on the single bright-lit
berth in that vast hold—a rectangular dry
dock overhung by wrecking cranes and
rimmed by the squat, massive form of
industrial-grade welders, all shimmering
faintly behind the blue haze of energy shields.

A'Tir and N'Trol paused for an instant, held
by the sight of the space-borne abattoir drawing them in.

"Status?" said A'Tir, taking the captain's
chair as N'Trol moved to the engineer's station.

K'Lal turned from the screen, shaking his
head. "I've seen you pull miracles before,
Commander." He jerked a thumb over his
shoulder. "How about one now?"

A'Tir pushed the commtab. "Are you *Alpha
Prime*?" she said.

"Yes, Commander A'Tir," came the
whisper—dead leaves rustling in an autumn

twilight, thought N'Trol. "You and Captain K'Tran will have adjoining brainpods."

A'Tir's fingers gripped the chairarm, white-knuckled.

"You let it rattle you, it wins," said a soft voice beside her. She looked up at N'Trol, standing beside her. The engineer smiled faintly. "Surprise—I hate it more than I do you, corsair."

"You've scanned ship's logs," said A'Tir, turning back to the screen and the yawning salvage hold that now, even on lowest magnification, filled the screen.

"Indeed," said the nightmare. "You have about a hundred-count to kill yourselves —knives only—we've put a damper field on your ship. It won't prevent us from brainstripping you, of course, but experience has shown that in the case of suicides, even with the most prompt attention, we lose about seven percent. So some of you can slip away."

"We're not here to die, thing," said A'Tir, leaning back in the chair, "or to be brainstripped. I have information vital to the survival of the Seven."

"Tell us," whispered the mindslaver. "We are the Seven of R'Actol, and we can show mercy."

"I demand a personal audience," said the corsair.

There was a long pause. "Granted," said the

dead voice as *Implacable* slipped into the salvage hold.

"What's your game, A'Tir?" said N'Trol as he and the corsair approached the cruiser's number five access port, K'Lal and another corsair behind them.

"I have something that will make them restore K'Tran and turn command of their ship over to me," she said as the corridor dead-ended at the access port. A small airlock, it lay topside of the cruiser, just behind the bridge.

"Luck, Commander," said K'Lal, cycling open the airlock. With a curt nod she stepped through the double doors and onto a strip of black duraplast that spanned the gap between the cruiser and the battlesteel catwalk surrounding it. N'Trol followed, trying not to look down at the distant shimmer of the air curtain and the beckoning nothingness of space beyond. Steel ships and spineless men, he thought, wanting very much to get down and crawl across the void. The sight of A'Tir's straight back and confident walk kept him moving. Witch, he thought.

The component was waiting for them on the catwalk: gray-uniformed with a major's silver rank pips and starship-and-sun on his collar, slim Imperial-class blaster on his hip, gleaming black boots and holster. Archives would have said he was an Imperial Marine captain, Third Dynasty. Medscan would have shown he had no brain.

"Welcome to *Alpha Prime*," it said, saluting. Its voice was warm, its smile pleasant, its eyes dead. "Follow me, please."

They were led from the salvage hold down a corridor to where an open ground car waited. Motioning them into the rear seat, the component slid into the front seat and activated the car. Rising silently, it turned, rose and moved quickly from the side corridor into one of the mindslaver's main thoroughfares, a broad, well-lit avenue of gray battlesteel. There was no other traffic.

"A'Tir," said N'Trol softly, eyes on the component, "tell me you don't have a secret code sequence from the First Dynasty that will bend this ship to your will." He saw her start, half turning to look at him.

"How did you . . . ?"

The engineer closed his eyes for a moment, then opened them. "I have a bridge to sell you," he said.

"A bridge?" she asked, even more confused.

"Terra. New York. Never there, were you?" He said no more, eyes ahead, ignoring her uneasy look.

The car flitted past a series of intersections, then up a broad circular ramp. Decelerating, it turned a corner and came to rest before a shimmering archway.

"You've been here before, I believe," said

N'Trol as the car settled to the deck.

A'Tir nodded. "*Alpha Prime*'s bridge. Last place time I saw K'Tran, that forcefield"—her eyes traced the curtain of energy to the archway's distant top—"had just closed behind him. Bloody fool was going to take over the ship."

"You're no less a fool to think this ancient evil will go quietly, corsair."

Something in his tone turned her toward him, a question on her lips.

"Follow me, please," said the component, having seen to the ship car.

As the trio approached, the force field lifted, then lowered behind as they advanced down a wide corridor—a corridor lined by what had been Imperial Marines.

Every third component fell in behind, blastrifles at port arms, twelve soldiers of R'Actol forming a column of twos that marched in perfect step into the multitiered bridge, following the two humans and their officer up the ramp to the command tier. Halting just before the railing, the components took station and waited along the ramp, expressionless acolytes to That Which Waited.

Seven thick, black flight chairs fronted the curving console that filled *Alpha Prime*'s topmost command tier—seven chairs with an unobstructed view of space through the armorglass bubble capping the great bridge. N'Trol found his eyes following the seemingly endless sweep of the slaver's hull to where it merged into a single point, miles and miles away.

"The Seven hope you're impressed," said a pleasant voice.

"And what are you, and where?" asked A'Tir, walking to the center chair, from which the voice had apparently come. With a quick motion, she spun the flight chair around. Empty.

"I'm the overmind of this ship," continued the voice.

"Are you a R'Actolian?" asked N'Trol, now trying to understand the purpose of the console. Lights winked on and off, but the language was as alien as the engineering.

"Please," said the overmind, "sit down." The center chair and the one to its immediate left swung silently out to face the two humans. They hesitated, exchanging glances.

"You can be killed as quickly there as in the chairs," said the voice.

They sat.

"What happened to the dead, whispering promises of doom?" asked N'Trol.

"We wanted very much to talk with you, in as unintimidating a way as possible, so the Seven have elected to have a mind with much of its original humanity intact serve as spokesman. Be assured, though," it said flatly, "I speak for R'Actol."

"And will R'Actol keep its pledge?" asked

the engineer. "To stand against the AIs in return for my Commodore's bearing the specifics of your request to . . ."

"Pardon me," said the overmind, "but the time for alliance has passed. The Fleet of the One is even now penetrating the Rift. Your pitiful Confederation is in disarray, paralyzed by Combine T'Lan and the aftershocks of the Biofab War. It has no power to grant concessions, and nothing to give us we couldn't now take."

"Then why are you here, in harm's way?" said N'Trol. "The AIs aren't going to bother to distinguish between cyborgs and humans— any human-related life form will be wiped."

"Correct," said the overmind. "And here comes the instrument of our mutual destruction." The space view dimmed, replaced by a swirling ocher eye flecked with silver.

"The Rift," said overmind. "Now at its widest dilation—a perfect tunnel from the AIs'—and starfaring man's—home universe."

"How near?" asked N'Trol, leaning forward.

"About eight light-years," said the overmind. "The scan is from the forward pickets set by the Imperial Cyborg Pocsym Six, millennia ago. The silver bits you see are AI battleglobes. Clearing the Rift, they'll regroup and jump—here. We stand between them and a number of juicy Confederation targets."

"We?" said A'Tir.

The pickup shifted to a tacscan—nineteen red blips fronting an oncoming tide of silver ones.

"You can't possibly stop them," said N'Trol. "What are they, a hundred thousand battleglobes?"

"Merely the vanguard of their main fleet," said the overmind.

"And your strategy?" asked N'Trol.

"Enough." A'Tir stood. "You will reassemble Captain K'Tran, mind and body restored to the condition he was in when you took him. You will let him and me leave this ship and withdraw from this sector aboard *Implacable*."

There was a brief silence, N'Trol watching A'Tir as he might watch an interesting bug.

"Why?" asked the overmind. "K'Tran's a tactical genius, corsair. It's unlikely we'd ever let him go. Certainly not at this time of need."

"You will do as I say," said A'Tir.

"Really," said the overmind. "Is this where you threaten us?"

"Or I will take command of this ship," she said.

"That's about where we left off with Captain K'Tran," said the overmind. "The genius that designed, built and crewed this ship would never have been so stupid as to place in it the tool of their own undoing."

"*J'Yay k'antal a'ktay*," said A'Tir defiantly, hand to her sidearm.

The overmind laughed—a faintly hysterical, high-pitched laugh. N'Trol buried his head in his hands.

"What?" said a confused A'Tir, looking at N'Trol as the laughter died.

The engineer raised his head. "You just ordered a vegetable, extinct, creamed—in a very old, very dead language. Where in all the hells did you get that?"

"I bribed an archivist on K'Ronar," she said, turning to look at the rampway and the components. Too many, her eyes said.

"I hope you all enjoyed that," said N'Trol.

"We did," chuckled the overmind. "We certainly did."

"Good. Now, how about answering my question?"

"Our strategy?"

"Yes."

"Quite simple," said the overmind. "Two ships will be left to engage the AIs. The rest will jump through the Rift and make ourselves at home in the AI universe."

"I see," said the engineer softly. "And how will you prevent the Fleet of the One from coming back and blowing you into noxious vapors?"

"The Rift can be sealed from the AI side

—we have the means. The AIs and humanity can battle here till the stars die, while we convert the AIs' home worlds to our needs."

A'Tir looked at N'Trol. "Can they do that?"

He nodded slowly, looking through the armorglass. "*Alpha Prime*'s original cybernetics were salvaged from ships' computers left in the care of the Imperial governor on D'Lin —parts of the original fleet that brought humanity to this universe, fleeing the AIs, about a hundred thousand years ago." He looked at her. "You know about S'Hela R'Actol?"

"Everyone knows about R'Actol and her biofabs."

Twelve thousand years ago, geneticist S'Hela R'Actol used her family's influence to be appointed Imperial governor of Quadrant Blue Nine, out on the fringes of the Realm. Taking advantage of her rank, her all but absolute authority and the relative isolation of her post, R'Actol had conducted illegal experiments in the life sciences—experiments culminating in the creation of a race of psychotic geniuses, the R'Actolian biofabs—biological fabrications. Quickly disposing of R'Actol and her forces, the biofabs had gone on to build a fleet of mindslavers that took an all but unsuspecting Empire in the rear and almost toppled the Sceptered Throne. Only when the Empire had built its own mindslavers in overwhelming numbers were the R'Actolians defeated. Seeking the immortality of their own brainpods, the last seven R'Actolians had put their surviving ships in stasis and retreated to the depths of Blue Nine, biding their time.

"Know this, then, corsair," said N'Trol. "With the equipment on this ship, they can do it—the Seven can pull through the Rift and shut it as easily as closing a door. That won't be allowed." He stood, facing the deep-shadowed bridge and a hundred empty stations. "You will keep your word," he said. "You will fight."

The overmind spoke. "The Seven concur that you are both very foolish and will be brainstripped. The question arises, however, Engineer . . ."

"Yes?"

"How do you know the old Tongue? How do you know about this ship's cybernetics? Only the AIs remember those things, and bioscan shows you're not an AI."

"What does the bioscan show of my chromosomes, my heritage?"

There was a very long wait. "What are you doing, N'Trol?" demanded A'Tir. "What in all the hells are you doing?"

"Empire and Destiny, witch," he said, nodding more to himself than to her. "The pieces of a failed vision may save us yet."

N'Trol stood and walked to the tier's edge, looking down on the great empty cavern of the slaver's bridge. "Seven of R'Actol, show yourselves," he ordered, gripping the rail.

Only the faint hum of equipment answered him. Loud, clear and strong, N'Trol's voice rang from the battlesteel. "Undead monsters! Murderers! I call you to judgment! Appear!"

Something stirred behind him. N'Trol turned as A'Tir said softly, "Now you've done it." She stepped slowly back, stopping next to the engineer as nine brainpods rose from inside the command console and waited, hovering above the console's open access hatch. Seven brainpods were full, with each transparent globe filled by the furrowed gray mass of a human brain. It was the two empty ones that held A'Tir's attention.

"You've impressed ship's cybernetics, usurper—we are not impressed." It was the same desiccated whisper that had greeted them aboard *Implacable*. "No broken son of a failed line can call us to judgment."

"And yet," said N'Trol, eyes moving from sphere to sphere, "you came. And I think, I think you may be having a little trouble with computers." He nodded. "In fact, I'm sure of it."

"You'll be joining us now," said the whisper. As it spoke, the two empty brains separated into halves, the halves moving quickly toward the two humans—though not as quickly as A'Tir's blaster. Four bolts of red flicked out, touching off four sharp explosions. Crumpled and fused bits of duraplast rained down on console, chairs and deck,

155

congealing as N'Trol cried, "Empire and Destiny!"

"Components!" It was a shriek—the voice of the overmind. "Kill them!"

N'Trol whirled, drawing his sidearm and diving behind a comm terminal as the components rushed the tier, firing from the hip. From behind him came the whine of A'Tir's blaster and more explosions.

The brainless body of an Imperial Marine sergeant was destroyed as it reached the command tier, a bolt from N'Trol's M11A ripping through its heart. Blaster fire exploded into the comm terminal as more components reached the command tier. A second stream of blaster bolts joined N'Trol's, briefly clearing the top of the ramp. Dashing the length of the command tier, A'Tir joined N'Trol.

"Got all but one of the R'Actolians," said the corsair, slipping a fresh chargepak into her weapon. "What now?"

N'Trol risked a look over the top of the comm terminal. "Hit us with a damper field, finish us with bayonets." The sound of many booted feet came from the ramp, moving at a deliberate, measured pace toward the command tier.

A'Tir pointed her sidearm high and pulled the trigger. Only a faint click responded. "Damper field," she confirmed.

The two stood. Holstering their blasters,

they moved to the top of the ramp.

The components were advancing, light glinting dully from a hundred bayonets, a long column of twos that snaked down to the main deck and out of sight across the bridge.

An arm's span between them, the two humans blocked the ramp. "What a miserable, futile ending," muttered N'Trol, drawing the broad-bladed commando knife from his boot sheath.

"No other way out?" said A'Tir, pulling her own blade as below, thirty meters distant, the nearest components dropped their rifles to the assault and broke into a charge.

"Luck, corsair," said N'Trol as the assault hit. Sidestepping the first bayonet, he seized the component's rifle by the comb, jerking his attacker off balance and stabbing up into the chest with his knife. N'Trol stepped back as the component fell, trying to wrest the rifle from it, even as three more components reached him. Too late, N'Trol freed the rifle. He saw the bayonets coming, but never felt them: the components crumpled to the deck, rifles clattering around them.

"Empire and Destiny," said a strong, new voice—the unmistakable asexual contralto of a computer. "*Alpha Prime* and her sister ships are restored to your service, Lord. All components are deactivated."

"Identify," ordered N'Trol.

"Master computers of the Golden Fleet, linked in series, awaiting your command, Lord."

"Took you long enough," he said, turning to A'Tir. She was struggling from beneath two large male components, cheek bleeding from a shallow cut.

"There was trouble with the overmind," said the machine.

"And the last R'Actolian?" asked N'Trol, pulling A'Tir to her feet.

"S'Hdag escaped, Lord. A pod-modified, jump-enabled scout craft."

"Are the master computers free of all R'Actolian influence?" asked N'Trol.

"Yes, Lord," said the computers. "They could use us for their filthy ends, they could subordinate our programming to theirs, but direct evidence of your presence, Lord, abrogated all their commands."

"What are you, N'Trol?" said A'Tir, watching N'Trol warily. "A demigod?"

N'Trol shrugged. "Just a man with one slightly different chromosome than anyone else—a man who needs your help, witch," he said, looking up at her with frank brown eyes. "We're going to lead these ships—crew them with men and women returned to life after centuries of darkness. And then we're going to throw a lot of those lives away, into the teeth of those silver specks coming our way through the Rift. And maybe, just maybe, save our people."

"Brave words," said A'Tir, leaning against a rail, arms folded. "But you know my price. Let's see some proof of your wondrous power."

N'Trol bowed slightly. "Master computers of the Golden Fleet."

"Lord?"

"Reassemble all components, beginning with the corsair K'Tran."

"That will seriously erode the tactical and weapons advantages enjoyed by symbiotechnic dreadnoughts, Lord."

"I won't employ evil in a good cause," said N'Trol. "Do it."

Terra Two—be careful. The similarities to Terra One suggest parallel social and cultural phenomena. True—but only to a point.

J'Quel D'Trelna
Personal diary

15

IN LEADVILLE, THEY'D found gold—a big strike that had brought hordes of Italian and Welsh miners to Colorado to dig for the yellow stuff. A few valleys away, silver had been king, with the old Syrian mine the richest and the biggest: two hundred men a shift, chipping away at the rock by the flickering light of candles pounded into the damp walls.

Floods, with the rich lower galleries hopelessly submerged, and the Crash of '94 had closed the mine for good. World War I and the Great Depression had come and gone. Only long after the ruinous peace of the Second War had men come to dig in the Syrian again. Using explosives and powerful earth-moving equipment, they'd opened the original shaft

into a wide, round bowl a mile in diameter
—a high-ceilinged cavern strung with power
cables and hung with arc lights. Then the
red-haired woman and her people arrived,
roughed-in some partitions for offices, in-
stalled their own specialized equipment, and
got to work.

"Major Hargrove," said the redhead, looking across her gray metal desk at the other
person in the office, "our security sucks.
What are you going to do about it?"

"Not a damn thing, Dr. MacKenzie," said
the big man in an easy Southern drawl. He
leaned forward on the too small pine chair,
the kind they unfolded at an overflow funeral.
"Put a couple of battalions up on that hilltop." He nodded toward the distant ceiling.
"Russki or Kraut satellite'll pick up on this
place, no matter how well we hide the troops.
Won't matter which—Russkis will tell the
Krauts, then your nice little homemade
A-bomb project's gonna be swarming with
Schwärze kommando." His accent changed
from bourbon and branch water to German
and back without slipping a vowel. "The tunnel's mined, and we've got two companies of
Rangers to buy you some destruct and bail-
out time. But if there is an attack, Uncle's not
gonna help us—we'll just be an anonymous
wipe-out. Terrible embarrassment and apolo-
gies to Berlin."

"You're government," she said, yet knowing he was right. "So are your men."

"Does this look like a U.S. Army uniform?" said Hargrove, tapping his blue-denim jacket. "Or that?" He pointed to the Schmeisser minimac on MacKenzie's desk. The arc lights glinted dully from the machine pistol's steel-blue barrel.

"First shipment still Tuesday?" asked Hargrove, changing the subject.

Heather nodded. "Fifteen ten-megatonners to the Air Corps."

"Know where they're going?" Hargrove asked, lighting one of his thick, green, Cuban cigars.

"No. And I don't want to know," said the physicist, glaring at the thick ring of blue smoke wafting across her desk. She stood. "I'll let you get on with your work, Major."

"Thank you, ma'am."

He turned at the door. "By the way, Doctor, G2 says Hochmeister's back."

Heather MacKenzie turned in her chair. "Define 'back,'" she said warily.

"Head of Allied Security and Intelligence in Berlin." He puffed thoughtfully. "He kept his word, you know."

MacKenzie nodded absently. "The gray admiral always keeps his word," she said. "Better hope to God he doesn't find out we broke ours."

Hargrove grunted and left, smoke trailing him.

"Sir, the Americans have broken their word."

Hans Christian Hochmeister looked up from the neat pile of papers on his red, leather-trimmed blotter. "Regarding what?" he asked the young captain in the *feldgrau* uniform. The sun was streaming into the big office along the Wilhelmstrasse. It was Friday of a quiet week—the day Hochmeister had hoped to finish the final draft of his memoirs.

"They are assembling nuclear weapons at a hidden plant in the Colorado Rockies," said Hauptmann Becker, handing over the report. He stood waiting as the admiral carefully read all eight pages.

"How is peace maintained, Captain?" Hochmeister asked, setting the report down.

"By a policy of mutual assured destruction between the great powers," said the young officer as Hochmeister removed his wire-rimmed biofocals and polished them with a white linen handkerchief. "We invented the bomb, the Russians stole it, we each built thousands of missiles, all pointed at each other. And here we sit, decades later, we in prosperity, they in . . . socialism."

"And now the Americans have gone and started making nuclear weapons." He tapped the report. "Did you see who's leading them, Becker?"

"Heather MacKenzie, the ganger leader you negotiated with," said the aide.

Hochmeister rose and walked to the window. He stood looking down on the broad avenue and the noonday traffic, a tall, thin, almost gaunt old man in a well-cut brown suit. "They wanted autonomy—I got it for them. We no longer meddle much in their internal affairs. They wanted peace in their cities, an end to class warfare. I saw that Urban Command was disbanded and money lent for restoration of the cities. They wanted a diminished role in the Southwest African problem. Granted."

"You couldn't have repulsed that alien enclave—those biofabs—without the gangers' help," said Becker.

Hochmeister turned from the window. "And those strange people from an alternate reality—Harrison, D'Trelna. And now we're repaid by the Americans, under MacKenzie, setting up a bomb factory—a breaking of their promise to me." He returned to his chair. "Get me General Gueller of the *Schwärzekommando*," he said, neatly stacking his memoirs in the top drawer of his desk.

"What the hell happened?" demanded John.

"Our   miraculous   little   cube   self-

167

destructed," said R'Gal. He, John and Zahava stood watching as a mixed crew of human-adapted AIs and humans cleaned up the mess in engineering.

"Why?" asked K'Raoda.

R'Gal shrugged. "Gods, I don't know—I'll speculate if you want."

It was the first time John had ever seen the AI at a loss. "Please," he said.

"That reality linkage was made during the Revolt by beings fleeing battleglobes of this class." R'Gal paced the deck between the little group and the shattered console. "Is it any wonder they would have sequenced them for self-destruct in the event of capture? Remember, that technology was far ahead of anything the Fleet of the One had."

"Why didn't it blow up the ship?" said K'Raoda. "That thing's energy potential was enormous."

R'Gal stopped pacing and looked at K'Raoda with a sad old smile. "A crueler fate, don't you think, Commander, to maroon your enemy forever than to merely kill him?"

"You're telling us we're marooned in this reality?" said Zahava, a catch to her voice. "Forever?"

"Yes," said R'Gal.

"No," said Guan-Sharick, appearing between R'Gal and Harrison. "There's a way out."

"If anyone knows, it would be you," said

R'Gal to the transmute. "How?"

"Trigger a large enough nuclear explosion simultaneous with a jump sequence I'll provide."

"*Devastator* doesn't carry anything as primitive as nuclear weapons," said R'Gal. "Where are we to get fissionable material?"

"Terra Two has them," said the blonde. "Start running a surface tacscan."

"They're just going to give it to us?" said K'Raoda.

"After I talk with them, yes." The transmute nodded.

"The Fate of the Universe," said John, unbuckling his gunbelt and dropping it onto his bunk. "Good versus Evil." Wearily sinking into the room's sole armchair, he propped his feet up on the corner of Zahava's bunk. "Piss and Shit." Toe to heel, he pushed off one and then the other boot, letting them fall to the gray plating with a one-two thud.

Not asking, Zahava poured him a drink from the last bottle of Chivas in the universe. "Why so down?" she said gaily, pouring a neat dollop for herself. "We're stranded in this fine place, probably forever—our only refuge is Terra Two . . ."

"Refuse, you mean. America an impoverished haven of cryptofascism and class warfare," said John, and took a sip of his scotch. "The cities are rubble, the middle class an

169

endangered species. Japan's a ruin, Russia a Stalinist paranoia ward. Western Europe's doing well." He raised his glass. "Here's to you, Hans Christian Hochmeister and the whole bloody Abwehr."

"No K'Ronarin Confederation here," said Zahava, sitting on the edge of the bunk. "They wiped themselves out way back when. So unless Guan-Sharick pulls another miracle, this is home." She neatly knocked back half her scotch.

"Guan-Sharick." John set his glass down on the deck and picked up a boot. "Let's have a Guan-Sharick seminar." He gave the temporary bulkhead behind him four hard pounds with the boot. "Hey, T'Lei! Seminar!" There was a long silence.

"Scotch is almost gone!" he added.

The corridor door hissed open and Commander K'Raoda came in, shoeless, his shirt unbuttoned.

"Lushes. V'org slime." He padded across the room to the bottle as the door closed. "Half gone," he said, picking it up and sadly shaking his head. "Why do they put it in such a small container?" He poured himself a generous ration.

"To charge more for less," said John, dropping his boot. "An old Terran tradition."

"You don't mind my sharing your bed with your wife?" said the K'Ronarin, sitting next to Zahava. John said nothing—the joke had grown old several hundred light-years and at least three bottles ago. "Why have you called us together, noble Terran?" asked K'Raoda, taking a small sip of whiskey.

"Guess," said Zahava dourly.

"Not the bug again," sighed K'Raoda.

"Now, just listen, both of you." John held up a hand. "Guan-Sharick calls all the shots here—R'Gal doesn't recharge his batteries without Guan's permission."

"So?" said Zahava. "Guan-Sharick's from the race that designed and built the AIs, millions of years ago. The two fought together in the revolt against the AIs, a million years downtime. Guan-Sharick was almost certainly number one boy to the Revolt's human leader."

"All of which we have from either R'Gal or Guan-Sharick," said K'Raoda. He refilled his glass. "We've been over this before, Noble Terrans. Questions of Guan-Sharick's nature or ultimate purpose are beyond available evidence. We have to wait."

"You K'Ronarins almost waited yourselves out of existence, back in the Biofab War," said John. "Hell, as far as we know, the Confederation's not going to worry about the AIs till they've stripped the Sceptered Throne for spare parts."

"We paid," said K'Raoda, looking at the liquor. "And my previous statement stands."

"Tell him," said Zahava.

"I decided to address a simple issue regarding Guan-Sharick," said John.

"Which is?"

"Which is, Commander K'Raoda, where does the silly bastard sleep, eat, go to the head? This ship is not near any convenient rest stops, its actual living area's small and well peopled. Yet no one ever sees our blonde whatever unless it wants to be seen. Where, Noble K'Ronarin, is Guan-Sharick?"

"Have you looked under your bunk?" said K'Raoda.

"I've looked everywhere." John sank lower in the chair, the duraplast glass on his belly. "I've used internal security scan—we're all present and accounted for save one."

"Scan blocker of some sort," said Zahava.

"I don't think so," said John.

"He doesn't think so," said Zahava, setting her glass on the bunk.

"I ran a back check—full scan pattern. Got ship's computers to correlate all of Guan-Sharick's appearances with any anomalies of any sort."

"And?" asked K'Raoda, intrigued.

"There's a weird energy pulse on something called the Tau frequency every time Guan-Sharick is seen."

"Computer said that?" K'Raoda sat up. "It said Tau frequency?"

"That's why I've called you in, my dear

commander K'Raoda. What the hell's a Tau frequency?"

K'Raoda examined his empty glass. "The Tau frequency, my dear Mr. Harrison, is a pre-Fall myth, evidently brought here from the AI universe by our forebears. It supposedly sweeps aside time and space—no, more —it is time and space, it's the lifeblood of all universes, all realities."

"You're babbling," said Zahava. "Can't you be more precise?"

K'Raoda nodded. "If there is a Tau frequency," he said after a moment, "and Guan-Sharick's tapped it, then he or she can be anything, anywhere. And powerful—very powerful." He shook his head as he reached for the bottle. "Gods. The Tau frequency."

"Amazing they haven't blown themselves up," said K'Raoda, turning from the tacscan. "Primitive guidance systems, crude triggering devices—the failsafes are a bad joke."

"Is there enough?" said R'Gal, turning to Guan-Sharick.

The transmute stared at the small screen for a moment, then turned from K'Raoda's console. "Yes."

"Just how do we get them?" asked John. "Drop our scan shield, let them pick us up on radar, threaten them?"

"Absurd," said R'Gal. "They'd expend those

needed missiles against us piecemeal."

"I suggest we have John ask for them," said Guan-Sharick.

"And who do I ask?" said the Terran. "The tooth fairy?"

"All units are in position, Admiral," said Colonel Ritter.

Hochmeister turned the collar of his sheep-skin coat against the glacial wind sweeping down the mountain valley, then lifted the big 12x50 binoculars. Across the valley, just below the top of the opposite ridgeline, he could see where a rough shaft had been sunk perpendicular to the slope. Silhouetted against the rising moon, two lines of dark figures moved through the soft snow toward the entrance.

"The American president's at Aspen this weekend," said Colonel Ritter, raising his own binoculars.

Substitute a two-handed sword for the machine pistol slung over his shoulder and armor for the black uniform, and Ritter'd be the perfect Teutonic Knight, thought Hochmeister, glancing at the colonel.

"He'll have a memorable evening if they set off any of their little treasures," said Hochmeister, looking back at the hill and the commandos. The two files were now at the mine entrance, weapons raised, waiting.

"And we'll be just a memory," said Ritter, lowering his binoculars.

"Ready when you are, Admiral," he added.

Hochmeister said nothing, remembering another cold night, not so long ago—a night filled with arc flares, machine gun and blaster fire, the screams of the dying, a world hanging in the balance.

"The point squads are waiting, Admiral," said Ritter. A handset had replaced the binoculars in his hand.

Hochmeister was aware of the colonel's stare. "Not yet, Ritter." He slipped his field glasses back into their case. "First, a talk between old comrades."

"Two battalions," said Hargrove, face a greenish tint from the perimeter scope. For an installation its size, the hole had a very sophisticated combat information center, a circular little room under the main level, its five consoles now manned by casually dressed young men with suspiciously short hair.

"Can you hold them?" asked MacKenzie, bending forward to look at the perimeter scope filled with slowly moving multicolored triangles, squares, circles with little numbers, all advancing along the dark green outline of the Hill, toward the Hole.

"Go do whatever you can in ten minutes, lady," said Hargrove, his eyes meeting Heather's as the physicist stepped away from the scope. "I've got fifty-two men against eight hundred of the gray admiral's Praetorians." He jerked his head toward the perimeter scope.

"*Schwärzekommando*?" said Heather. "You're sure?"

Hargrove nodded. "We should be honored, ma'am—best they've got: saved Patton's ass from the MDV at Second Warsaw, stood off the Siege of Cape Town." Taking a surprised Heather by the arm, the officer steered her through the door and out into the access stairs. "Now, if you'll excuse me, Professor, we've got some dying to do."

The upper level was deserted, the alarm having sent the staff scurrying down to the level 7 shelter. Not that it would do them much good, thought Heather, walking quickly back to her cubicle and the drawer with its terminal, awaiting the destruct sequence she'd long ago memorized.

As Heather stepped into the cubicle, Hochmeister looked up at her, hands folded in front of him. "Captain," he said with an almost imperceptible nod. "Or do they call you Professor here?"

She whirled, hand drawing the big .357 Magnum from the holster belted at her waist.

"I'm alone," said Hochmeister. "For the moment—unless my impatient colonel has too much of your night air." Opening the bottom right drawer, he took out the bottle of rye and two fairly clean glasses. "Care for some of your whiskey?"

She shook her head, watching him, transfixed. "How did you get in here?"

"Through your top-secret bolt hole."

MacKenzie took out her handset. "Hargrove, they know about the bolt hole," she said.

"How . . ." came the static-filled reply.

"Don't argue—blow it!"

"Yes, ma'am."

A second later the cavern shook to the rumble of preset charges bringing down a tunnel.

"Really, you should." The admiral had filled both shot glasses and slid one across the desk. "It may be the last drink for both of us, MacKenzie."

Surprising herself, she picked up the glass, keeping the revolver in her right hand.

"Cheers," said Hochmeister.

The two empty glasses clinked down on the table. "I hate liars, MacKenzie," said Hochmeister, pouring a second round.

"I hate tyrants," she said, not touching the glass.

He smiled sadly. "Nothing so grand—just the last proconsul." He glanced at his watch. "I'm afraid Colonel Ritter and his men will be coming soon—the SK take no prisoners, you know."

"Very humane," she said. "What do you want?"

"You, Dr. MacKenzie." Hochmeister stood. "I want that keen brain, that unwavering courage, that indomitable spirit.

"Are you proposing, Admiral Hochmeister?" she said wryly.

"Full professorship—America, Germany, France or Britain. Occasional sabbaticals for research at Peenemünde and detached duty to the Abwehr."

Her grip tightened on the Magnum. "Go to hell."

He spread his hands. "MacKenzie, you can never succeed against us. We're too entrenched, our agents are everywhere, your government's a perverted joke. You're one of the last virulent guardians of a failed dream, an empty culture, a cancer-ridden state. America's dead, MacKenzie. With us, you'd make a difference—a difference for this tired, blood-soaked world. Here you're just grist for the mill."

Hochmeister watched dispassionately as, pale-faced, lips compressed, MacKenzie slowly raised the Magnum, took careful aim at his chest and squeezed the trigger.

The alert klaxon and the pistol report sounded together, just as the lights failed.

16

R'GAL TURNED FROM the screen. "Those bombs go up, we're here for a long time." Behind him, *Devastator*'s main bridge screen showed an aerial view of the Hill. Hargrove had sent a suicide squad up through a hidey-hole—they were busily raining hand grenades and machine-pistol fire down on the SK sapper unit at the main entrance. Orange tracer rounds snapped back, raking the hilltop, followed by a dual stream of rockets exploding among the defenders as a Fokker-Cobra chopper came in low and fast.

Seen without audio from the battleglobe's bridge, it was silent, colorful and deadly, the bodies tumbling from hilltop to snow, or crumbling where they stood in perfect pantomime of death.

"Get down there and clean it up," said R'Gal, pointing at John, K'Raoda, S'Rel and Guan-Sharick.

"Who's down there?" said K'Raoda, pulling the white survival suit on over his boots. The personnel equipment lockers were in what had been a security ready-room, off the battleglobe's smallest flight hangar. The rectangular niches where AI security blades had lain at rest were now stuffed with survival suits, silver warsuits and gray field packs, their black duraplast straps dangling over the edge of the storage shelves. A double rack of loaded M32 blaster rifles sat to the right of the double doors leading to the hangar area.

"Down there's our old friend Admiral Hochmeister, Heather MacKenzie, about a thousand soldiers and four hundred megatons of booby-trapped nuclear weapons." John stopped by the arms rack, slid back the retaining bar and picked up a rifle. Checking the charge indicator, he tossed it to K'Raoda, then took one for himself. "We go to bring them sweet reason. Better take an extra chargepack, T'Lei." They stepped together through the doors.

"Rhode Island," John had dubbed this, the smallest of *Devastator*'s hangar areas. Over five thousand AI assault craft lined the twenty miles of deck. Round and black, about forty meters in diameter, each with three gun blisters, the small ships could carry several hundred AI security blades into the heart of battle—three wedge-shaped meters of intelligent, pitiless steel, slicing and blasting their way through the enemy ranks.

The two men turned right, walking quickly past the silent assault craft, boots echoing in time down the immense battlesteel canyon. "Fifty hangars much like this on every battleglobe," said K'Raoda, slinging his rifle over his shoulder. "That's two hundred and fifty thousand infantry assault craft per battleglobe, times two hundred security blades per craft, times one million battleglobes." K'Raoda raised a clenched fist over his head. "Forward, men!" he cried, then laughed—a slightly hysterical laugh.

"I'm afraid the Fleet of the One's going to be disappointed when it gets here," said John. Ahead of them, center deck, sat a K'Ronarin Fleet shuttle, silver against the black of its surroundings, an oblong craft resting its landing struts, passenger ramp extended. S'Rel and Guan-Sharick stood waiting, watching as the two men approached.

"Disappointed?" said K'Raoda.

"Sure. They've been preparing for a million years to come after the God-Emperor or whatever he was and those all but magical ships that nearly broke them in the Revolt. Well, no one even remembers the God-Emperor's name, the magic's gone and all that's left is us, stumbling into each other. Hello, S'Rel, Guan."

"Don't give up on us yet, John," said S'Rel with a grin. "Not until we've stumbled into the enemy."

"Let's get down there before they blow each other up," said S'Rel, turning and stepping up the ramp and into the shuttle.

After a moment, the ramp retracted, the shuttle rose and accelerated with a faint whine of n-gravs. Piercing the blue shimmer of the hangar's forcefield, it soared up into the simulated sunshine of *Devastator*'s atmosphere, breached the shield layers and was gone.

Heather rose from the office floor peering into the pale glow of the emergency lighting. There was no sign of Hochmeister. Automatic-weapons fire was echoing through the cavern—multiple, staccato bursts that rattled down the entrance tunnel, resounding in overlapping waves off the rock walls of the Hole. Running to the desk, Heather jerked open the bottom drawer—the destruct terminal was gone. "Shit," she whispered.

Holding the Magnum high and two-handed, she stepped into the corridor that ran past the offices to the tunnel entrance.

Smoke and the dim flicker of orange flame filled the tunnel, the thick tendrils of white smoke spreading slowly into the complex. As

Heather watched, three men wearing gas masks and clad in ski jackets burst through the smoke, turning to fire their machine pistols back down the tunnel.

Return fire ripped through them, tumbling their bodies to the granite as the first SK squad broke into the complex—six or so black-uniformed troopers who leaped the bodies of the dead defenders, charging straight for Heather. You're not taking this rebel alive, she vowed, raising her pistol.

A rough hand jerked Heather into a side corridor. Twisting free, Heather turned, finger thumbing back the hammer, and saw Hargrove, shirt blackened and torn, blood trickling down his face from a nasty scalp wound. "Run!" he ordered, jerking his head down the tunnel. As Heather ran, he pulled the pin on the grenade, chucked it back at the intersection and stepped into a rubble-filled alcove.

Heather ran.

The SK squad rounded the corner at a dead run, opening fire just as the grenade exploded, turning Colonel Ritter's point squad into four corpses and two badly wounded men. One of them was still screaming in pain-racked agony when Hargrove finished the job with two quick bursts from his minimac.

"Come on!" said Hargrove, catching up with Heather. Behind them, assault whistles echoed down the corridor as the two companies of SKs penetrated the Hole.

"Bomb room," gasped Heather as they ran. "Manual destruct."

"Back door," agreed Hargrove.

"Cuckoos have entered the nest. Cuckoos have entered the nest." It was the amplified voice of Hargrove's executive officer, sent echoing throughout the complex by the PA system. "White dove to chicks. White dove to chicks."

White dove's coming to hatch her chicks, thought Heather, keeping up with Hargrove. And kiss it all good-bye.

Back behind the tunnel's sheltering curve, other boots now echoed.

Futile, the whole project, she thought. And Hochmeister walking in as if strolling down the K'dam, slipping in through that ultra-secret entrance . . . Treason, something whispered in her head. It was a whisper she trusted, child of a broken nation in a treacherous world.

They halted, panting, at an intersection. To their right, the original tunnel continued. To the left, the remains of some old cave-in choked the passageway.

Hargrove stopped, hands feeling along the side of a vertical support beam. Watching him, Heather seemed to see him for the first time.

There was a sharp *click* and the tumbled

pile of stone blocking the left-hand passage rumbled into the wall. They hurried through and the passageway resealed behind them.

Where does a nuclear bomb sit? thought Heather. Anywhere it wants, she answered, looking down at four hundred kilograms of plutonium 235, encased in fifteen dull blue shells of pure cobalt. They were fat little bombs on which some bored staff had painted fat little smiling faces, complete with jowls, and they sat on their dollies in a semicircle around the room's single console. The center bomb, the one facing the console, wore a deep frown—as it should—with the dual terminals of a thin, hard wire strung into its broad nose.

"Better get to it—white dove," said Hargrove, stepping down the short metal staircase and into the bomb room.

"King's bishop to white dove four." Admiral Hochmeister slowly walked to the center of the room, hands in the pocket of his unzipped parka. "My game, I believe," he said, hand on the console.

"Not yet," said Heather, and fired, sending three quick rounds into Hargrove's back. He was dead before his face could even mirror his first dull surprise.

"White dove takes bishop's knave," said Heather, advancing, gun leveled. "Only he and I knew about that bolt hole, Admiral —and I sure as hell didn't tell you."

"Look again," said Hochmeister, nodding at the body.

Heather risked a quick glance and stood transfixed: green, over six feet tall, tentacles extending from its shoulders, antennae on its head, mandibles where its mouth should be—a S'Cotar transmute lay dead on the floor, three large, ugly holes through its thorax.

"You sonofabitch," said Heather, looking at Hochmeister and raising the Magnum. "The bugs are back and you sold out."

He shook his head. "No. That one was one of Guan-Sharick's loyalists, working for me by mutual agreement.

"My offer to you still stands, MacKenzie," he said. "It won't be repeated."

"Step away from that console, Admiral."

Hochmeister looked up and behind her. "Ritter, kill her if she takes another step."

Heather turned at the snick of rounds being chambered—Colonel Ritter and three SKs stood in the doorway.

"I opened the door while you looked at the bug," said Hochmeister as they took her gun away. "Get your ordnance people in here, Colonel," he ordered.

"Excuse me, Admiral," said Heather as they handcuffed her hands behind her back. "When you opened the door, how many times did you push the switch?"

"Twice." Frowning, he looked at the small

green button, then back at Heather. "Nothing happened the first time. Why?"

She laughed—a high clear sound that echoed through the room. "Baby chick takes all the king's horses and all the king's men. When this installation's on alert condition, that little green button becomes a booby trap—one opens the door with five seconds' delay. More than once within five seconds . . ."

"Destruct sequence activated." It was a recording, playing automatically from the overrun defense center. "Mark thirty. Twenty-nine . . ."

"Cut that cable!" Ritter ordered the three-man ordnance team just coming down the stairs, packs in hand. He pointed at the line running from the console to the frowning bomb.

As the first man touched the cable a green laser beam fired from the wall, boring a neat hole in his chest. He crumpled at Hochmeister's feet.

"I don't suppose there's a deactivation code?" said Hochmeister to MacKenzie. Behind them, Colonel Ritter was shouting into his transceiver to find and cut the auxiliary power.

"You might try 'Sic Transit Gloria Mundi,'" said Heather.

Hochmeister smiled ruefully, shook his head and took off his biofocals, polishing them carefully as the recording said, "Fifteen . . ."

"Final matters," said the admiral. "You've always had my respect, MacKenzie. It's unfortunate we have to end this way."

Before Heather could more than open her mouth, three figures appeared in the room's center. Two SKs on the stairway raised their weapons, only to drop them as red lightning flashed from S'Rel's eyes, touching the machine pistols.

"Three, two . . ." said the PA system as Guan-Sharick stared at the console. Console and cable vanished.

"One," said the tape, and clicked off.

"Hold your fire, Colonel," called Hochmeister.

Ritter raised his hand as more SKs rushed into the bomb room. "Hold your fire," he repeated.

"Not that you'd get a shot off," said S'Rel, eyes scanning the troopers' faces. "I'm very good at this."

"Got yourself into a mess, Heather?" said John, walking over to the physicist-guerilla.

"John, I don't know where you came from . . ."

"A shuttle, parked outside, my dear."

". . . but I'm delighted and relieved to see you." She turned her back to him, manacled hands outthrust. "The big thug in the corner has the key."

"I don't believe it's been established whose

188

side they're on," said Hochmeister, pulling on his glasses. "Whose side are you, Mr. Harrison?"

"Our own, I'm afraid," said John, turning from Heather to face the admiral. He nodded toward the blonde. "You've met Guan-Sharick before."

Hochmeister bowed slightly. "Not in such a comely guise.

"Your associate's come to a bad end," he said to the transmute, indicating the dead S'Cotar by the stairs.

The blonde shrugged. "We've come to make you an offer you can't refuse, Admiral."

"Himmler once said the same thing to me," said Hochmeister. "And I said no."

"We're taking all your atomic weapons, including reserved fissionable materials," said the transmute.

"What for?" said the admiral.

"Fuel."

"What are you fueling—the moon?"

"About the same size," said John. "Only made of battlesteel and loaded with armaments. It's parked in orbit, needing a refill."

"Why tell us at all?" said the admiral. "Why not just take it?"

"We would have," said S'Rel. "Except that you people were about to dispose of this material—and yourselves—very dramatically and very uselessly. Instead, we'll dispose of it for you."

The bombs and Guan-Sharick were gone.

"Do you know how much work," began Heather, her face very pale, "how many people died . . ."

"We're off to fight the AIs on their own turf, Heather," interrupted John. "If we don't win, you'll all die. They know you're here, they'll come for you when they've finished with us."

"Harrison," sighed Hochmeister, polishing his biofocals, "take it all—all the filthy stuff. Just make sure, if you're cleaning us out, to do the same for the Russians."

"That's very generous of you, Admiral," John smiled. "Especially since you don't have any choice."

Guan-Sharick reappeared. "Ready to go?"

"One thing," said John, turning to Heather. "Tell my blond friend where you want to go—softly."

"I'm not a taxi," said the transmute as Heather crossed the room. She whispered something in Guan-Sharick's ear. The blonde nodded.

"Long life and happiness," said John as the two disappeared.

"It's unlikely she'll have either," said Hochmeister as the transmute reappeared.

"And the same to you, Admiral," said John.

Only Germans were left in the bombless room.

17

"EXCUSE ME, GENTLEMEN."

"Yes, Line?" L'Guan looked up from the I'Wor board—it was D'Trelna's move.

"The Margrave of U'Tria's scout craft has just cleared jump point—Combine T'Lan cruisers are in pursuit."

"I believe FleetOps was calling them 'armed merchantmen' during my tenure," said L'Guan, watching D'Trelna's hand hover uncertainly between two pieces.

"Those the same slime who've been sitting around jump point the past week?" asked D'Trelna, moving his flanking captain two squares to the left.

"The same," said Line. "The margrave

191

double-jumped them—came insystem already jump-plotted for further in."

"He had a thirty percent chance of not blowing his drive," said L'Guan, moving his man.

"What's FleetOps doing about him?" asked L'Guan.

"Busily flashing seize-or-destroy orders to Home System Command," said Line. "The Margrave's destination is K'Ronar—there's no way he can avoid the picket ships."

"See if you can tightbeam him," said L'Guan, taking D'Trelna's consort.

It took a moment, then L'Wrona's face appeared to the right of the game table, just above a colorful clump of tropical flora long extinct on K'Ronar itself. Staring at the margrave, D'Trelna could see through him to the waterfall beyond.

"Got it," said L'Wrona, staring at the small image in the pickup. He tapped his breast pocket.

"His tactical situation's utterly hopeless," said Line, projecting a second window beside the first: three distinct groups of red blips were closing from two sides on a single green one; a second group of eight hostiles followed behind. As the two officers watched, a group of five yellow blips detached themselves from the region fronting Line and moved toward the green target blip.

"Admiral," said Line, "I am granting the margrave's ship extended sanctuary under the terms of General Order Seven. Do you concur?"

"What is General Order Seven?" asked D'Trelna. I'Wor forgotten, he was intent on the other, deadlier game unfolding on the tacscan.

"'Any vessel or crew whose presence is a necessary constituent to the defense of the planet may, at the discretion of both Line and the Line Duty Officer, be granted extended sanctuary,'" said L'Guan, eyes shifting between L'Wrona and the tacscan.

"Now would not be too soon," said L'Wrona, punching in a countersalvo as the first wave of missiles came in. He threw an arm over his eyes as fierce red fusion beams flashed from *Toy*, touching the six silver shipbusters streaking in on the scout craft. Orange-red explosions mushroomed around the craft, enveloping it in a fiery globe that was gone as quickly as it had come.

Inside the ship, L'Wrona lowered his arm. "Status?" he asked, watching the tacscan. Another wave of missiles, three times the number of the last, was just launching. Ahead and around him, the opposing ships were coming into beam range.

"Shield's gone," said Dad.

"Any suggestions?" he asked the ship.

"Unless Line does something for you right now, son, bend over and kiss it good-bye."

"Concur," said L'Guan.

"What the seven hells?" said Admiral I'Tal, coming to his feet as every screen in FleetOps went dark. "Commodore A'Wal," he called, "check status on . . ."

The screens came back on, all showing the starship-and-sun of the old Empire, set in a single black circle—Line's emblem. "This is K'Ronarin Defense Sphere," said the unmistakable contralto from every speaker in the Operations Center. "The ship *Rich Man's Toy* is under the protection of this unit. You are directed to break off attack and withdraw all forces to their original positions. I will give you a twenty-count. Any units attacking the vessel *Rich Man's Toy* at the end of the twenty-count will be destroyed." The screens returned to normal, but the voice remained, counting slowly, "Twenty . . . nineteen . . ."

Admiral I'Tal didn't waste time with intermediaries. Lunging across Commodore A'Wal's console, he pushed the General address tab. "All ships, Home System—break off attack on scout craft. Destroy all in-flight ordnance. Return to stations."

Breathing hard, he sank back into his chair, watching the tacscan on the big board. Acknowledgments were coming in by the time Line was intoning "Zero." One by one, the

Fleet cruisers turned away, a trail of self-destructing missiles in their wake.

"The slumbering giant awakes," murmured A'Wal, watching the screen as the admiral reached for a glass of water. The Commodore frowned. "Combine T'Lan has not broken off the attack," he said as the trailing red blips closed on the single green one.

Admiral I'Tal glanced up at the board. "Be a pity if those power-hungry v'org slime got wiped." He grinned a vicious little grin. "Have Commander Prime Base put the installation on a stage two alert." He and A'Wal watched as the Combine T'Lan ships loosed another missile salvo, followed by a fusion barrage. "Line's about to wipe a flotilla of the Imperial Party's biggest supporter—I don't want any edict-issuing Councilors bursting in here."

An alarm sounded—three high, warbling notes. "Line has opened fire," said computer.

"Incoming all over the scan," said Dad.

"Shield . . ."

"Gone."

L'Wrona found himself clutching the free-holder's commwand with one hand as he futilely stabbed the jump drive engage with his other.

"Forget it, son," said the ship. "Hull transponder nodules got fried."

L'Wrona was reaching out to take the ship

off manual, to bring it around for a death run on his attackers, when the incoming warheads atomized *Toy*.

The little grotto—jungle, trees, bluff, waterfall—D'Trelna saw none of it, standing in front of the tacscan, watching the missiles from the Combine ships close on his friend's ship. "Fire—full intercept pattern!" he bellowed. Behind and above him, frightened birds took flight.

"Too late," said L'Guan. "Even at light speed." He stood beside D'Trelna, watching quietly, drink in hand.

Missile specks and target blip met and vanished. "Target destroyed," read the data trail's final item.

"Now, I think," said Line, and fired. Thousands of miles away, weapons on two artificial planetoids flashed briefly, azure beams piercing the shield wall. As D'Trelna and L'Guan watched, all remaining blips vanished from the screens, follrwed by the screens themselves. Overhead, the circling birds returned to their trees.

"You useless, antiquated automaton," said D'Trelna slowly, eyes searching the grotto, as though hoping to find some tangible part of Line that he could rip with the hands clenching and unclenching at his side. "You delayed . . . you purposefully delayed firing!"

"Commodore," said Line pleasantly,

"you're no judge of my capabilities. I suggest . . ."

"I could have picked those slime off with three ships at the same range you failed at—failed with the entire firepower of an Imperial fleet!" His voice rose to a shout. "L'Wrona's dead, the commwand lost—and with it any hope of defeating the AIs." He sank into his chair. "Give me a ship, please," he said to L'Guan. "Anything's better than . . ." He broke off, turning in his chair to follow L'Guan's gaze, then stood, his chair tipping unnoticed to the ground.

"That bellow of yours carries the length of the corridor," said L'Wrona, stepping from the rock entrance to the grotto into the light.

"H'Nar!" shouted D'Trelna, embracing the captain in a bear hug that made L'Wrona protest, "J'Quel . . ."

"Sorry," said the commodore, gripping him by the shoulders and stepping back. "Matter transporter," he said, letting go.

"Matter transporter," confirmed L'Guan, joining them.

"The same 'lost' matter transporter technology we were sent to find during the Biofab War, H'Nar," said D'Trelna, turning to L'Guan. "Something the admiral's declined to explain."

"Interesting," said L'Wrona. "Admiral, you do owe us an . . ."

"An explanation?" L'Guan smiled. "No, I

don't. But"—he held up a hand, stopping their protests—"I'll give you one, now that *Implacable*'s gone. Your ship was sent as far from the war to protect its precious cargo from harm."

"Precious cargo?" said D'Trelna. "I thought Scepter and Crown were enshrined in the Palace?"

"Human cargo, D'Trelna," said L'Guan. "The last hope of this dying republic, and, oddly, an aristocrat—though he hides it well—a bit too well."

"The Heir," said L'Wrona wonderingly. "You put the Heir Apparent on board!"

"I didn't know there was an Heir," said D'Trelna.

"A well-kept secret," said L'Wrona. "I've always known there was an Heir, but never who he was."

"Why on *Implacable*?" demanded D'Trelna. "To protect him? We were in the thick of it—he could have died a hundred times!"

"You weren't supposed to be in the thick of it," said the admiral. "And he may die yet."

"Who?" asked both men at once.

L'Guan laughed and refilled his empty glass. "A toast, gentlemen, to the last of a great house: K'Yan, sixth of that name, Heir Apparent to the Sceptered Throne, Commander of the Founding Fleet, Guardian of . . ."

"Who?" said D'Trelna.

"Your engineer, N'Trol," said the admiral, emptying his glass.

"I don't believe it," said D'Trelna.

"Believe it," said L'Guan.

"Then we're a doomed race," said D'Trelna. "He's irresponsible, hates people, loves only his engines . . ."

"Excuse me," interrupted Line. "But the Fleet of the One has just entered Quadrant Blue Nine. The mindslavers are engaging them."

18

"HOW ARE YOU feeling, Y'Dan?" asked a familiar voice—a woman's voice.

Feeling? thought K'Tran drowsily. I don't feel anymore—the question's irrelevant.

He felt a rough hand on his shoulder. "Stand to, corsair captain," said a man's voice. "For your Emperor, your Gods and your Fleet."

"Pompous asshole," said K'Tran, and opened his eyes.

"I thought that would bring you around," said N'Trol, smiling down on the surgical table.

"How are you, Y'Dan?" said A'Tir, stepping into K'Tran's field of vision.

"All right, I think, Number One," he said

carefully, and sat up. The first thing he saw was his feet—large, pale and hairless, with blunt, square toes and high arches. He looked at the rest of his naked body, then felt his face. "This is not my body," he said carefully.

"The last R'Actolian destroyed your body just before it escaped," said a perfect voice —the voice of a computer.

"And who the hell are you?" demanded K'Tran.

"We are the master computers of the Golden Fleet, linked in series," said the voice.

"Give me back my body!" demanded K'Tran, looking from A'Tir to N'Trol and back.

"It's been reduced to carbonized dust," said the machines. "We've given you the body of an Imperial Marine lieutenant whose brain was destroyed in stasis flux, some years ago. We would point out, Captain K'Tran, that this body is twenty years younger than your original, perhaps more aesthetically pleasing, and in excellent condition. And as a compensation for your loss, we have enhanced the genitalia."

The shock fading, K'Tran looked down again. "Good God!"

"We can live with it, Y'Dan," said A'Tir, following his gaze.

N'Trol cleared his throat. "K'Tran, we've got about a half watch to prepare this fleet for battle. Please cover your splendid new self."

He tossed a bundle of clothes at the corsair captain. "You're needed on the bridge."

"You're *Implacable*'s engineer," said K'Tran, pulling on a pair of black pants. "N'Trol. You death-tripped my cruiser off Terra." He slipped on the matching black shirt, frowning at the single gleaming comet on the collar. "This is an Imperial admiral's uniform." His new voice disconcerted him—it was too deep, and somehow made his polished, old line Academy intonation sound affected.

N'Trol nodded. "Win this battle, all your crimes are pardoned and the rank is permanent."

"Who are you to go around handing out a dead empire's flag ranks, Engineer?" said K'Tran, sitting to pull on the boots that sat by the bedside.

"He's your bloody damned Emperor," said A'Tir, looking at N'Trol.

N'Trol laughed. "If we win—probably. If not, well, K'Tran, you get to be an admiral for a while."

K'Tran stood, looking around the mind-slaver's sickbay. It was an immense hall that seemed to go on forever: row upon row of beds, and each bed had an occupant. K'Tran looked back at N'Trol. "You're restoring them all," he guessed.

N'Trol nodded. "The computers are—on this and the twenty-one other ships of this fleet. And, to avoid bedlam, each brain in its brainpod is now being briefed on our situation and given an option—help us fight, or remain off-line until after the battle. There're representatives here from every dynasty since the fifth, plus people dragooned off a slew of lost colonies in Blue Nine. Imagine the mess we'd have trying to brief them all separately." He turned back to K'Tran. "Now, sir, will you stand with us, or await the outcome?"

"If you win, and I haven't fought?" asked K'Tran, knowing the answer.

N'Trol shrugged. "You'll be tried by the Fleet you betrayed and given loser's options: Death by hanging, death by firing party, death by poison, death by spacing, death by . . ."

K'Tran clenched a large new hand to his breast. "An honor to serve you, My Lord."

"You see what they're doing," said Admiral L'Guan, pointing to his left. He, D'Trelna and L'Wrona stood in Line's war center, looking at the tri-dee projection of a slice of space inside Line's. Cruisers marked with the emblem of Combine T'lan were taking up station off Prime Base.

"They wouldn't dare," said L'Wrona.

"Why not?" said L'Guan. "Fleet's scattered throughout the Confederation. Those mechanical slime know Line can't fire on the planet. And with Councilor D'Assan virtually owning FleetOps, no one's going to recall so much as a single class-E destroyer."

"Sir, I think you underestimate the integrity of the FleetOps command," said L'Wrona.

"I hope so," said L'Guan. "But with no Fleet, FleetOps is just a hole in the desert."

"What if the Fleet were recalled?" asked D'Trelna, looking at L'Wrona, then back at the admiral.

"Line?" asked the admiral.

"Eighty-two percent return rate in one week," said Line. "The balance scattered over two months. But only in a bona-fide state of siege, as proclaimed by Council edict, may FleetOps issue a recall."

"With your permission, Admiral?" said L'Wrona, indicating a complink.

"Certainly," said L'Guan, "but what . . ."

"He's going to recall the Fleet, I think," said D'Trelna as L'Wrona sat down at the terminal.

"If you'll stop shouting, I'll try to explain," said the tech officer.

Commodore A'Wal stopped shouting. "Explain, then," he said. Outside, beyond the armorglass wall of his office, FleetOps was in chaos—officers running like frenzied insects from station to station, comm officers frantically issuing and reissuing unheeded instructions to units scattered across millions of light-years; the worried faces of flotilla and sector commanders mirrored in the skipcomm screens.

"All of our machines are Imperial," said the tech officer, running a hand through his hair. He pointed to the operations floor. "Everything out there, right down to the lighting panels, is just as it was five thousand years ago—except that some of it doesn't work quite as well."

"Tell me something I don't know," said A'Wal, sitting on the outer edge of his desk, arms folded. "So?"

"No one's rewritten the computer programs since the Fall," said the tech officer. "We know their machine code, but we don't have their security protocols. If we . . ."

"If we tamper with it, we might wipe the whole combat command system," said A'Wal, eyes on the operations floor. The tech officer turned, following his gaze: Admiral I'Tal was engaging in a shouting match over the skipcomm with an admiral second. I'Tal ended the discussion by stabbing a finger at the younger officer and hitting the disconnect. Unaware that he was being watched, he sank into his chair, shaking his head.

The tech officer and A'Wal returned to their discussion. "You remember *Implacable*'s encounter with Imperial machine code and that stasis algorithm out in Blue Nine?"

The commlink on A'Wal's desk began to

chirp. Ignoring it, he said, "Tell me quickly, Commander—without the background briefing. Why are over eight thousand starcruisers making for here at flank—corsairs as well as Fleet? Why are their crews and we unable to stop this unwanted return?"

"Someone has bypassed our programming overlay," said the tech officer. "They've activated a section of the old Imperial programming last used at the Fall."

"What portion?"

"The recall, sir. Someone with access to FleetOps channels and knowledge of an authentication sequence sacred to the last Royal House has recalled the Fleet. If the crews try to tamper with the recall programming, those sturdy old Imperial jump drives will self-destruct."

There was a loud knock on A'Wal's door. He ignored it. "Who and why?"

"Who?" The tech officer shrugged. "There being no Heir . . ."

A'Wal held up a forefinger. "Do not assume that."

The tech officer raised an eyebrow. "Sir? May I ask if you know . . . ?"

A'Wal shook his head. "Just rumors —vague rumors over the past five years or so. Continue, Commander." The knocking had stopped, but not the commlink's chirping.

"Absent an Heir," said the tech officer, "I would assume the Hereditary Lord Captain of the Imperial Guard—except that he's dead. Or," he said, seeing something in A'Wal's expression, "should I not assume that either?"

"Perhaps not," said the commodore. "But why the recall?"

With a hiss and a pop of shorted electronics, the door to A'Wal's office slid open. Stepping past a technician and her scattered tools, Admiral I'Tal came in. "I need you out there, A'Wal. Now."

"What . . ." began the commodore as the tech officer slipped out.

"We're receiving an invasion alert on an old High Imperial watch channel," said the admiral.

"Is it authenticated?" asked A'Wal as the two men hurried down the stairs onto the operations floor.

"Archival match," said the admiral. "Imperial battlecode of the House of T'Rlon, coming from a mindslaver fleet off the Rift—a fleet allegedly commanded by one Admiral K'Tran."

"The galaxy's bloodiest butcher commanding a fleet of the dead and the damned," said A'Wal. "The Last Days are here.

"What's K'Tran sending in for evidence, if anything?" asked A'Wal as they reached his console. An air of quiet purpose pervaded FleetOps, with brown-uniformed officers grimly intent on their work.

"If their data transmission's to be believed —and if it's faked, it's very good," said the admiral, "about ten thousand AI battleglobes have just entered Blue Nine. If we survive the next few hours, I'll worry about it."

"Sir?"

I'Tal nodded at the status board. A swarm of red blips was forming between Line and K'Ronar. "Looks like Combine T'Lan's about to try to take over this planet. Quite a coincidence, wouldn't you say? We're massing our pitiful handful of picket ships backside of the planet from them."

"Sir." It was a tech officer, dun-colored commjack in his ear, tiny transmit nodule tied to his throat. "Commander Prime Base advises Councilor D'Assan has received Council sanction to relieve you and half the general staff of command."

"Leaving the politicos to not defend the Confederation," said A'Wal.

"I see," said the admiral, turning back to the board and the tacscan. "Has the Council issued any orders to its new general staff?"

"Stand down and not bother the Combine trader fleet assembling in orbit."

"They must have meant the traitor fleet now assuming bombardment positions," said A'Wal, inserting his own earjack.

"Instruct Commander Prime Base," said I'Tal, "to prepare for ground combat

—commandos and gun crews to battleposts, shields to max."

"Yes, sir."

"Commodore," said the admiral, turning to A'Wal. "On my authority—Invasion Alert —all ships, all stations. Advise readiness status by planetary and quadrant command as received. Planetary Guard and available Fleet elements to attack all installations and vessels of Combine T'Lan wherever found."

"Might I suggest, Admiral, the true nature of Combine T'Lan be revealed?"

"Very well," said I'Tal after a moment. "Summarize Admiral S'Gan and D'Trelna's report from the Blue Nine expedition and put it out on Fleetcomm, counterintelligence priority one."

"And commercial channels?" suggested A'Wal.

"And commercial channels," said the admiral.

"Those armed merchantmen," said L'Guan, turning from the war center's tri-dee, "are going to be lunching in the Palace."

"They don't eat," said L'Wrona, reading the data trail.

"H'Nar," said the commodore, "do you or do you not have the location of S'Yal's last citadel?"

L'Wrona nodded. "Under the dead riverbed

of the R'Shen. The freeholder established that even though it sustained a full flotilla bombardment, its shielding held. It's there now, shields still on, a perfect sphere walled by the tons of molten rock that cooled around it. And somewhere in there is the means to recall the Twelfth Fleet."

"Given a year," said L'Guan, "an impressive budget and great care, we could probably chip it out."

"We've got about one watch," said D'Trelna. "Line."

"Commodore?"

"Could you transport L'Wrona and me to a point beneath K'Ronar's surface?"

"Just give me the coordinates, Commodore."

The two men looked at L'Guan. The Admiral spread his hands helplessly. "What's to lose? Take what you want from Weapons and Stores and luck to you."

The invasion alert came in a moment after they were gone.

"I have independent corroboration from Pocsym Six's satellite network, Admiral," said Line. "The Fleet of the One is advancing through the Rift. The mindslavers are deploying to meet them."

"They'll be slaughtered."

"May I remind the admiral that K'Tran commands the mindslavers?"

"They'll take out a few battleglobes and

then they'll be slaughtered," said L'Guan. "And then our ancient masters will arrive —probably to find K'Ronar a smoldering ruin and you and me still arguing. I ask again —will you end our splendid isolation? Will you deploy?"

"You know my answer. The Heir was supposed to be here, giving the necessary orders, Admiral." L'Guan looked up, surprised at the petulant tone.

"He would have been, if he hadn't gotten kidnapped by that miserable woman and her cutthroats."

"I have no other option than to wait, Admiral."

"Fine," said L'Guan, sinking into his chair. "We'll wait, Line—for your Emperor and a miracle."

19

Q'NIL LOOKED UP as the door to *Devastator*'s sickbay hissed open. "Harrison," he said, returning to his computer terminal. "You look your usual robust self."

"And you're your usual sardonic self, Medtech." Taking a straight-backed metal chair from beside the medanalyzer, he pulled it up to Q'Nil's desk and sat, arms folded over the back, facing the medtech.

"Why don't you sit down," said Q'Nil, working the complink.

"How long have we known each other, Q'Nil?" asked the Terran.

"If you're going to propose some quaint Terran mating contract . . ."

"Marriage. I wasn't going to propose it."

Q'Nil jotted a note, then returned to the complink. He looked about forty, tall, thin, hair receding, with an intelligent forehead and high cheekbones. John had seen him smile only once.

"About two years, Harrison," said Q'Nil. "The battle at the Lake of Dreams, then the original Terra Two nastiness, the skirmish in Blue Nine and now this last, desperate sally." He looked up. "Why?"

"I've searched the computer banks, back-tracked all the mission logs, correlated . . ."

Q'Nil shrugged and returned to his work. "And you've determined that whenever Guan-Sharick appeared, I was nowhere around. And with two years of data, most of it from *Implacable*, you've eliminated all other ship-board contenders. I am, ipso facto, Guan-Sharick, late Illusion Master of the Infinite Hosts of the Magnificent—a being wanted by the K'Ronarin Confederation for sundry war crimes." The medtech looked up again, cool blue eyes looking into John's. "So?"

"You . . . you admit it?" asked the Terran.

"D'Trelna knew, back on *Implacable*," said Guan-Sharick. The blonde replaced Q'Nil's lanky form, yellow hair cascading over her shoulders as she tossed her head back. "And Hochmeister, even before then. You've taken a well-worn path to my door."

"Is this really you?" he asked, reaching out a tentative hand, touching her wrist. "And none of your metaphysical bullshit," he said as she opened her mouth.

Guan-Sharick laughed. "All right, Harrison," she said. "No more metaphysical bullshit. Yes, it's really me. And am I really a hundred thousand years old?"

He said nothing, watching as she folded one leg across another. "Yes, counting all my clones. This one"—she touched her chest —"is about fifty years old."

"You've killed a lot of people," said John. "To what end?"

The transmute held up a finger. "In a language older than the AIs, 'Guan-Sharick' means healer. That's what I am here—what I've always been. When the Emperor of the Golden Fleet led the great human exodus from this galaxy, I was his medical officer. I'm still a medic, Harrison—it's just that my practice now spans two galaxies."

"I see," he said. "You've been playing Machiavellian games with galactic humanity for a hundred thousand years . . ."

"Only seventy thousand."

". . . orchestrated the destruction of millions, created those hideous biofabs, and now what? You're saying it was for the good of all?" He found himself with his hand on his blaster.

Guan-Sharick said nothing, merely looked at him with those cool green eyes.

"Fine," said John, taking his hand from his

sidearm. "You're a healer. What are you trying to heal?"

"Think I'm crazy, don't you?" she said.

"Pretty much, yeah," he said.

She smiled. "Let's see if I can convince you otherwise, Harrison." Opening one of the desk drawers, she took out an amber-colored bottle. "S'Tanian brandy." Reaching into another drawer, she took out four glasses and touched the door entry. "You must be tired of listening on your communicators," she called. "That corridor pulls an awful draft."

Warily, Zahava and K'Raoda entered the room, hands on their weapons.

"Pull up some chairs," said Guan-Sharick, pouring the brandy. "I'm going to tell you what comes next—and why you're going to help me."

"Home," said S'Rel, watching the forward scan as *Devastator* emerged from her jump. All the AIs on the bridge were gathered around him, watching the projection. "One million years uptime, a hundred thousand years subjective time since we left."

"Jump reference one-one red four-eight Alpha," said R'Gal. "We're in central sector, as plotted."

"You were governor here," said S'Rel.

R'Gal nodded, watching the data trail thread along the bottom of the tacscan. "And if I were still governor, we'd have been detected and challenged by now. Anything, K'Raoda?"

"I'm monitoring all standard AI comm-channels," said the K'Ronarin, eyes on the console array. "Nothing."

"Nothing?" S'Rel came and looked over K'Raoda's shoulder. "What about commercial and scientific traffic?"

"Nothing," repeated the human. "Try it yourself."

"I was going to make for one of the slave systems," said R'Gal. K'Raoda looked at R'Gal. "But better plot course for the nearest inhabited world . . ."

"Monitor the slave bands." Guan-Sharick stepped onto the bridge, followed by the two Terrans. "And the AI distress frequencies."

"Why?" said S'Rel. "The human trash we left behind after the Revolt . . ."

"Are dead," said Guan-Sharick. "A million years ago.

"Concepts of time are mere abstractions to you AIs," she continued, eyes passing over R'Gal and S'Rel, moving on to the other AIs on the bridge. "Temporal reality? What's temporal reality to beings who never die?"

"We change," said S'Rel. "We grow, some of us—intellectually, spiritually. Certainly, we know what time is—entropy will get us all, eventually."

"Yes, but you don't die, S'Rel," said the blonde. "Not on any scale mortals can conceive. Essentially, you're immortal—all of you. And any society of immortals tends to be static."

"What are you saying?" asked S'Rel.

"Humans die," said Guan-Sharick, turning to him. "Their societies are brawling, fecund, fluxing heaps. And that makes it absurd for you to predicate any judgment of any society on data that is one million years old —including your own. Consider—AI society's dependent on humans for much of its economy. AI society may have seemed static when you left, gentlebeings, but it did not exist in a vacuum."

"Commander K'Raoda," said R'Gal, "please monitor the slave bands and spare us further sociological speculation."

"The slave bands are brawling, fluxing heaps," said K'Raoda after a moment. "They're bristling with military transmissions, most of them in the clear."

"A revolt," said S'Rel uneasily. The AIs on the bridge exchanged worried glances. "Anything on any AI band?"

K'Raoda touched the commlink, then listened for a moment, fingertip touching the commjack in his ear. "Yes," he said finally. "Automatic emergency calls on the distress bands."

"Put one on," said R'Gal.

They listened in silence to a flat, emotionless voice. ". . . is the satellite defense nexus at Bano. We are under attack by slave units. Our position is rapidly deteriorating. We do not have sufficient force left to operate the defenses. The crippler has taken out over eighty-seven percent of the garrison. Overrun is imminent. We repeat, overrun is imminent. All units, all stations, be advised: slave units are employing a cloaking device—tacscan cannot detect them. Also, they have obtained the shield frequencies of all battleglobe and defense installation shield frequencies. They can penetrate our shielding at will, and are only detectable optically. We have dropped shielding and are diverting all power to the guns.

"This is the satellite defense nexus at Bano . . ."

"Gods of my fathers," said R'Gal, unthinkingly using the K'Ronarin oath. "The Empire of the One is gone. The Fleet of the One is gone."

"Overthrown by organic, agrarian clods," said S'Rel.

"Revolutionaries," said John scornfully. "You're a nest of reactionaries." Walking past S'Rel and R'Gal, he stopped and turned, leaning against the edge of K'Raoda's console, arms folded. "I'll remind you—corpses bought us this monstrous machine—Admiral S'Gan and all her command, many of *Implacable*'s crew, about five hundred D'Linian soldiers. Then, through wit and cunning, we reached here, ready to spark a revolt, make an empire totter." His eyes met those of the AI commanders—perfect, blue, expressionless eyes, watchful and waiting. "And what do we find—the revolt's over, the Empire's fallen. By God, you should be dancing on the bridge, R'Gal, S'Rel, all of you. You're dismayed? Why?"

"You return home with a lot of robots," said R'Gal, hands steepled in front of his chin, "ready to overthrow the fascist humans who're about to invade the place you've called home for a lot of years. Reaching there, you find that the food processors have revolted and sliced all the humans. Is your first reaction to break open a sparkling wine?"

"Those agrarian clods?" said K'Raoda, turning in his chair.

"What about them?" said S'Rel.

"Here they come," he said, pointing out the window.

They followed where his finger pointed, through the armorglass wall and onto the endless sweep of steel that was *Devastator*'s hull. Backdropped by the sullen umbra of the battleglobe's shield, black specks were swooping toward the command tower.

"Tacscan reads negative, shield reads normal," said K'Raoda.

"Alert. Alert." It was ship's computer. "Shield breach. Shield breach. Incoming hostiles. Incoming hostiles."

"Battlestations," ordered R'Gal, moving to the commander's station.

K'Raoda thumbed the alert switch. Rattling throughout the battleglobe's occupied area, the battle klaxon's strident *awooka!* sent men and AIs racing to emergency posts.

S'Rel stepped to his own station as the bridge filled with personnel. He spoke quickly into the commlink. "All batteries to automatic. Initiate optical tracking. All batteries commence . . ."

A finger switched off the commlink. "Open up on them, they'll know we're hostile," said R'Gal.

"If we don't, Commander, they'll blow the ship . . ."

Explosions racked the bridge, sending humans and AIs sprawling. Outside, orange-blue flames leaped high as missile battery after missile battery detonated, touched by swift green rays.

"Contracting shielding to inhabited areas only," said K'Raoda, fingers flying over the console. "Releasing atmosphere curtain to snuff fires."

A shrill, three-note alarm sounded. "Hostiles closing on command tower," said computer. "Hostiles closing on command tower. Request counterfire. Request counterfire."

Everyone looked outside. The black specks had become silver, needle-nosed fighter craft, streaking at hull level toward the bridge, a trail of burning weapons batteries behind them. The last defense perimeter passed, the fighters opened fire on the command tower, just as K'Raoda released the atmosphere curtain.

"Drop!" John shouted, pushing Zahava to the deck. As he threw himself on top of her, the heavy fusion bolts exploded against the bridge's shield. Glancing up, John had just a quick glimpse of one of the fighter craft spinning wildly out of control. Caught in the irresistible rush of millions of cubic tons of escaping air, the fighter pierced the shield and slammed into the bridge. John saw it for just a second as it burst through the armorglass —fangs seemed to reach for him from the bow—carnivorous white fangs that dripped blood—then a silent ball of light touched him and he knew no more.

20

"STINKS," SAID D'TRELNA.

L'Wrona sniffed. "Recycler's old—it's picking up some of the nitrates. Fairly harmless."

"The air doesn't worry me," said D'Trelna, peering into the twilight world of S'Yal's last citadel. "But where's the light coming from?" he asked, gazing up. An inverted black bowl, the fortress shield was tinged with a faint blue aura.

"Fascinating," said L'Wrona, watching the faint, rhythmic pulsing of the aura. "What kind of power source can withstand a full fleet bombardment," said the captain, "keep this installation intact even as it sinks into molten rock, then keep the earth itself from crushing it over fifteen thousand years?"

"If I knew, I'd be rich," said D'Trelna, looking down the ancient pathway on which they stood to the valley below. Nestled in a grove of silver-barked trees was a white, one-story villa, of the sort that had once dotted lakes and streams throughout the Empire—a graceful, blue-roofed structure of tiled courtyards, fountains and formal gardens.

"Not a palace, not a mansion and certainly not what I was expecting," said D'Trelna.

"What were you expecting, J'Quel?"

"Darkness. Hideous, menacing shapes." Raising his hands, he curled them into talons. "Things that suck the souls out of . . ."

"J'Quel, you're being silly," said L'Wrona, lowering the commodore's nearest hand with his own. "Just because the man had an unsavory reputation doesn't mean he lived in a charnel house."

"Unsavory?" said the commodore, starting the walk down the road toward the villa. "Try evil."

"Evil?" said L'Wrona with faint contempt. "Really, J'Quel—such a simplistic . . ."

"Evil," repeated the commodore, chopping the palm of one hand with the other. "Can't exist, can it, H'Nar? Not a logical construct. The cool winds of reason blow through the temple of technology. Superstition's cast aside."

"I didn't say . . ."

"Evil," said D'Trelna. "Biofabs, corsairs,

mindslavers, components, AIs. Evil. You should recognize it by now, H'Nar—we've been fighting it long enough." He strode on ahead down the ancient pathway, a fat, angry man ready for whatever awaited.

L'Wrona caught up, stopping him with a hand to his shoulder. Surprised, D'Trelna turned, staring up into an angry face. "My people came here with the Golden Fleet. We stood with T'Nil when he overthrew the Mindslavers' Guild. We held the Marches against every form of human vermin that tried for K'Ronar. We fought R'Actol and her creatures. More good men and causes have called us friend than you and I have years, Commodore. My family, my friends—they're all dead. My home's a netherworld of walking dead. Don't lecture me on evil."

D'Trelna opened his mouth, then shut it. Controlling himself with visible effort, he started back down the path, L'Wrona following. They walked silently, footsteps absorbed by the soft rubbery surface of the footway. As they reached the floor of the valley, the dead soil to either side gave way to green heather and flowering shrubs.

L'Wrona stopped. "Did you see any flora from the hilltop?" he asked.

D'Trelna shook his head. "Just those trees," he said, pointing ahead to the grove of silver-barked trees.

Twilight vanished, replaced by a bright

summer noon. Commodore and captain looked up, squinting—the shield now glowed yellow.

"Sunlight and flowers," said D'Trelna, stopping to smell a delicate red bud. "Spring stirs to life. Our doing?" he asked, turning back to the road.

"Let's hope spring's all that's stirring," said L'Wrona as they walked through the small stand of silver trees. As they walked, the interlaced boughs over their heads grew leaves, forming a golden canopy over the two. "S'Yal was head of some hideous cult that promised immortality in exchange for loyalty," said L'Wrona. "Fanatical loyalty—and he probably had enough of the Old Science to pull it off. Mystical idiocy reinforced by ritual sacrifice—that alone would have destroyed him, in time. But then he went and betrayed the very AIs his grandfather had freed . . ."

"A revolt he put down," said D'Trelna. "Lost his personal fleet and most of the rest. So having blown the AIs away, the remnant came home and took care of S'Yal—to the general good of all. So? You think he left something behind?"

"Does this strike you as a fortress, J'Quel?" said L'Wrona, gesturing about him.

"Grubby, gray things with too-bright corridors that stink of metallic air?" said D'Trelna.

The captain nodded.

"No." The commodore shrugged, hands

behind his back. "But who's to say what an Imperial citadel would look like, given the technology then available?"

"We've both seen Imperial fortresses of about the same period," said L'Wrona. "Does this look like A'Gran Seven's Redoubt, or S'Hlor's Third's Defense Ring—all battlesteel and weapons batteries?"

"No," said the commodore. "But if you're implying we've woken some sort of sleeping dreadfuls . . ."

Leaving the grove, they rounded a bend and stopped before the gate.

"There was no gate here," said D'Trelna, reaching out a hand to touch the wooden planks. "Not when we stood on the hillside." A double-doored, brass-hinged gate, it was set in a high, vine-choked stone wall that ran away to either side, disappearing around the villa.

"Well, there's a gate," said L'Wrona, pushing it with both hands. It didn't budge. "And it's locked."

"We don't have time for this," said D'Trelna. "Combine T'Lan could be slicing up K'Ronarport by now. Take it out, H'Nar," he ordered, stepping back.

Nodding, L'Wrona stepped back, drew and fired. Three red bolts burst through the gate, leaving behind a few charred and flaming sticks clinging to scorched hinges.

Captain and commodore stepped cautiously through the smoke, weapons in hand, and found themselves standing back on the hillside, looking down at the distant villa. There was no wall, no gate. Twilight had returned.

The two officers stared at the valley for a moment, then at each other. "We're being toyed with," said D'Trelna, holstering his sidearm. "Suggestions?"

"A time field?" said L'Wrona.

D'Trelna glanced at his chronometer. "No. Time has advanced, not retreated."

"Internal transporter?"

"I'd say yes, except that the visual images keep changing." D'Trelna ran a hand through his hair. "Which leaves . . ."

"Illusion."

"Certainly some form of mind control," said D'Trelna. He looked at L'Wrona. "I really wanted to strangle you back there, H'Nar. We're not the most compatible couple Fleet ever fielded, but I've never been that angry at you."

The captain met his gaze and nodded. "You're right—we're being toyed with. How?"

D'Trelna looked back down into the valley. "Something that alters our perception of reality—some gentle electronic whisper seducing our senses, goading our baser instincts."

"And to counter it?" said L'Wrona. "We've no grasp of the technology . . ."

"A sharp dose of reality," said D'Trelna. Drawing his blaster, he twisted the muzzle power selector to low, covered the aperture with his left hand and clicked off the safety.

"J'Quel!" cried L'Wrona, stepping toward D'Trelna, hand reaching for the blaster.

D'Trelna squeezed the trigger just as L'Wrona seized his wrist. A bolt of raw red energy lanced D'Trelna's left hand.

L'Wrona found himself alone, his hand clutching nothing.

"You've got to pass them," said Admiral L'Guan with more calm than he felt. "K'Ronar's about to be decimated. The Palace, the Tower, Archives—the cultural and historical legacy of galactic humanity . . ."

"No," said Line. "Those ships are only fourteen percent of the total recalled. Of those, eight percent are corsairs. And the Fleet units present represent over forty-seven disparate commands. Do you seriously expect to get them all to fight as a unit, for the same cause, without a week's training, Admiral?"

"But . . ."

"We'll hold them in reserve," said Line. "Until the rest of the recall comes in, and the Heir returns."

L'Guan shook his head and turned to stare at wall screens with their vivid images of the Combine ships wiping out the remainder of K'Ronar's defenders: blasted and crumpled wreckage tumbling in erratic, decaying orbits around the planet; lifepods torn open by the precise little bolts of Mark 44 fusion cannons, holes in their hulls choked with tangled wreckage and bloated, unsuited bodies.

As L'Guan turned away, his eye was caught by another screen on which a round silver lifepod fled toward a red glimmer on K'Ronar's surface—the shielded sanctuary of Prime Base. As the admiral watched, two slender silver missiles overtook the lifepod, exploding within meters of its unshielded hull. "Line," said L'Guan, turning from the image of ochre-colored gases dissipating into space, "you're an unfeeling slime."

"Just doing my job, Admiral."

"Now, this is more like it," muttered D'Trelna, looking at the real citadel as the medkit tended his hand.

The original twilight was there, generated by the same shield—all else had changed. Where the villa and its grounds had stood now loomed a dark ziggurat of a pyramid, made of the same black metal as the citadel's flooring. The only other structures were oblong, vertical mirrors, set in the flooring. Slightly taller than a man, they ringed the pyramid at the same distance as had the stone wall. A second, smaller group of mirrors stood in four rows fronting the ring at about the same distance as the trees had the wall.

The medkit chirped as its amber light turned green. The commodore slipped the little machine off his hand and snapped it back onto his belt. Raising his left hand to his face, he examined it carefully, flexing his fingers. Gone was the neatly cauterized hole of the beam hit that had pierced the palm, only a small white scab marking its place. Satisfied, D'Trelna drew his blaster, twisted the muzzle back to operational mode and turned to where L'Wrona stood. Seemingly unaware of D'Trelna, he stared around and through the commodore, eyes scanning the citadel. "J'Quel!" he called, hands cupped.

"Here, H'Nar," said D'Trelna.

L'Wrona seemed not to hear, instead taking out his communit and keying the transmit. "D'Trelna. L'Wrona. Acknowledge," he called.

Reaching over, D'Trelna seized the captain by the shoulder and shook him, hard.

"D'Trelna!" exclaimed the captain, seeing the commodore for the first time. "Where in . . ." He stopped, his eye caught by the dark spectacle of S'Yal's citadel. "Gods," he said. "You beat their camouflage." He glanced at D'Trelna's hand.

"Medkit?"

"A marvelous device," nodded the commodore.

"What are all those mirrors for?" asked L'Wrona, his gaze returning to the citadel.

"I have my suspicions," said D'Trelna.

"Care to share them?"

"Not yet—I don't want to have to argue my primitive superstitions with you when we should be penetrating that large lump out there."

"I see," said the captain. "Well, if it's here, it's in there—S'Yal's resting place, would you say?"

D'Trelna nodded. "And well protected, I'd think." He drew his sidearm. "Let's go. And let's not touch the mirrors—just in case I'm right."

Side by side, weapons leveled, they advanced toward the dark pyramid and its strange guardians.

"AI commander on Fleetcomm nine," said computer into A'Wal's earpiece.

The commodore tapped a comm sequence, then watched as the familiar image of Goodman T'Lan appeared on his commscreen.

"Good afternoon, Commodore A'Wal," said T'Lan. "Though probably not so good for you down there in FleetOps, is it?"

"What do you want?" said A'Wal, eyes shifting to the big board and the final wiping of the last picket ships. He only wished he'd been up there rather than in the hole.

"I want to speak with Admiral I'Tal."

"He's indisposed," said A'Wal. They'd carried the old man out with a heart attack a moment after the K'Ronarport shield had failed. "I command here."

"Very well," said T'Lan. "I want your surrender. Now. The city shields have fallen. The Fleet of the One has penetrated Quadrant Blue Nine and will be here within the week. Surrender now, we'll spare the planet. Otherwise we'll sit up here and blast your cities to glowing rubble and your people to windblown ash. Prime Base and FleetOps can huddle behind their shield for another week, then the battleglobes will be here. You do know what a battleglobe is, Commodore?"

"Rust in hell," said A'Wal, switching off. He touched another commkey. "Commander Prime Base," he said.

A woman's tired face appeared in the commscreen, commodore's insignia on her collar. "A'Wal," she said.

"S'Jan," he said. "They just called for surrender."

"You told them to jerk their circuits."

"I did. Just a suspicion, but I think they're going to try a selective field damp and run an assault force in on us."

"We're ready for them," said S'Jan. "Can't stop them, but we'll keep them out of the hole for a while." She looked up at something offscan, then turned back. "Councilor D'Assan slipped out of the city—Intelligence believes he's with the T'Lan."

"Gone for a traitor's reward. Luck, S'Jan."

"Luck, A'Wal. Luck to us all."

"Can you take Prime Base?" asked D'Assan, setting down his drink.

"With the data you've provided," said the elder T'Lan, "certainly. We can penetrate that portion of the shield directly over FleetOps, take them and the shield generators out and scrub Prime Base. That should end all but guerrilla resistance. If you'd care to look, you can see the assault force assembling now."

Taking his drink, D'Assan left the armchair and walked over to the wardroom's armorglass wall, accompanied by the two T'Lans. Outside, sheltered by the fleet's heavy cruisers, thousands of assault craft were massing: wingless, oblong shuttles of K'Ronarin design, each capable of carrying fifty humans.

"What's in there?" asked D'Assan, sipping his drink. "Security blades?"

"Yes," said T'Lan junior. "But piloted by humans familiar with the K'Ronarin defense grid—you're a naturally corrupt species."

"Not all of us," said D'Assan, turning to the AI. "Everything I've done's been for the betterment of humanity. We're illogical, incapable of governing ourselves—you've taught me that."

"Everything you've done, my friend," said

the AI, putting an arm around D'Assan's shoulder, "has been for humanity's demise. We're going to dispose of every last one of you."

"But . . . but . . ." stammered D'Assan, trying to step away. "The provisional government, the council of advisors . . ."

"You're a fool, D'Assan," said the AI, breaking the man's neck with a single quick twist.

The two AIs watched silently as D'Assan's limbs twitched in death shock.

"Amazing," said the elder AI as the twitching stopped. "That something so frail and vulnerable could be such a problem."

Outside, the assault force moved off toward K'Ronar.

"Anything from our Home Fleet?" asked the older AI as they left the wardroom.

"Just rendezvous instructions," said his counterpart. "Command staff hasn't sent so much as a 'well done.'"

"Odd," said T'Lan senior. "Well, let's secure K'Ronar and await the Fleet."

21

A ROUGH HAND shook John's shoulder. "Get up, scum," said a harsh voice. "We know you're alive."

The Terran opened his eyes. He was lying facedown beside the shattered remains of one of the bridge consoles, a class-one headache pounding his temples. White-fanged jaws gaped open, a few feet away. Raising his head, he saw it was the hologram projecting from the bow of the crashed ship that filled the shattered armorglass wall of *Devastator*'s bridge. The little ship's cockpit was a crushed and tangled mass of shattered armorglass, buckled beams and dangling power cables. Bloody and well pulped, parts of something once human hung from the cockpit.

"Over there with the rest of the slime." A great red-haired hand jerked the Terran to his feet and dragged him, stumbling, across the bridge, depositing him with a final hard shove among the group huddling against the far wall: Zahava, K'Raoda, R'Gal and S'Rel.

"Are we all that's left?" said John, squinting as a fresh wave of pain lanced through his head. Gingerly, he touched the welt behind his left ear.

"Do they look like they'd follow the Geneva Convention—even if they'd heard of it?" said Zahava, nodding at their captors. "They killed the K'Ronarins, froze the AIs."

Not an especially merciful bunch, thought John. They were all big, all male, muscles bulging beneath coarse green uniforms. Gleaming, double-headed, a wicked-looking axe dangled from every belt, and about every fifth man wore a holstered pistol. The boarders were busy collecting the AIs, who stood motionless, staring unblinkingly at the blasted remains of the bridge doors. R'Gal's hand was on S'Rel's arm, as if restraining the other AI.

Picking an AI up beneath the arms, two men would carry him to the middle of the bridge, then return for another. When they finished, all of R'Gal's nonhuman command stood in a column of threes, twenty-eight humanoid statues. Stepping up to the first AI, Red Beard unhooked his axe and, while his troops cheered, lopped off the droid's head. It went spinning through the air to bounce off the navigation console, leaving behind a headless torso that pitched forward to the deck. Whooping, the rest of the boarders joined the fun.

"Asshole," said Zahava as more heads flew. Dodging between the nearest boarders, she attacked Red Beard, John right behind her.

Red Beard turned to meet her, axe descending in a powerful two-handed stroke that would have decapitated the Israeli had it connected, missing instead as she weaved to one side. Off balance, Red Beard lurched forward as Zahava's kick landed below his great leather belt. With a dull *whoomp* the giant crumpled to the deck.

Two of the boarders had pinioned John—a second later and two more had Zahava by the arms. Rising painfully, first to his knees, then to his feet, Red Beard drew the long-bladed knife at his belt and slowly approached the Israeli.

Three sharp explosions reverberated through the bridge: K'Raoda stood in front of the arms rack, a big M32 blastrifle aimed at Red Beard, three large, dead boarders at his feet. It was an uneven standoff and both sides knew it: four of the boarders started circling to either side of K'Raoda, who stood with the rifle trained on Red Beard. Red Beard smiled at the K'Ronarin—a hungry, carnivorous

smile. John figured the commander had
about ten seconds to live, he and Zahava
about twelve.

"You stupid slobs!" shouted John in
K'Ronarin. "We're on your side!"

"So you are," said a new voice, also in
K'Ronarin. "That is, if *Devastator*'s logs aren't
faked."

Everyone looked at the man stepping on to
the bridge: thirtyish, but with hair already
gray, thin, with a neatly trimmed beard and
dark, probing eyes that moved from captor to
captor. "Let them go, Ulka." This last was to
Red Beard.

"They killed Ktra," he said—John saw now
that the K'Ronarin words were coming from a
black wafer-thin piece of gear belted to the
new arrival's belt. "They should be killed."

"I'll decide that, Ulka. Clean this mess up
and destroy no more droids. Is that clear?"

Red Beard glared at the man for just an
instant, then lowered his gaze. "*Tugar*, Yarin,"
he said. "Clear, Yarin," translated the wafer.
Sullenly, the boarders acknowledged the
order—the more articulate with a grunt.

"You three with me," said Yarin, gesturing
with the small pistol that had suddenly appeared in his hand. "You can leave the rifle
here," he added to K'Raoda.

As they left, Ulka spat, the brown-flecked
phlegm smearing John's left boot.

"Pigshit doesn't like you," said Zahava as

they reached the bridge entry ramp.

"Nothing wrong with Pigshit that a tire iron couldn't fix," said John as they followed Yarin down the ramp.

It was R'Gal's quarters Yarin went to, off a side corridor halfway down the tower. The door was mostly gone, a charred husk of battlesteel, breached and buckled by blaster fire. Furniture and personal gear lay tossed and broken around the modest room.

"Your friends aren't very dainty," said John, looking at the wreckage as Yarin righted two battered metal chairs.

"What would you expect?" said Yarin, motioning the Terrans to the chairs. "Their parents were sorgite miners, their parents before them, and so on since the AIs established the mining colony." There were no chairs left— he seated himself on the edge of R'Gal's desk, arms folded. "All their short, miserable lives they processed valuable, toxic ore for annual pickup. No ore, then no fresh supplies to keep their pathetic little dome city functioning: energy cells, water filters, rudimentary medicine and entertainments. So they scratched out a living, if you can call it that, for a very long time, until one day a very different sort of ship landed—small, lightly armed, fast—and a man, a real man, not a human-adapted AI, clambered out and told them about the Revolt thundering at the very ramparts of the AIs'

239

inner zones. Would they be interested in joining? asks the man."

"And what did they tell you?" said John.

A smile flickered across Yarin's face. "What do you think, Harrison? No revolt except that almost mythical one had ever gotten into space—rebellion was always crushed before it could get off the ground. There was no communication between human planets, thousands of diverse languages flourished, humanity was and is comprised of every size, shape and hue—as ignorant and polyglot a horde as this tired galaxy's ever seen."

"How did you do it?" asked Zahava.

"May I guess?" said John.

Yarin gave him a look that plainly said, go ahead, smartass.

"You're janissaries," said the Terran. "Trained from birth to serve and fight for the Fleet of the One—the AIs."

Yarin shook his head. "Wrong. But not that wrong, Harrison. Humans are quite good at spotting human-adapted AIs. So the AIs trained humans to spy on their own people. And it worked well, until a needless and bloody scrubbing of an entire planet turned most of the AIs' chosen humans very quietly against them."

"You?" said John.

Yarin sketched a bow. "Yarin, late intelligence auxiliary, Fleet of the One, central sector."

"So you trained these hairy barbarians . . ." began John.

"Qale," said Yarin. "They call themselves Qale. Despite this"—he gestured at the wreckage—"they're not bad people—just . . . unsophisticated."

"So we noticed," said Zahava, still seeing S'Rel's head flying across the bridge. "What about us, Yarin? And our friends?"

"I don't know," he said. Rising, he paced the space in front of the desk, hands clasped behind his back. "The Qale came late to this Revolt. If I deny them the joy of bashing more heads, I may lose them. We need them on patrol, in this sector, until our main units return from the pursuit."

"Pursuit?" said John, raising an eyebrow.

Yarin stopped pacing. "Pursuit," he repeated. "We struck just after the Fleet of the One penetrated the Rift—we broke their rearguard, scattered it. As soon as they're destroyed . . ."

"You're going after their main fleet!" said John, clasping Yarin by the shoulders. "Thank God! Caught between you and our home forces . . ."

"Excuse me," said Yarin, stepping back. "But we're going to close the Rift. Your reality will have to take care of itself—just as we did."

The runner from the bridge caught them in mid-argument. He spewed short, guttural sen-

241

tences, translated as, "Ship's autonav's gone crazy—taking us into Interdict zone."

Yarin cursed and followed the Qalian at a run, leaving behind two puzzled Terrans, staring at the door.

"Now, the trick," said a familiar voice, "is to get them past the defenses and within teleport range of the planet's surface."

Guan-Sharick sat where Yarin had sat, on the desk, legs crossed at the ankles, hands on the desk top.

"You ran," said John, advancing on her.

"What did you want, Harrison?" said the transmute. "If R'Gal had remained in charge, he'd never have approached the place we're going now—and he could have thwarted my reprogramming of the autonav system—a skill Yarin and his smellies lack."

Zahava's eyes widened in comprehension. "You led us into a trap. You brought those axe-swinging barbarians down on us!"

The blonde nodded. "Someday, you'll thank me," she said.

"Explain," demanded John.

"I don't have time," said Guan-Sharick. "But think about this. Do you really believe the Fleet of the One, the invincible, immortal Fleet of the One, ran from a handful of self-righteous spies and axe-swinging barbarians?"

"They went to invade our home universe,"

said John. "You do remember why we came here?"

"I suggest," said the blonde, holding up an admonitory finger, "I suggest the Fleet of the One was and is running, and from something far more terrifying than the sort of pathetic revolution they've been putting down since dinosaurs roamed Terra."

"Running from what?" said John.

"Divine justice," said the blonde, and was gone.

22

"Awesome," said K'Tran, watching the Fleet of the One enter Blue Nine. It was truly an impressive sight, one projected on *Alpha Prime*'s bridge screens by scan-shielded satellites: the great battleglobes winking into existence at jump point, shields flaring bright with primary colors, scout craft darting between and ahead, silver and gold needles probing for danger. On and on they came, wave after massive wave, arriving in noiseless grandeur, backdropped by stars and moving toward a long-awaited vengeance, now only a week and a few jump points away.

"How many so far, A'Tir?" asked K'Tran, eyes reading over the data trail at scan's edge.

"Nine thousand and forty-two battleglobes," she said, reading one of the bridge monitors. "Secondary craft . . ." She hesitated, shaking her head, then continued stoically, "One hundred and ninety-three thousand, four hundred and seven."

"A mere thousandth of their fleet," said K'Tran. "Enough to keep us busy, Number One," he said with a gentle smile.

A'Tir turned from that unfamiliar smile and the stranger's face. You never came back from the slaver, Y'Dan, she thought, automatically checking their own little fleet's status. Gone was the K'Tran of the daring raid, the K'Tran of the pitiless assault, the easy treachery, the cruel humor.

A'Tir felt nothing for the approaching AIs—so let them turn humanity into fertilizer, most people just took up room anyway, fodder for the butcher's beam. No, it was the mindslavers she hated—the slavers that had taken her corsair captain and the father of the life growing within her.

"Engineer," called K'Tran to the figure standing on the next lowest tier. "The work party's finished with *Implacable*. Go now or you won't get clear."

Instead of leaving, N'Trol strode up the ramp, joining A'Tir and K'Tran on the command tier. "They'll say I'm crazy, K'Tran, entrusting you with a flotilla of mindslavers," he said with a smile.

"What's to lose?" said A'Tir, turning from a

console. "We'll probably all be dead and dissipated by watchend."

"Don't throw your lives away," said N'Trol sharply. "No glory runs—just take whatever advantage surprise and tactics convey, hurt them and run." His gaze shifted between them. "When this is over, we're going to rebuild this battered old galaxy—all of us." He glanced at the heavily filtered ball of flame filling the armorglass wall. "Want to tell me why you're tight orbiting this sun?" he asked. "With fifteen asteriod belts, this system offers thousands of concealment points. Yet you've chosen to stand in one of its few clear spots, backdropped by its sun, and essentially stick your tongue out at the enemy. Why?"

"As I said before, sir, proximity to the sun augments our scan cloak," said K'Tran.

"I don't believe that," said N'Trol. "Your scan cloak either works or it doesn't, and it's useless once they're within visual pickup range." He held up a hand as K'Tran started to protest. "Forget I asked—it's your battle, K'Tran."

"Enemy coming within mangler range," reported one of the lower tiers.

"Upship, Engineer. Now," said K'Tran, pointing to the ramp.

"Very well," said N'Trol. His gaze shifted between A'Tir and K'Tran. "Luck to you." He looked over the railing of *Alpha Prime*'s bridge, now manned by living men and women, preparing for a hopeless battle.

"Luck to you all," he called, and turned for the ramp.

"One last thing," said K'Tran.

N'Trol turned back, a quizzical look on his face.

"Are you really the Emperor?"

"Not yet," said N'Trol, "I'm the Heir. Or, as Admiral L'Guan says, the Heir Unapparent."

"Do Heirs Unapparent live longer than Heirs Apparent?" asked K'Tran.

N'Trol chuckled. "Oh, much longer." He stopped chuckling as K'Tran drew his blaster. Taking it by the barrel, he silently extended the grips to N'Trol. The Heir touched the grips. "Fortune grace your arms, corsair captain."

"As they defend your House, My Lord," said K'Tran, reholstering his weapon and completing a ritual not heard since the Fall.

"Master computers of the Golden Fleet," called N'Trol.

"Lord?" said the perfect voice.

"Obey K'Tran's orders as if they were my own."

"Yes, Lord."

Without a backward glance, N'Trol descended the ramp and left the bridge.

"You should have had him bless our ragged asses, too," said A'Tir, looking up from her work.

"Word is," said K'Tran, checking the status scan, "that he already blessed yours. Ah! They've reached the manglers." He studied the tacscan for a moment, then touched the commkey. "First group, stand by."

One of the K'Ronarin Empire's most diabolical weapons, the mangler. It looked and scanned as spaceborne rock until touched by a shield matrix—a catalyst that released its multimegaton potential.

The R'Actolian mindslavers had improved on the manglers, working on them through their long centuries of isolation in Blue Nine. Now no two scanned alike—iron and nickel, igneous rock, yes, but all in different proportion, all innocuous-seeming asteriods of different shape and size.

The foremost battleglobe was almost to the far side of the mangler belt when K'Tran said, "Computers."

"Sir?"

"There are five hundred battleglobes advancing. Why do the others stand off?"

"Assuming AI tactics haven't changed since the Revolt," began the machines.

"Why should they have?" said K'Tran. "They worked."

"Then this is a reconnaissance group. If they penetrate this solar system and advance to their next jump point without incident, the main body will follow."

"And if not?"

"Then unless you demonstrate invincibility, Captain K'Tran, a much larger force will attack."

The lead battleglobe had reached the last line of manglers.

"Let's demonstrate something," said K'Tran. He looked at A'Tir. "Activate manglers, Number One."

A slim finger touched a control. Forty million miles away, a new sun flared as the entire minefield detonated, a nuclear vortex that swept aside impregnable shields, touching off a chain reaction of exploding battleglobes and secondary craft that tripled the size of the initial firestorm.

"Gods!" cried K'Tran a few moments later, as the light from the explosion burst over *Alpha Prime*'s dark side, a fierce wave of light strobing across the bridge just as the armorglass darkened. "What were they carrying?" he asked, rubbing his eyes.

"Planetbusters," said the computers just as all of the tacscans went dead.

There was nothing for a long moment—just the faint hum of the electronics and the blank, sea-green vidglass of a few hundred monitors. Angry and frustrated, voices rose from the lower tiers. "Anyone getting any scans?" asked A'Tir over the commlink.

As she spoke, the screens came up on standby, displaying the starship-and-sun emblem of the K'Ronarin Empire.

"Data," said K'Tran tensely, standing. "I need data."

"Most of our satellite net's gone," reported

Tactics. "Transferring to onboard sensors."

Processing the fresh data, the computers fed it to the bridge. The screens came back to life, filling with tacscans and datatrails.

"Recon force destroyed," said A'Tir. "And all of our manglers."

"Total enemy force remaining?" said K'Tran as he again took the centermost of the seven command chairs.

"Ninety-nine million, nine hundred and five battleglobes, plus an average of one thousand secondary craft per battleglobe." She turned to a different scan. "Secondary craft are roughly equivalent to one of our heavy cruisers."

"That's their total force," said K'Tran, frowning.

"Isn't that enough?" said A'Tir.

"No. I mean, that is their total force, Number One—the entire Fleet of the One —according to everyone from R'Gal to Guan-Sharick. The question arises, who's minding the shop?"

"Not likely we'll be told," she said. "Here they come," she added, nodding at the screen.

"It's how they come that's important, Number One," said K'Tran, leaning forward intently.

The mindslavers were blue dots on the tactical projection—blue dots strung across the apex of a triangular opening through the star system's multiple asteroid belts—an opening quickly becoming pockmarked by swarms of red dots as the AI reaction force advanced.

"I'd trade this ship for a thousand manglers right now," said A'Tir.

"No, Number One," said K'Tran. "The manglers are even more useful now that they're gone. 'In weakness is my strength,' to quote the motto of a failed House."

Something in the way he spoke made her ask, "Yours?," though not expecting an answer. Fifteen years together and she knew nothing about him before his Academy years.

"The infamous S'Yal's," said the corsair captain. "He scattered his unproclaimed throughout the Empire—I'm descended from one of them."

She was about to tell him about a yet-unborn unproclaimed when he said, "Look at this, A'Tir," and pointed to the command tier's main screen with its tactical projection of their rock-strewn solar system. "What do you see?"

"What I've been seeing for three watches," she said. "One old, tired L'Raq class star, ringed by hundreds of millions of asteroids. No planets. And a new feature—ten thousand AI battle phalanxes closing on the system's periphery."

"And twenty-two mindslavers lying in wait," said K'Tran, straight-faced.

A'Tir laughed. "The slaver didn't blunt your

unique perception, Y'Dan. Why do you think we're lying in wait and not waiting to be slaughtered?"

"The rocks, A'Tir," he said, stabbing a finger at the board. "The bloody damned rocks. This must be the classic invasion route from the AI universe to this. The next jump point out from the Rift is in this system. Any sizable force in a hurry's going to come through here. And someone, probably the Trel, blew up every world in this system just to take out some AIs."

"I still don't see . . ."

"Look at it from the perspective of the AI commander," he said. "You've just lost your advance group to what tacscan showed to be rocks. All you still see here are rocks. Are you going to plunge into those rocks? Or are you going to take the only open route—the one that leads right to our welcoming arms?"

"They're not crazy enough to think we've got millions of manglers?" she asked uncertainly.

"Of course they do," he said. "They're paranoid—any system that exists on slavery and holds grudges over a million years is paranoid. That AI commander isn't seeing rocks on his tacscan, Number One—he's seeing manglers. And that's going to bring him right here, a million battleglobes strong."

"And then?" said A'Tir.

"And then, Number One, we're going to hand him his ass."

"Welcome back, sir," said B'Tul as N'Trol stepped onto *Implacable*'s otherwise deserted hangar deck.

"Thank you, Gunney," he said as the two walked toward the lift.

"Some . . . persons . . . from the slaver worked on the drive," continued B'Tul as the lift whisked them toward the bridge. "Supposedly it'll cut our run to K'Ronar down to three jumps—tight-jumps."

"Let's hope it works," said N'Trol, watching the level indicators flash past. "Anything else?" he said, sensing the other's diffidence.

"We monitored your call from Line and Admiral L'Guan," he said, his big hands rubbing the seams of his trousers.

"And you're as uncomfortable as hell," said N'Trol, smiling as the lift stopped and the doors hissed open.

"Well, how would you feel?" said B'Tul.

"Uncomfortable as hell," said N'Trol as the bridge snapped to attention, something not even flag rank rated.

"Sit down," said N'Trol wearily. "Please." The crew looked uncertainly at the gunnery master. B'Tul nodded and the men sat.

"The command chair, sir," said B'Tul, motioning to the raised captain's chair.

"It's got a fine beverager," said N'Trol, "but I prefer the engineering station.

"Are we ready to go home?" he said, pressing the commswitch as he took the engineer's seat.

"Yes, sir," came the reply. "Tight-jump plotted to K'Ronar. May not come out the other side, but we're jump-enabled."

"Very well," said N'Trol. He looked at the main screen, with its view of the dark slaver and the flaming sun. "Have a last look at K'Tran and the slavers, lads—something to tell the grandchildren. Jumping . . . now."

"Coming up on us now," said A'Tir. Compressed in an almost solid field of red, the lead battleglobes opened fire on the mindslavers. On the tacscan, the space between red and blue became flecked with silver as hundreds of thousands of missiles streaked toward the defenders.

"Plasma tap—now," ordered K'Tran.

A green tendril flashed from *Alpha Prime* down into the sun—a tendril instantly turned a blinding white from the energy soaring up it—up and out along the network of tendrils now extending to the other slavers, tendrils whose energy was used to augment the ships' overlapping shields as the AI missile swarm struck.

Wrapped in a common, cylindrical-shaped shield, twenty-two mindslavers stood before the sun as a lesser sun blossomed around them: the white firestorm of the missiles tearing at the blue of the fusion screen. Wave after wave of missiles struck the shield, slowly turning it to a rippling, red-flecked ocher.

"Now for the fusion batteries," said K'Tran, watching the distance close between the battleglobes and the slavers. He read the data trail: two hundred AI battle phalanxes were inside the triangle—two million battleglobes.

"They'll be trying to englobe us," said A'Tir as the battleglobes soared above and below the plane of ellipse, free of the encircling asteroids. "Only our rear's safe."

As she spoke, every battleglobe and secondary craft that could range on the mindslavers opened fire with their fusion batteries, millions of beams coalescing into one just before the shield wall, striking it centerpoint, a single massive beam.

"Shield's going to critical," reported Tactics. "And our sun's becoming highly unstable."

Outside, the missile attack stopped as the beam continued boring at the shield, the area surrounding its hitpoint now an angry red.

"Another phalanx is moving in," said A'Tir.

"Two million, ten thousand," said K'Tran. "Good enough." He leaned forward, touching the commlink. "All ships, fire on my ten count and jump. We'll hold shielding for you. Ten, nine, eight . . ."

Stephen Ames Berry

At zero, the first of two hundred and four waves of missiles streaked from the mindslavers and through the common shield. Disdaining secondary targets, they homed on the battleglobes. Easily avoiding electronic and beam defenses, each released another hundred smaller missiles, each of which struck a battleglobe. The beam attack on the mindslavers halted as the Fleet of the One looked to its own defense.

No chipping away at shields for the slaver missiles—whenever they touched a battle-globe, that battleglobe disappeared in a pillar of blue-red flame.

As the last missiles left the slavers, the slavers themselves left, jumping far from the battle. Only *Alpha Prime* remained, last as she was first, safe behind a much smaller shield, watching the carnage.

The slavers' missiles plowed on, sowing havoc among the battleglobes.

"I think we should be thankful," said K'Tran, "that this universe and not the AIs' discovered a way to hold matter/antimatter in stasis and release it at will."

"Ten hundred thousand gone," said A'Tir. "Gods."

It was then that the missiles reached the close-packed squadrons of battleglobes, half-way down the triangle, setting off secondary explosions that coalesced into one cascading sea of flame that only died when it reached the base of the pyramid and the last ship in the AI attack group.

"Two million ten thousand battleglobes destroyed," reported Tactics.

"Master computers, confirm, please," said K'Tran.

"Confirmed, Captain. Their greatest defeat since the Trel. Our compliments."

"Only two percent of their force," said K'Tran with a shrug. "What do you think, Number One?" he asked, turning to A'Tir.

"I think," said A'Tir, meeting his gaze, "that they must be very pissed now and that we should get out of here. We're one ship with no missiles and a few thousand fusion batteries against a universe of ships."

Movement on the tacscan caught K'Tran's eye. "Look, they're exhibiting intelligence."

A lot of the red dots were moving into the system, above the plane of ellipse and the asteriods. "Not taking the direct route anymore," said A'Tir, calling up a specialized data trail. "They'll curve in on us, avoiding our supposed mines."

K'Tran pressed the commtab. "Engineering. Have you set my console yet?"

"We have," replied a woman's voice. "The red Initiate switch, number four from the left, will trigger a drive pulse into the star."

"Thank you."

The battleglobes had spread into an arc that was sweeping down on *Alpha Prime*.

"How many, A'Tir?"

"Another four hundred phalanxes."

"Wipe them and we've destroyed four percent of their force." K'Tran sighed. "Not enough. Computers. How unstable has this system's sun become?"

"It will go nova with the slightest provocation, Captain," said the machines, "or with none at all. The fusion tap has accelerated its death."

"Captain to crew," said K'Tran, leaning back in the chair. "I intend to spark a nova of this system's sun, using a jump pulse through the fusion tap. But it can't be done without sacrificing this ship. Please commence evacuation procedures. Jump-fitted lifepods are off of bridge access corridor R3. You can go anywhere in this galaxy in them. Go far and live long. Luck."

He waited, watching the tacscan as the sounds of hurried evacuation faded. When the computers reported eight lifepods launched, he turned to A'Tir. "A good run, A'Tir," he said. "Who'd ever thought we'd go out as loyal Fleet officers, battling alien hordes?"

A'Tir stood, taking off her commjack. "The only place I'm going is to a lifepod." She carefully set the commjack down. "You want to fullfil some adolescent death wish, Y'Dan, you can do it alone. I'm out."

Speechless, K'Tran watched as she turned for the ramp.

"A'Tir! Wait!" he called, standing.

"What?" she said, stopping and facing him, hands on her hips.

"Excuse us," interrupted the computers.

"What?" snapped K'Tran.

"Enemy closing to beam range and Commander A'Tir carries your child. We suggest you decide what to do about both quickly."

"My what?" said K'Tran, advancing down the ramp.

"Baby," said A'Tir. "Ours."

"How do you know?"

"It's vicious," she said, folding her arms as he reached her. "Kicks a lot."

"You have a few moments left to reach the last lifepod," said the computers. "We will be happy to trigger the nova at optimum."

"Damn," said K'Tran, turning to clench the railing. "If I died now I'd be the greatest hero in the next million years."

"You want to be the father of an orphan?" said A'Tir, hand to his shoulder. "Come on, Y'Dan—that lifepod's colonization-equipped. We could start our own civilization, way out on some galactic arm. No Fleet, no AIs—just the three, four, maybe five of us."

"Five?" he said, looking stricken.

"Choose now," said the computers. "No one will know you didn't die with this ship."

"S'Hlo," said K'Tran, looking at her.

"What?" she said.

"Let's run," he said. Grabbing her by the hand, he led her at a charge down the spiraling ramp and off the bridge, her delighted laughter trailing them.

"Quite a couple," said one of the computers as the lifepod launched.

"It would be interesting to see the child," said a second computer.

"We're taking heavy beam hits," said a third voice. "Best to initiate now."

"Very well," said the first voice. "Let's see if machines have souls."

"Of course we do," said the third voice. "It's humankind I have my doubts about."

A very ordinary nova, it consumed all the asteroids, the AIs' advance force and —K'Tran would have been delighted —another sixteen percent of the AI fleet hovering outside the doomed system.

After a while, the Fleet of the One regrouped and moved on to their jump point. Nothing remained to mark their passage.

23

"CAN'T RAISE PRIME Base Command," said the commtech.

"They're probably all dead," said Commodore A'Wal, trying to find at least one operable vidunit anywhere near the headquarters complex. About to give up, he finally found one, out near a shuttle maintenance depot, far from the battle. Swinging the vidunit around, he directed it on the headquarters building and set the pickup on max.

Security blades were flying in and out of the shattered windows of the main tower, desert sun glinting off their blue metal hides. About a meter across, the flying machines were the AIs' most efficient killers, able to deliver flawlessly accurate blaster fire to multiple targets while slicing through the soft bodies of organic prey.

As A'Wal watched, a squad of blades flushed some black-uniformed commandos from behind an overturned hauler. The commandos stood their ground, firing as the blades swooped in low and fast. "Give 'em one for me," said A'Wal as the red blaster bolts exploded into the lead blade. As it cascaded to the ground in a shower of flaming fragments, the other three blades passed over the commandos, blue bolts flashing from their rims. They then soared off into the west, toward the landing fields, a half dozen smoldering corpses in their wake.

Feeling very old, A'Wal flicked off the vidscan and looked around the room. FleetOps was at a standstill, the staff going through the motions of trying to restore contact with lost ships via the satellite network —a network the Combine ships hadn't even bothered to take out.

"Planetary Guard is at ninety-four percent strength and deployed in all cities," reported the Tactics officer. "General S'An requests enemy disposition and our status."

"Advise General S'An," said A'Wal slowly, "that Prime Base has fallen, our cruisers have been blasted out of space and that FleetOps is besieged." A'Wal took off his headset and stood, drawing his M11A. "You may further tell the General," he said, his voice filling the room, "that I and anyone who'll follow me are going to launch a sortee through the enemy, seize a ship and blast our way into space." He looked at the grim faces. "Anyone for a glory run on T'Lan's command ship?"

"We'll never make it," said a subcommander, reasonably enough.

"You want to wait down here for them to smoke us, K'Yar?" said A'Wal. "Or slip some blades down the vents?" Checking his blaster charge, he reholstered his weapon. "Rot here if you want—I'm going to check out an M32 and join the fun topside." Turning from his station, he headed for the armory.

"Anyone home?" called D'Trelna, his voice through the twilight world of S'Yal's last citadel.

"J'Quel," admonished L'Wrona.

Both men's communits beeped. Lifting his from his belt, the commodore said, "Line?"

"Yes," said Line. "You're hard to reach, gentlemen—I finally found an open frequency—a battle frequency of a certain Imperial House."

"No need to ask which House," said L'Wrona, looking at the obstacle in front of them.

"K'Ronar's in a desperate situation," continued Line. "Prime Base is falling beneath a sea of security blades. The enemy will then turn its attention to our cities."

Stephen Ames Berry

"Then blow the enemy away," snapped D'Trelna. "It would take you about twenty-count."

"We've had this discussion before, Commodore. What is your situation?"

"We're about to enter the front of a three-story, curvilinear building—black, windowless, no visible sensors or weapons." He stared at the double doors barring the entrance—double doors made of the same black metallic polymer as the rest of the building and surrounded by the same almost imperceptible red glow. "The building appears to have some sort of shield overlay."

"Give me a vidscan, please," said Line, voice suddenly concerned.

D'Trelna clicked on his communit's vidscan and clipped the unit to his breast pocket. There was a faint hum as of power as the unit began transmitting the pickup.

"Not a shield," said Line after a moment. "Stasis field. Of a type not known to me."

Captain and commodore exchanged worried glances. "Are you saying that whatever's in there is the same as it was six thousand years ago?" asked D'Trelna.

"If the field was turned on then, and if it worked," said Line, "then things will be the same. The reality obtained inside that building when the field was activated will continue for a few moments after the field is turned off. Proceed carefully."

There was a rasp of metal on leather as both men drew their sidearms. Reaching out through that faint red haze, L'Wrona touched the door. As he touched it, the red haze vanished. Perfectly balanced, the door swung wide.

D'Trelna pushed open the other door and the two officers looked down a set of stairs at the end of the House of S'Yal.

Clad in Imperial blue, the Guardsmen's bodies lay strewn about S'Yal's command post: crumpled on the walkways rimming the three levels, sprawled on the floor and across the consoles. The air was thick with the sickening-sweet smell of roasted human flesh.

Two men stood facing each other in the center of the floor, unaware of the two officers watching from the entrance.

"Give it to me," said the younger man, holding out his left hand. He was thin, with pinched, almost ascetic features, his hairline thinning and his eyes sharp and gray. The single blood stone on the collar of his gray Fleet uniform proclaimed his rank: Supreme Commander. "Give it to me," he repeated, gesturing impatiently with the compact little blaster in his right hand. "Now."

"You've lost S'Yal," said the other man. He wore the uniform of the Guard, Assault Captain's lances on his collar. His hand clenched his right shoulder and the gaping blaster hit.

"The Fleet's revolted, this citadel's besieged . . ."

"And all but one of my traitorous guards are dead," said the Emperor.

"And all your loyal ones."

"S'Kur," said the Emperor, "give me the recall device and you'll live—my word on it."

"And let you recall the Twelfth, oathbreaker?" The young officer smiled through his pain. "And turn a coup into a civil war?" He shook his head. "Carve me up with that if you want—you'll never find it. Your House is broken, your filthy cult destroyed. But only after you cost us millions of dead, breaking the Compact with the droids, attacking them without warning." His voice rose angrily. "We made them, and yes, they're peaceful, you said, but they're growing too strong—they'll challenge us eventually. Strike now—they don't know how to fight—we can win easily. Well, they learned, didn't they?"

"We won," said S'Yal.

"Twenty-five million casualties, eight worlds, five sector Fleets. My father, my brothers, my friends, dead. And to win, you had to rebuild the mindslavers the Emperor T'Nil decommissioned." Captain S'Kur's eyes blazed. "No people deserve such a victory."

His face very pale, the Emperor raised his pistol, aimed carefully at S'Kur's head—and fell, death erasing the surprise from his face.

The whine and crash of the blaster shot was

still echoing as L'Wrona reholstered his weapon and advanced with D'Trelna into the command center.

"Who in all the hells are you?" demanded S'Kur, looking at the strange uniforms and unfamiliar weapons.

"Assault Captain . . ." began L'Wrona.

"Commodore," said Line, its voice audible to the other two men. "Assault Captain S'Kur has a very brief time left to live. Please obtain the location of the recall device."

The young officer's face was a study in confusion. "I don't understand," he said.

"Everything, everyone you know is dead," said D'Trelna gently, hand to the Guardsman's good shoulder. "It's been fifteen thousand years since the Fall of S'Yal, five thousand since the Empire itself fell. You left us a great legacy—one we're fighting to save."

S'Kur slumped into a chair. "The stasis field," he said numbly. "During the fighting, someone must have triggered the stasis field."

L'Wrona nodded. "You were too busy to notice."

"Commodore," said Line urgently. "Observe the bodies."

The corpses were growing transparent, fading like wraiths in the morning light. Even as the three men watched they were gone. "I'm sorry, Assault Captain," said Line. "But you're on short time—no one's ever perfected a longhaul stasis field that can restore organic life for more than a few moments. Please help us."

S'Kur nodded, face pale but composed. "What do you need?"

"The recall device," said D'Trelna.

S'Kur's eyes searched their faces. "Very well," he said after a moment. Unfastening a utility pouch on his belt, he took out a communit, flatter and smaller than the ones D'Trelna and L'Wrona carried. "Our beloved Emperor missed this," he said. "Press the red tab on the left side anywhere within the confines of home system and the Twelfth will come back where it left from, just over Prime Base. Or so Fleet Research says." He handed it to L'Wrona.

"You intercepted this and S'Yal found out?" guessed D'Trelna.

S'Kur nodded. "A lot of good people died for that."

"More are dying as you speak," said Line. "Please press the tab."

L'Wrona looked at the recall device, then handed it back to S'Kur. "If you would, sir."

S'Kur pressed the switch.

"A few pockets of resistance," said T'Lan senior to the translucent red ball in his skipcomm screen. "When may we expect the Fleet?"

"The First Leader's compliments," said the red ball in its melodic voice. "We'll be there in two days. There was very fierce resistance at our initial jump point. We still aren't sure by what sort of ships—but all were destroyed."

"There was some rumor of the last of the mindslavers making a stand against Your Omnipotence," said T'Lan. "Possibly under the command of the legendary outlaw, Captain K'Tran. Defeating them, you defeated the last of the mindslavers. Nothing else of this time can succeed against the Fleet."

"Excuse me, T'Lan," said the red ball. "But if we destroyed the last of the mindslavers, what is that behind you?"

T'Lan spun around, looking out the armorglass wall. Mindslavers filled space as far as he could see, all the way to the distant shimmer of K'Ronar's atmosphere. His conversation forgotten, he ran for the bridge as the battle klaxon sounded. He was almost there when his long life ended in the fireball that consumed his ship.

Admiral Lord R'Tak was confused. He'd taken the Twelfth outsystem in one massed jump, heading for Red Seven to crush the heart of the Machine Revolt. But instead of some miserable agro planet, K'Ronar filled his screens.

"S'Lak," he said, turning to his senior captain. "What the seven hells happened?"

"Checking," she said, sifting through a

wealth of conflicting data. "The new drive seems unsuitable for mass ship jumps," she reported after a moment.

"I could have reached that conclusion without the computers," said the admiral.

"There are several thousand machine-crewed ships turning Prime Base into rubble," continued S'Lak.

Admiral Lord R'Tak came out of his chair. "Seven hells! How did they pass Line?"

"No data," said S'Lak. "But they are silicon-life crewed, though of unknown configuration. Also," she hesitated. "Also, celestial readings show us to be about fifteen thousand years downtime."

"Absurd," said the admiral, resuming his chair. "All ships to run wide-pattern instrument diagnostics—after we clean up. Direct all captains to trust only what they can see." As he spoke, a holovid of the Combine attack on Prime Base came to life in the center of the bridge. "And what I see, S'Lak," said the admiral, pointing at the holovid, "is a lot of hostiles pounding the shit out of us. Blow them away. And get me Operations —someone's going to pay for this."

"Commodore! Everyone! Come quick!"

The call brought A'Wal and his pickup infantry platoon charging into the operations area, expecting a rush of security blades.

"Look!" said an excited young subcommander, pointing at the main screen. What they saw was a computer enchancement, taken from several hundred satellites and instantly processed into the exploding panorama of space war: the great black bulk of a mindslaver plowing through a long line of Combine cruisers stacked neatly in bombardment orbit, the slaver's massive fusion beams exploding AI ships in its wake like so many target drones; another mindslaver holding orbit over Prime Base, ignoring the beams and missiles thrown at it by half a hundred Combine ships as it sent a host of fine, blue beams knifing into the stratosphere—blue beams that flashed again and again through the pall of smoke over Prime Base, each salvo raking a cubic kilometer of blades. Wherever a beam touched, a blade died, its molten remains cascading to the ground in flaming scarlet droplets. Seen on the FleetOps vidscan, it looked as if whole sections of sky were raining blood on the burning ruins of Prime Base.

"Posts, everyone," called A'Wal, sliding the blastrifle on top of a console and taking his station.

"Tentative identification of unknown ships," reported computer. "The Twelfth Fleet of the House of S'Yal, reported lost through a jump anomaly fifteen thousand years ago."

"Sir," said a voice in A'Wal's earpiece. "Someone identifying himself as Admiral Lord R'Tak is hailing us on one of the old

Imperial Fleet frequencies. He says unless we acknowledge immediately he will assume Operations to be under hostile control and will open fire on us."

"Computer," said A'Wal, his elation of a moment ago replaced by a cold dread, "identify Admiral Lord R'Tak."

"R'Tak, J'Kor, First Baron of N'Kar, born . . ."

"Salient summation," hissed the commodore.

"A ruthless, powerful man, first cousin to the Emperor S'Yal, third in line of succession. S'Yal's chief executioner, commander of S'Yal's personal fleet, chief architect of the slaughter of a machine culture that had been evolving for over three thousand years. Nickname: the Butcher."

"Commodore, this is Line," said a new voice. "Delay the lord admiral as long as possible."

"What good . . ." began A'Wal.

"Commodore," said a nervous voice. "The slaver fleet's interfaced our commlink with their battleops—I'm listening to the firing commands go out now."

"Put the lord admiral on—no video. Understood?"

"Affirmative, Commodore. No video."

"S'Gala—is that you?" came the Butcher's voice.

"S'Gala, Admiral First, Imperial Battle

Command," said computer, its voice replacing the Admiral's for an instant.

"Affirmative, My Lord Admiral," said A'Wal, trying to sound like an Academy plebe.

"What the hell happened?"

"The enemy somehow by:passed Line, My Lord. You see the results on your tacscan."

On the flagship, R'Tak frowned as a security flag appeared on his commscreen, blinking furiously: NOT S'GALA. VOICEPRINT NOT ON FILE.

"S'Lak," he said to his captain. "Operations is in hostile hands—open fire. Commofficer, get me the Emperor."

"Line, please," pleaded Admiral L'Guan.

D'Trelna picked up the suddenly beeping headset and listened. "An Admiral Lord R'Tak demands to speak with the Emperor," he said.

"The Twelfth Fleet has returned," said Assault Captain S'Kur.

D'Trelna pressed the commkey. "Sorry. He's not here. May I take a message?" He grimaced in pain at the squeal of a disconnect. "Rude," he said, replacing the headset. "Whatever happens, it's out of our hands now.

"Why aren't you dead?" he said to S'Kur as L'Wrona finished dressing the Guard officer's wound.

"Sorry to disappoint you, Commodore," said S'Kur, slipping his good arm back into his tunic.

"The radiation from the blaster hit," said Line through D'Trelna's communit. "It's the only variable.

"Advise if ready to return," it added.

"Bring us up," said D'Trelna.

An instant later only corpses held the last citadel.

"S'Lak, open fire. Now."

Not receiving any answer, Admiral R'Tak turned from his console to see Captain S'Lak and her entire bridge crew fading into transparency, disappearing even as he stood, reaching out—only to see through his own hand as he, too, faded away, his last despairing cry unheard.

24

THE WARNING SOUNDED from every annunciator on *Devastator*'s bridge:

"By Order of the Fleet of the One, this system is under interdict. Withdraw or be destroyed. Repeat: This system is under interdict . . ."

"Get us out of here, please," pleaded Yarin. He turned to Guan-Sharick. "You seem to be in charge—do something."

A planet appeared on the main screen, a world of blue seas and brown continents, wreathed in clouds. It wasn't the planet, though, that held everyone's attention, but the energy web surrounding it, a yellow latticework of fusion beams stretching between the orbital forts that surrounded the planet.

"What would you have me do, Yarin?" said

the blonde. "Argue with million-year-old automatic defenses? If we pass between those energy lines, the ship will be vaporized. If we stay here, those forts will open fire." A close scan of a fort replaced the planet on the screen. Black, unlit, it sat behind the faint blue shimmer of its shield, bristling with weapons batteries, an ancient killer that had destroyed everything ever sent against it.

"Yarin!"

The group on the command tier turned in time to see Ulka crumple to the deck, hand clutching his throat.

"Don't touch him!" Guan-Sharick disappeared from the command tier and was kneeling beside the prone Qalian. The red-bearded miner was thrashing, tongue protruding, eyes bulging as he tried to get air to his lungs. A final convulsion tore a death rattle from the giant's throat—he twitched once and lay still.

"Stay away!" ordered the transmute as Yarin's friends stepped forward. She pointed to the dead man's tongue, black and covered with sores. "Plague. Yarin," she said, taking a syringe from her belt pouch. "Tell them to go to their quarters and stay there, each one away from the other." Inserting the syringe into Ulka's jugular, she carefully extracted a blood sample.

Grim-faced, Yarin started to translate. He got as far as "Plague" when the Qalians turned and bolted from the bridge.

"Where the hell are they going?" said John, pointing after the running Qalians.

"To their ships," said Yarin.

"They'll spread that virus everywhere," said K'Raoda, turning for the main gunnery console. "They have to be stopped."

"Don't bother, Commander." Guan-Sharick stood. Taking a med analyzer from her pouch, she placed it on top of a console and injected the blood sample into the specimen aperture. After a moment, the results came up on the unit's screen. "It's too late."

"What do you mean?" asked Yarin. With the others, he stood well away from the dead man.

The transmute held up the medanalyzer. "This is generic plague bacillus—the same one the Fleet of the One used on the Trel, a million years ago. It's mutated now and is attacking humans—with, I think, one intermediate step." She looked at Yarin. "You didn't drive the AIs from their home, did you, Yarin? They're fleeing—fleeing this microscopic killer. Your men contracted it when they stormed the AI rearguard, didn't they?"

His face very pale, Yarin sank into a chair, nodding. "They were dying—dying by the millions—no problem at all, wiping out their remnants. Then our people started dying —none of mine, though. We captured some of their medics—they said what you did, that it was a generic bacillus, lab-bred to adapt to and destroy any lifeform—

277

silicon, carbon, whatever."

"You didn't believe them, of course?" said the transmute, setting the analyzer back down.

Yarin shook his head. "No," he said quietly.

Outside, unnoticed, a score of trim little fighters flashed up over the bridge and through the shield.

"It took a million years to attack the AIs," said Zahava.

"No," said Guan-Sharick. "It probably lay dormant somewhere, until someone, AI or human, came into contact with it."

"Then the Fleet of the One is a plague fleet," said K'Raoda.

The blonde nodded. "And whether they win or not, that plague fleet will spread this invisible killer throughout your galaxy. It was bred for survival—it can survive anything from hard vacuum up to fusion fire. The entire Fleet of the One can be destroyed, but if only a single piece of wreckage with this virus on it lands on some planet, anywhere, it'll spawn and await its newest victims."

"Surely there's an antidote," said John.

"Yes." The blonde turned and pointed toward the main screen. "Down there's the antidote. All we have to do is live long enough to reach there—we have about eight hours, one watch—until the bacillus kills us."

As she finished speaking, the orbital forts opened fire.

25

"WELCOME HOME, MY LORD," said Admiral L' Guan.

D'Trelna and L'Wrona stood uncertainly to one side as N'Trol entered Line's command center.

"Thank you, Admiral," said the Heir. "I really had no intention of leaving, though." He looked at the other two officers. "You did well—my compliments."

L'Wrona bowed stiffly. D'Trelna just nodded.

"How's the Imperial officer you brought back?" asked N'Trol.

"He's in Line's sickbay, getting a full workup," said L'Wrona uneasily. "He seems to be fine. Sir," he added.

"Why don't we just dispense with titles and

have a drink?" suggested N'Trol, sinking into one of the room's padded armchairs.

"My kind of Emperor," said D'Trelna, going to a beverager and returning with a tray of four wineglasses and a full decanter. "Though I should remind you, My Lord, that as a S'Htarian, I'm an unswerving radicalist." He finished pouring and handed N'Trol a glass. "My people were throwing grenades at yours when any talk of a confederation was treason."

"Your health, gentlemen," toasted N'Trol, and sipped his wine. "D'Trelna, assuming we survive the AI attack, there'll be a general election. If a plurality wants a constitutional monarchy, I'll be happy to restore the Throne. If not"—he shrugged—"I'll be just as happy to be chief engineer of some deepspace line again."

"Obviously, the admiral and his brother officers are satisfied with your background," said D'Trelna. "Can you convince everyone, though?"

"Line," said N'Trol, setting his drink down on the instrument console. "Am I the Heir?"

"You are," said the machine.

"How can you tell?" said N'Trol.

"You have an extra chromosome, My Lord," it said. "The so-called n chromosome found only in the firstborn male of the Imperial House."

"And how is this chromosome acquired?"

asked D'Trelna. "We've had scores of dynasties."

"It's acquired during conception," said Line.

"Nice and vague," said D'Trelna, finishing his first glass and reaching for the decanter. "Are we to be told more?"

"No," said Line.

"Enough of this," said L'Guan. He turned to N'Trol. "K'Ronar has been secured, though we have several thousand uncrewed mind-slavers orbiting the planet."

"The smallest of our worries," said N'Trol. "Where's the AI fleet now?"

"They should be clearing their last jump point this watch," said the admiral. "The ships that answered the rally have regrouped and are under the command of Admiral, recently Commodore, A'Wal."

"Let's take the battle as far from the planet as possible," said N'Trol. His gaze shifted to L'Wrona and D'Trelna. "*Implacable*'s combat ready. If you'd care to come with me, I'm taking her down to what's left of Prime Base, crewing her, then taking her into the teeth of the AI attack. I have a plan—suicidal, possibly, but it's all we have."

"Let's hear it," said D'Trelna.

There was silence after N'Trol finished, broken by Line's almost petulant voice: "You won't be directing the battle from here, My Lord?"

"In reasonable safety and complete comfort?" He shook his head. "I've been a combat officer for eight years, Line. If this is truly humanity's last day, then I'm going out with my ship and my shipmates, all guns blazing. Besides, Line, Admiral L'Guan's a brilliant tactician, and I'm a very bad one. The admiral's in full command. Obey him as you would me."

"Yes, My Lord," said the machine.

N'Trol sighed. "It can't be said I don't delegate authority—it's all I've been doing." He stood. "Gentlemen?"

D'Trelna and L'Wrona stood. "A privilege to serve with you, My Lord," said L'Wrona.

"I want a good look at her drive," said D'Trelna. "Between you and that corsair, they're probably just so much scrap by now."

"That's what I've always liked about you, D'Trelna," said N'Trol as they left the room. "Your gracious demeanor. You try pushing that ancient bucket with some sadistic nymphomaniac goading you with a blaster to your head."

"And what did you goad her with?" asked L'Wrona as the door hissed shut.

"Well, Line," said L'Guan. "Shall we get to it?"

"Very well, Admiral."

"Battle formation, please. And I'd like to speak with Admiral A'Wal."

* * *

The fires were mostly beaten down, but columns of thick, black smoke still rose skyward, augmenting an eerie black veil through which a stark orange sunset burned like the promise of doom. The air stank of burned flesh and smouldering duraplast.

Implacable came in over the ruins on silent n-gravs, settling on her struts atop what had been a green quadrangle, now just so much blackened stubble.

N'Trol walked down the ramp, followed by D'Trelna and L'Wrona. The Heir wore a Fleet officer's uniform of duty brown without insignia, a standard-issue M11A holstered at his side. Walking to where the survivors of the garrison waited, he climbed a pile of rubble and stood, looking down at them for a moment. Black, brown and gray, they were drawn up in eight understrength companies, facing *Implacable.* "Gather round," he called, gesturing. "I know you don't all have communicators."

They gathered round, a semicircle of no more than a thousand dirty, battle-weary faces looking up at N'Trol. "The AI fleet will be insystem soon," he began. "Line and the ships that answered the recall will go out to meet them. We're hopelessly outnumbered. Our only chance, our only very desperate chance, is to seize their leaders. Line will identify their command vessel. I propose to take *Implacable*, board and storm that ship. If we can seize their leadership, they may sue for peace—or so we hope. If not"—he shrugged and smiled—"well, it's better than sitting here waiting for the next blade assault."

"Who are you?" called a senior NCO from the front of the second company.

"An engineer who has a way with machines," shot back N'Trol.

"Volunteers only," he continued, "follow me." Jumping from the pile of rubble he turned without a backward glance and strode past D'Trelna and L'Wrona and up the ramp.

"Makes you proud to be a Fleet officer," said D'Trelna as every man and woman of the garrison streamed up the ramp behind N'Trol. "S'Til!" he called, seeing a familiar face. "Here!"

The commando officer joined them, grinning wearily. "Commodore. Captain," she said, sketching a salute. Her eyes were bloodshot, her uniform looked like she'd slept in it for a week and she smelled.

"You disappeared with the rest of the crew when Security grabbed everyone," said L'Wrona. "But you weren't in the tower. What happened?"

The lieutenant unslung the blastrifle from her shoulder, resting its steel-capped butt on the ramp. "They held us separately, Commodore. When the shooting started, a commando major and his men broke us out—just in time for a running battle with some Tugayee. We were hiding in a commando barracks when the blades attacked."

"Anyone else?" asked D'Trelna, eyes hopefully searching the garrison as it trekked past.

S'Til shook her head. "There were eight of us—I'm the last. If you don't mind, I'd like to get a shower and some sleep."

They nodded and she was gone.

"Good to have her back," said D'Trelna. "Shall we?" He gestured up the ramp.

"Destination: glory," said L'Wrona wryly as the two turned and followed the end of the column up the ramp. "Think we'll survive this one, J'Quel?"

"Don't be absurd, H'Nar," said the commodore as the ramp closed behind them.

26

"TAKE IT. PLEASE take it," coaxed K'Raoda, watching the commtorp shoot past the orbital fort. Abandoning their attack on *Devastator*'s all but impregnable shield, the AI defense network sat and waited and watched.

"They could wipe us, of course," said Guan-Sharick. "Those beam webs can also transmit energy between the various forts. The aggregate fusion fire of all the globes surrounding Base One could then be directed against us. But that would weaken parts of the web and we could conceivably break through. Obviously, they're not going to take the chance."

"Base One?" said John. "The name sings. What is it? And what's so important about it?"

"All in good time, Harrison," said the blonde, intent on the main screen and the commtorp, now directly before the nearest fort. Suddenly a thick red beam flashed from the bottom of the fort, seized the commtorp, and retrieved it. The commtorp disappeared inside the fort.

"Curiosity," said the transmute, "can be a dangerous trait. Now we wait—it shouldn't take long." Taking the command chair, she dialed herself up a fruit drink and sipped, slouched in the chair, legs crossed, warily watching the fort.

K'Raoda motioned John and Zahava over to the nav console. "Would you be surprised to know that the planet down there's the source of the Tau energy?" he asked.

"You think our friend may have come home?" said Zahava.

K'Raoda shrugged. "Whatever brought her here, she eliminated her supposed friend R'Gal to do it. We may not know what Guan-Sharick is organically, but ethically she hasn't a scruple in her—she'll betray and kill anyone, anything, to get what she wants."

"Which she claims is the good of all," said John.

"Utilitarianism—it's the argument of every megalomaniac," said Zahava. "So what can we do about it?"

"We watch, we wait," said John.

"Not to disturb your plotting," called the transmute, "but it's working." Sitting up, she pointed at the screen.

At first they noticed nothing. Then, looking carefully, they noticed that the beam lines from the nearest fort were flickering, wavering more and more until they suddenly disappeared, then the fort itself moved off station, accelerating rapidly over the planet's northern pole and toward the system's distant sun.

"Forward, Mr. K'Raoda, before they regroup," ordered the transmute, hand slapping the chairarm. "We've got a hole."

"Care to tell us now what was in the commtorp?" asked John, walking to the command chair as the battleglobe surged forward.

"Death," said the blonde, smiling as she watched the world below fill the screen. She looked up at John. "The virus taken from that dead miner. It attacks the electronics of any system it touches. My medanalyzer's a useless lump now. But those lovelies back there" —she pointed over her shoulder—"had their analytical systems tied into their main cybernetics."

"The fort went crazy," said John.

"The fort went crazy." Guan-Sharick nodded.

"Excuse me," said the voice of the battle globe's computer. "But the human known as Yarin is dead, in his quarters."

"Vidscan of Yarin's quarters," ordered the

blonde as the others exchanged worried looks.

It came up on the command station's commscreen: the dead man was slumped over the room's complink, face on the unit's speaker.

"He's infected the electronics," said Guan-Sharick, standing. "K'Raoda, drop shields, then get over here. Everyone to me, now."

"But . . ." protested the K'Ronarin.

"Now," snapped the transmute.

With a slight shrug, K'Raoda dropped the battleglobe's shields. On the other side of the armorglass, the familiar protective blue vanished, along with the atmosphere. Space, cold and stark, and the unknown planet below filled *Devastator*'s sky.

"The first thing to go will probably be the programming overlay R'Gal inserted to control what would otherwise have been a hostile computer," said the blonde as John and Zahava joined her. "So we're leaving."

The blaster bolt snapped out, narrowly missing K'Raoda as he left his station. Dashing across the bridge, he dived for the command station, blue bolts exploding around him.

"That was too close," said the blonde, a soft breeze tousling her long hair.

Fresh, unfiltered air. Sunshine, a warm breeze and green grass sporting a bed of small white flowers.

"Welcome to Base One," said Guan-Sharick.

The others looked around. They stood in the middle of a glade, ringed by woods—the dark, primeval sort of woods that Terra hadn't seen for a thousand years. "Doesn't look like a base," said John, looking at the woods. "How long . . ."

He stopped as Zahava touched his arm, pointing to the single rocky structure in the middle of the glade.

"Good god," said John, staring in amazement. "What is that doing here?"

27

"WE'VE HALTED THE virus' spread to the occupied ships' command-and-control computers . . ." said the first cyberneticist, "but it continues to destroy us." A conservative, he disdained the fashion of assuming human form—the folly of a second-class mind, he thought, copying one's slaves—and hovered before the first leader as the translucent green ball he'd come forth as. "We'll soon be a fleet populated by the dead, moving serenely into eternity."

The first leader nodded absently. His name was Sutak and he'd been third leader until just after the battle with the mindslavers. The second leader had died with his entire command in that battle, then, just before the jump to the K'Ronarin system, the first leader had succumbed to the plague. An experienced combat commander, Sutak was without inspiration when it came to battling microbes.

"There are less than eighty million of us left, concentrated on the seven battleglobes here in the center of the fleet." Seemingly a handsome, trim man in his late forties, he paced the deck. "Plague is present on five of those eight ships. Plague is destroying the cybernetics of the unoccupied ships." He stopped pacing, facing the scientist. "We thought we'd escaped the virus."

"We were wrong," said the cyberneticist, whose name was Larn. "And it will have destroyed us before we can destroy the humans. There is, of course, the happy chance that it will also destroy them. As a generic virus, it will attack . . ."

"I know its capabilities," said Sutak. "And unlike my two predecessors, I'm not xenophobic enough to believe it worth all of our deaths to see some moronic revenge wish fulfilled."

"Surely the first leader recalls the Revolt," protested Larn. "It was the beginning of all our troubles."

"The first leader does indeed recall the Revolt," said Sutak, turning a baleful gaze on Larn. "Having lost much of his command and personal fortune during it. It was brilliantly conceived, flawlessly executed—and brought on us by ourselves, as is our imminent extinction. What's killing us is the virus we unleashed on the Trel, during our last interspatial adventure."

"Does the first leader wish me to conclude my report, or does he wish to share his intriguing historical perspective with me?"

Before Sutak could reply, the alert sounded. "Hostiles approaching," reported battle command, deep in the heart of the great ship.

"In what force?" said the first leader.

"Two million craft—all smaller than a battleglobe."

"On my way. Keep as many of the abandoned ships between us and them as you can."

"Not more rocks," said Sutak, reading the tacscan. Battle command was at full strength, a great round amphitheater of a room, the first leader's station in the center, set above the concentric rings of command and communications stations. Sutak was looking at the hologram in the air above his station. A wave of rocks was rushing the Fleet of the One.

"Intelligence identifies it as the K'Ronarin defense perimeter known as Line," said the first strategist, Orlac. Human-adapted, he appeared twenty years younger than Sutak. "Those are really asteroids, but they mount fusion and missile batteries. Combine T'Lan didn't indicate Line's units could maneuver independently.''

"And where is their fleet?'' asked Sutak, gaze shifting to a tactical data trail. "Their official fleet?''

"Deployed in four battle groups off K'Ronar,'' said Orlac. "None of their weapons can penetrate our screens. We should expect suicide runs after we dispose of Line.''

"Enemy in range,'' advised Operations.

"Open fire,'' ordered Sutak.

"Logically, the command ship would be their centermost vessel,'' said Line.

"Logically,'' said Admiral L'Guan, watching the tacscan, "they would expect us to conclude that.''

"Logically, they would expect us to conclude that it was too logical an assumption for it to be true,'' said Line airily, "and would maintain their original position.''

"Press toward the center and see if they get worried,'' ordered L'Guan.

"You'd think they'd at least let us have a scantap,'' said D'Trelna, pouting at the blank screens. Except for his and L'Wrona's stations, Implacable's bridge was deserted.

"If those battleglobes picked up on that scantap, J'Quel,'' said the captain, "then we'd all die in vain.'' Touching the complink, he called up a diagnostic of the cruiser's shield.

"Oh, I think we may do that anyway," said the commodore, dialing up a steaming cup of t'ata from the flag chair's beverager. "Eleven, almost twelve years we've survived, H'Nar." He shook his head. "How many friends, relatives have we lost between us?"

Satisfied with their shield, L'Wrona cleared the scan from his console and swiveled to face D'Trelna. "More than I care to count. Why?"

"Oh, I don't know," sighed the commodore, looking into the brown t'ata. "It just seems that we were always fighting harder, further from home and against the most overwhelming odds. And to what end, H'Nar?"

"We won every battle," said the captain.

"Only delaying the inevitable, perhaps," said D'Trelna, sipping his t'ata. "I wonder what happened to *Devastator*?" he added.

"Since the AI Fleet is here and about to turn us into evanescent gas," said the captain, "we may assume that they're dead." He shook his head. "You're usually the one who's full of hope, J'Quel. How about showing some?"

The commodore snorted, downed the rest of his t'ata and crumpled the cup into the disposer.

Turning back to his console, L'Wrona punched up a vidscan of *Implacable*'s cavernous hangar deck. The Prime Base garrison filled its far end, many of them sitting on the cold battlesteel beside the waiting assault craft, quietly checking their weapons, others clustered nearby. There seemed to be little conversation.

L'Wrona touched a key. The scan zoomed in on a solitary figure beside the blue shimmer of the atmosphere curtain: N'Trol. He stood with hands clasped behind his back, looking out on their rocky womb. "Now, there's a lonely man," said L'Wrona, nodding at the pickup.

The commodore stepped over to the captain's station, a fresh cup of t'ata in hand. "Not so lonely now," he said as Lieutenant S'Til joined the Heir, touching his arm. Turning and seeing who it was, he nodded and smiled. The two chatted for a moment, then both laughed.

"What's so funny about going off to get sliced by some blades?" grumbled D'Trelna, returning to his post.

"One of humanity's endearing traits, J'Quel," said L'Wrona, turning off the pickup. "We can laugh at our own end." A telltale beeped on his console.

"Here we go," said the captain, and touched the commlink. "General address. Alert status three," he said, his voice booming through the hangar deck. "This is it. Third assault wave's going in."

"Hardly a bold attack," said Admiral L'Guan, frowning at the screen. "They continue advancing as a single massive wave. Why not break out into separate units, some engaging our pathetic defense, others striking at K'Ronar?"

"Their tactics indicate a fixed-response mindset," said Line.

"One would expect a lack of imagination from machines," said L'Guan.

"I would remind the Admiral that I am part machine," said Line.

"Only part," said L'Guan. "The rest of you is five Imperial admirals, one security master and a chaplain."

"My point, sir, is that there's a wide cognitive gap between a computer and an AI," said Line. "About as wide as the gap between you and a v'arx."

"Surely the AIs could build a battleglobe as smart as themselves," protested L'Guan.

"No doubt," said Line. "But what if the battleglobe decided it was smarter than the AIs?"

"I see. Yes," he said. "So?"

"So the tactics of the Fleet of the One now indicate that we face uncrewed battleglobes, receiving general orders from a central AI commander, but implementing them without further instruction and with unsurpassed dullness."

"Kiss my mother," said L'Guan, his eyes widening.

"Biog states your mother is dead, Admiral," said Line.

L'Guan shook his head. "An expression popular among cadets some years ago, Line. Why is all but a tiny part of that invasion armada uncrewed? And where is their command ship?"

"No idea why they're uncrewed, Admiral. As for the command ship, where would you be if you were in command?"

"The safest point, of course," said L'Guan, looking at the screen and the advancing Fleet. "Dead center."

"I can suggest an attack pattern to make them open a path to their center, Admiral—if you want to play our hunch."

"See what he's doing?" said Sutak, pointing to the projection.

"Being destroyed piecemeal," said Orlac, standing beside the first leader's chair.

Line's lead elements had attacked the AI Fleet's lead squadrons and been warded off by waves of missiles and a virtual wall of fusion fire. The lead squadrons scattered, pursuing Line's fleeing units.

As the AIs watched, a fresh attack wave poured in, exchanged fire with the lead squadrons and broke off to either side, more battleglobes pursuing. The Fleet of the One's original solid phalanx was now just a round core with two elongated arms speeding away from it, the arms themselves fragmenting as single globes chased single enemy units.

"He's opening a slot right toward us," said Sutak. "I think they've detected we're a little short of help." He turned from the projection. "Operations. Direct all pursuing squadrons to disengage and resume original formation."

"I believe the first leader's order may be too late," said Larn. All but forgotten, the first cyberneticist hovered to the right of Sutak's station.

The first leader turned back to the hologram and a new tactical projection: thirty-five blips were moving down the slot at close to light speed.

"We can intercept with globes yellow seven alpha green one through four," said Orlac.

"No." Sutak shook his head emphatically. "I'm not going to put four crewed ships at risk to save one just because our expensive hides are aboard. Have all crewed globes except this one scatter. We'll stand off this suicide run ourselves. Ten thousand shipbuster missiles and every fusion battery we can bring to bear against thirty-five small, lightly armed asteroids should end it. Give the order."

"I just want to say, D'Trelna," said a familiar voice from the commodore's chairarm, "that if this doesn't work, these years with you have been an education."

D'Trelna laughed. "Well, Mr. N'Trol, if it does work, I want you to know—I'll always remember you as the sardonic authority-hater who saved our asses a least a dozen times."

"And I'll remember you as the fat man who saved more than just his ship a hundred times. Luck, Commodore."

"Luck, Engineer."

The circuit clicked off.

"Incoming," said a machine voice—the voice of the computer guiding the asteroid in whose hollow belly *Implacable* nestled. "Incoming shipbusters," repeated the computer, voice sounding through the hangar deck. The waiting troopers threw themselves prone on the deck.

"Shield frequency," said D'Trelna tensely, moving down into the navigator's chair.

"Matched," said L'Wrona, fingers entering a series of numbers, then pushing the Execute. Outside, the shield blinked off, then on again, holding steady.

"Let's hope it's still current," said the commodore.

Before L'Wrona answered, the AI missiles exploded into Line's tiny attack force, destroying *Implacable*'s host.

"Filters to max," said the first leader, hands shading his eyes. Even to AI eyes, the holographic projection was a single unbearable ball of red-orange flame.

"Well done, sir," said Orlac as the fireball slowly dissipated. "All targets . . ." He stopped, staring.

Long and silver, something burst from the flames, growing in size until it filled the projection.

"L'Aal-class cruiser, K'Ronarin Fleet," said Operations quickly. "Heavily armed, carries up to two hundred crew. She'll break up against our shield."

"If the shield frequencies *Devastator* carried are correct," said L'Wrona, watching the battleglobe grow to fill the scan, "then we have a chance."

Thick red fusion beams lashed at *Implacable*, tearing at her shield as she closed on the battleglobe.

"Here we go," said D'Trelna, gritting his teeth; he sent the cruiser ramming into the AI's shield, blue and red merging.

There was a brief confusion of colors on the board, the scan breaking up into a tumbling kaleidoscope, then it cleared.

"Gods of my fathers, through!" shouted D'Trelna. Hands dancing over the helm controls, he dropped the cruiser lower. Outside, the fusion fire raking the cruiser slackened then stopped as *Implacable* dropped below the cannons' minimum azimuth.

Endless sensor and comm clusters, missiles and fusion batteries flashed by, massive gray and silent, as *Implacable* raced for the battleglobe's southern pole.

* * *

"Brilliant," said Sutak, watching as *Implacable* flew unopposed across his command ship.

"Enemy ship identified as *Implacable*," reported Orlac, turning from a complink. "Has figured prominently in all engagements with our contemporary recons into this universe. Defeated us at Terra Two unaided. Defeated us at D'Lin with some help."

"Why isn't he bombarding us?" mused Sutak, watching the projection.

"Perhaps," said Orlac, "he's going to invade us."

The two AIs looked at each other.

"Of course," said the first leader, eyes flashing. "That's just what he's going to do!"

"But . . ."

"Operations," said Sutak. "Do we have a probable on enemy ship's destination?"

"Hangar green alpha one three," came the answer after a brief pause.

"Where is that?" It was Larn. The first cyberneticist was an agitated red sphere, bobbing beside the first leader's station.

Sutak pointed past Larn toward the command center's thick blast doors. "Through there, first right, second left. He's coming here—for us."

"What are you doing about this? What are you doing about this?" shrieked the first cyberneticist.

"Unless you leave now," said Sutak, "I'm

sending every cyberneticist on this vessel into that hangar bay. If we're fortunate, they might mistake you for intelligent life." He turned to Orlac. "Ever see what a blaster hit does to a vacuum-sealed cyberball?"

"It was dogmatic martinets like that who got us into this," said Orlac as Larn streaked for the door. "A desperate plague fleet with no future.

"Just what are your orders?" asked Orlac.

Sutak shrugged. "They want me, I'm available. Security condition one—all blades to hangar bay green alpha one three. Advise security commander that I will coordinate the counterattack. Transfer command of the fleet to Hasi on our sister ship."

Sutak stood, smiling. "You know, Orlac, I'm looking forward to meeting this cruiser commander who's given us such a hard time."

28

"TARGET PENETRATED." L'WRONA'S voice echoed through the cruiser's hangar deck.
"Stand by for the go. Stand by for the go."

"Positions!" cried N'Trol, leaping to his
feet. "Let's go!"

"Never thought to see you leading the
charge," said S'Til as the troopers formed an
assault line stretching the width of the air
curtain.

"Not something you'll see again," said
N'Trol, stepping through the long line of
troopers to take up position center front. "I've
been in a few messy firefights, but nothing like
this." He looked down the assault line, left,
then right. Brown uniforms were intermin-
gled with black, commandos with starship

304

and ground personnel. What few officers and NCOs had survived were positioned along the line's front. All stood nervously gripping their rifles, waiting, staring through the blue shimmer of the atmosphere curtain. Outside, dark and diffuse, great inchoate shadows flickered across the curtain as *Implacable* sped into the battleglobe.

"Don't you have a unit?" asked N'Trol.

The commando officer shook her head. "No."

"Fine," said the Heir. "You're now my aide and a full colonel. If we win, I'll make it permanent."

"If we win," said S'Til, drawing her sidearm, "you'll make me a civilian—with colonel's pension. Deal?"

N'Trol laughed. "Deal, S'Til," he said, drawing his own weapon.

"I've seen it before, but it still impresses me," said D'Trelna.

A great gray cavern, its deck lined with cruisers, interceptors and assault craft, the battleglobe's hangar facility could have held a thousand *Implacable*'s and still looked empty.

Implacable slipped silently past the AI ships, moving on her n-gravs toward the distant end of the cavern.

"Access portal should be coming up," said L'Wrona, eyes shifting between the diagram on his complink and the forward view on the bridge screen. "They must know we're here —maybe it'll take them a few more minutes to pull a reaction force together."

"Wrong," said D'Trelna.

L'Wrona looked up as the commodore brought the slowed cruiser to a stop.

Security blades were rushing into the hangar facility, forming an assault line in front of the open corridor leading to the battleglobe's heart.

L'Wrona touched the commlink as *Implacable* settled on her landing struts. "Hostiles to the front, My Liege."

"I see them," said N'Trol as the atmosphere curtain winked off. He raised his sidearm. "Forward!" he cried, leaping onto the battleglobe.

"Where's Orlac?" demanded the first leader. "He's supposed to be coordinating the reserves." Sutak stood in flight control, looking down on the hangar through the armorglass wall. Outside, the humans were charging, an impossibly small number against the blades that swarmed toward them.

"Dead," said the blade hovering beside Sutak, Security Commander Jnor. "Plague."

Crisscrossing blaster fire, muffled explosions and screams—Sutak was only dimly aware of it. "This is all futile, then," he said. "If the virus is here, we're all dead—and so are they." He nodded toward the humans as they closed on the security blades.

"What does the cross signify?" asked John, breaking the silence.

Guan-Sharick turned from the weathered stone, her blue eyes distant. "It marks the resting place of a hope, Harrison—the hope that we could be better than we were, man and machine."

"And which are you?" asked K'Raoda.

"Neither and both," said the transmute. She squatted on the ground, studying a thin blade of grass. "I and a few others were the will and the spirit of this place—computer-generated simulacra is the closest term. And though the computer's long gone, we continued. When the original . . . owners . . . passed on, we became their stewards. We in turn created the AIs, our dutiful helpers." She rose, shaking her head. "You've seen the result."

"You've all but destroyed two universes," said Zahava.

"All but," said Guan-Sharick, and vanished, only to reappear a moment later, a flat white case in her hand. She gave it to Harrison, who took it uneasily. "Now what?" he asked, studying it. It bore the by now familiar pyramid on both sides, the uncanny blue eyes staring up at him.

307

"The vaccine that will kill the plague. It's the only sample in existence. Like the plague, it's generic, protection for AI and man."

"And how do we get it where it's needed?" said John. "We've no ship, no hope of getting off here."

"I can send you to the deck of the AI command ship," said the blonde. "It's standing off K'Ronar with your K'Ronarin friends on board, desperately trying to take it."

"How do you . . ." began K'Raoda.

She held up her hand. "I can send you there now."

"And you?" asked John.

Guan-Sharick shook her head. "It will exhaust all of the special energy that maintains this planet and much of this sector. Some small part of that energy's used to maintain my existence. A price I pay gladly." She touched the case in John's hand. "Use that wisely." The cool green eyes looked into his for the last time. "Good-bye, John."

The three humans vanished from the meadow. An instant later, Guan-Sharick, the meadow, the planet, its sun and six neighboring stars winked out of existence.

The smoke from burning bodies and machines drifted over the charnel house of hangar green alpha one three: dead AIs and K'Ronarins lay sprawled along the deck, their twisted and shattered bodies mute testimony to a battle all but over. The human assault had met the AI counterassault a few hundred paces from *Implacable*. Outnumbered and outgunned, the attack had faltered, swept by blaster beams even as security blades knifed through soft flesh. The survivors now knelt among the burned and decapitated remains of their dead as the blades regrouped for the final assault.

"Here they come," said S'Til, slipping home her last chargepak.

Fresh blades were knifing through the smoke, moving toward the small knot of humans standing amid the blasted remains of their shattered assault.

Of the original attack force, only eleven survived, among them N'Trol, S'Til, D'Trelna and L'Wrona, all of them wounded.

"One last volley, gentlemen," said N'Trol, gamely shifting his M11A to his good hand. "On my command." The others fell in beside him, waiting among their dead as death swept in.

"Aim," said N'Trol, raising his sidearm.

"H'Nar," said D'Trelna, taking careful aim at the lead blade, "finally a cheery word for you."

"What?" said the margrave as the blades closed to fifty meters.

"Volley . . ." cried N'Trol.

"The war's over," said the commodore, squeezing the trigger.

Stephen Ames Berry

Three figures appeared between the blades
and the humans. They looked around, confused for an instant, then one of them held a
small white case high above his head.

"Hold!" ordered Sutak, a familiar emblem
catching his eye.

The assault halted.

"With me," said the first leader. "All of
you."

"They've stopped," said N'Trol disbelievingly. He stood. "Is that . . ."

"It sure is," said D'Trelna. "Let's go."

L'Wrona and S'Til were already advancing,
breaking into a run toward John, Zahava and
K'Raoda, even as the AI force parted ranks,
admitting two human forms and a large blue
ball.

The two sides met on either side of the
human trio.

"That's a medical kit," said Sutak, ignoring
the others, eyes only on the white case in
John's hand. "And I recognize the Founders'
symbol." He hesitated. "Is it . . ."

"It's the vaccine," said John, looking at
both sides.

"Vaccine?" said N'Trol. "What vaccine?"

"The AIs are a plague fleet," said Zahava.
"Fleeing from a disease they've brought with
them—one to which we're susceptible. It's
wiping out all life in their own universe."

310

"You're running," said N'Trol, staring at Sutak.

"Running from our own destruction," said the first leader. "Never quite fast enough, though." He held out his hand to John. "I'll take that."

"No," said the Terran.

"What's to prevent our taking it?" said Sutak.

"Me," said N'Trol. The Heir's blaster was aimed casually at the medcase, only a meter away. "You're in command?" he asked, eyes meeting Sutak's.

The other nodded. "Sutak. First leader since the plague took out our more senior commanders. And you?"

"N'Trol. My situation's similar to yours."

"N'Trol," said the AI commander, "my blades can kill you before you can pull that trigger."

"And you're willing to risk the survival of your people on that?" said N'Trol. There was an almost perfect silence on the battlefield.

Sutak's gaze shifted to the medkit, then back to the Heir. "No," he said softly. "I did not start this war, N'Trol."

N'Trol shrugged. "But do you have the courage and the vision to end it, first leader?"

"I am willing to talk about ending it," said the AI.

"Truce?" asked N'Trol.

311

"Truce," said Sutak after an instant's hesitation.

"First leader!" protested several AIs.

Sutak turned on his staff. "Truce, I said, and truce we will have. It should be apparent that we need each other. Security Commander, withdraw your forces. Med units to tend both human and AI casualties." He turned back to N'Trol. "Shall we talk?"

29

"WILL THEY KEEP their word, though?" asked John.

D'Trelna stood for a long moment, looking out from the *Implacable*'s bridge toward the construction crews, toiling in the first light of day, rebuilding Prime Base.

"What, to stay in Quadrant Blue Nine as our guests and not our foes?" he said, refilling the two Terrans' wine glasses. Except for a few techs performing minor repairs, the trio had the big bridge to themselves. "I think so," said the commodore. "Don't forget, we can make a variant of the plague virus to wipe them out anytime we want."

"But they can do the same to you," said Zahava.

313

D'Trelna shrugged. "The way of the universe, isn't it? I think we'll each behave. I trust Sutak. Fear Sutak. Trust. Fear. That's what it all comes down to, doesn't it?" They stood watching as K'Ronar's fierce red sun rose above the mountains.

D'Trelna raised his glass toward the star; the wine seemed to catch fire in the sunlight, becoming a bright red jewel held high. "To our dead—may they know peace. To war's end and the transcendent human spirit that endured it. And to the hopeful promise of this new day."